distress.

And it would upset her parents. On top of his money worries, it might very well kill her father. Money worries. If only Teddy had not gambled so heavily. If only her sister had not flirted with Andrew Ashton. If only she herself did not love Mark quite so much. Dear Mark. He did not deserve to be embroiled in scandal from any direction. How was it all going to end?

AUTHOR NOTE

The quandary central to my main characters may seem strange to modern readers, who would not hesitate to break off an engagement if they realised the love they had hoped for was missing, but in the period in which my story is set the social mores were different. Love was not the only or even the main reason for marrying. Title, wealth, status, the wishes of one's family and the need to keep an unbroken hierarchy all played a part. Divorce was only for the very wealthy and required an Act of Parliament, and an engagement was a solemn undertaking. A lady might brave the censure of Society and break her promise to marry, but a gentleman never could. It was a dishonourable thing to do and laid him open to being shunned by Society as a man who could not be trusted to keep his word.

My story is a love story, and my hero and heroine are deeply in love, but the customs of the time prevent them from being together. She has her loyalty to her family and he has his honour, both of which must be satisfied before they can have the happy ending we all look for.

SCANDAL AT GREYSTONE MANOR

Mary Nichols

Printed and bound in Spain
by Blackprint CPI, Barcelona

MILLS & BOON®

Published in Great Britain 2014
by Mills & Boon, an imprint of Harlequin (UK) Limited,
Eton House, 18-24 Paradise Road, Richmond, Surrey, TW9 1SR

© 2014 Mary Nichols

ISBN: 978 0 263 90952 4

Born in Singapore, **Mary Nichols** came to England when she was three, and has spent most of her life in different parts of East Anglia. She has been a radiographer, a school secretary, an information officer and an industrial editor, as well as a writer. She has three grown-up children and four grandchildren.

Previous novels by the same author:

RAGS-TO-RICHES BRIDE
THE EARL AND THE HOYDEN
CLAIMING THE ASHBROOKE HEIR
  (part of *The Secret Baby Bargain*)
HONOURABLE DOCTOR, IMPROPER ARRANGEMENT
THE CAPTAIN'S MYSTERIOUS LADY*
THE VISCOUNT'S UNCONVENTIONAL BRIDE*
LORD PORTMAN'S TROUBLESOME WIFE*
SIR ASHLEY'S METTLESOME MATCH*
WINNING THE WAR HERO'S HEART
THE CAPTAIN'S KIDNAPPED BEAUTY*
IN THE COMMODORE'S HANDS*

**The Piccadilly Gentlemen's Club* mini-series

And available through Mills & Boon® Historical eBooks:

WITH VICTORIA'S BLESSING
  (part of *Royal Weddings Through the Ages*)

**Did you know that some of these novels
are also available as eBooks?
Visit www.millsandboon.co.uk**

Chapter One

April 1817

'Stand still, Issie, do,' Jane said. 'How can I pin this hem if you will keep dodging from one foot to the other? And stop admiring yourself in the mirror. We all know what a beautiful bride you will make.'

It had taken weeks of indecision about colour and style before the heavy cerise silk had been bought and then they could not decide on who was to make it up. 'You do it,' Isabel had told her sister. 'You are every bit as good a seamstress as any London mantua-maker and a great deal better than poor Miss Smith.'

Jane laughed at the compliment. 'Very well, but we'll ask Miss Smith to do the plain stitching. She could do with the work.' The elderly spinster came from the village three times a week to make petticoats for the ladies as well as repair torn garments and mend the household linen.

Jane had been doing as much as possible towards the wedding to save a little on the expense. Her mother was determined it would be the wedding of the year, in spite of Sir Edward's pleas they should not be too extravagant. Jane was perhaps the only one of the family to take any notice of him, but that did not mean Isabel's wedding would be anything less than perfect if she could help it. She had taken great pains with the gown, making sure it fitted perfectly. It had the fashionable high waist, long sleeves, loose at the top but tight from the elbow down, a heart-shaped neckline and a flowing skirt, trimmed with lace and embroidered with white-and-pink roses. All that was left to do now was stitch up the hem and add the decoration to the neckline and sleeves—yards of ribbon and lace, interspersed with tiny coloured beads. Sewn on by hand with minute invisible stitches, they were going to take some time to do. She did not begrudge the time, nor her sister her happiness, not even at the sacrifice of her own.

Isabel was to marry Mark Wyndham, heir to Lord Wyndham, who lived with his parents less than three miles away at Broadacres. The families had known each other for years and often visited each other, so the girls and their brother had grown up in close proximity and there was no formality between them. A marriage between Mark and Isabel had been talked about for years as if it were a foregone conclusion, though Mark had not formally proposed until he came back from the Peninsular War, where he had distinguished himself as an aide to Sir Arthur Wellesley, now the Duke of Wellington. The engagement pleased both families and it had relieved the girls' father, who did not want Isabel to go the way of Jane and become an old maid. To have two unmarried daughters was not good for his self-esteem, and nor, come to that, his pocket.

Jane was perhaps the only one of the family, apart from her father, who realised that they were living beyond their means, trying to maintain a status and lifestyle not commensurate with income. The estate was run down, fences needed mending, ditches needed cleaning out, some of the cottages needed repairs and the house itself was in urgent need of refurbishment. Greystone Manor was a lovely old house, solidly built to withstand the ravages of the east wind that blew in off the German Ocean, but that didn't stop it being draughty. Its large withdrawing room was icy in winter and cool in summer; its huge kitchens and dairy with their stone floors were hard on the servants' feet. The family tended to use the smaller parlour as a sitting room and the break-

fast room as a dining room except on formal oc-
casions. Today the girls were working in Isabel's
bedchamber, whose window overlooked the front
drive. Outside the spring sunshine was warm and
inviting and everyone hoped that this year there
might be a good harvest, which would make up
for the terrible failure of the year before.

'There, that's done,' Jane said. 'You can take it
off now and I'll get Miss Smith to stitch the hem
while I gather the flounces for the skirt.'

She helped Isabel out of the gown and carefully folded it ready for the seamstress when she
came that afternoon.

Isabel hugged her. 'You are so good, Jane, I
wish I could be more like you. You are clever at
whatever you do, sewing, cooking, managing the
servants and you have such a way with the village children. You ought to be getting married,
too, and having children of you own.'

'We can't all be wives, Issie.' At twenty-seven,
everyone, including Jane herself, knew she was
well past marriageable age. Her role in life was
to be a helpmate to her mother, to busy herself
with the arrangements for her sister's wedding,
to calm her other sister's excitable nature and try
to curb her brother Teddy's profligacy. Added to
her good works in the nearby village of Hadlea,
it was enough to keep her occupied. She had little
time to bemoan her single state.

'But you must wish for it sometimes?'

'Not really. I am content with my life.'

'Did you never have an offer?'

Jane smiled, but did not answer. There had been someone once, ten years before, but it had come to nothing. Her father had disapproved on the grounds that the young man had no title and no fortune, no family of any standing and no prospects. She could do better than that, he'd told her. But she never had and the only other man she had come to have feelings for had not reciprocated and her foolishness was a deeply held secret which she had never told a soul. She was not beautiful and, compared with her younger sisters, she was plain Jane.

How their parents had managed to produce three girls so different from each other, Jane could not fathom. Jane and Isabel were both dark haired, but there the similarity ended. Jane was taller than average; she had strong features, well-defined brows and a determined chin. Isabel, six years younger than Jane, was considered the beauty of the family. She was a little shorter and more curvaceous than Jane, and her face was rounder and very expressive; she was not one to hide her feelings. Tears and temper were often displayed, but she soon recovered and became her usual sunny self. Jane was more circumspect and kept her feelings to herself. As for Sophie, she was fair-haired and blue-eyed and, at seventeen, had not yet shed what her mother chose to call her puppy fat.

'I am doing the right thing?' Isabel asked suddenly, sinking on to her bed in her petticoat.

'Whatever do you mean?'

'Marrying Mark.'

'You are surely not having doubts now, Issie?'

'It's such a big step. I keep wondering if I shall make him happy, or if I shall be content with him.'

'But you have known him all your life. You know he is tall and handsome, that he is thoughtful and considerate, that he has deep pockets and likes nothing better than to indulge you. What more can you ask?'

'That's just it. Perhaps I know him too well. And perhaps I've missed someone else, someone for whom I could feel the grand passion.'

'Isabel, you are talking nonsense, the grand passion is a myth, dreamed up by romantics. It's much better to marry someone dependable, someone you know won't let you down.' Isabel's sudden doubts were having a strange effect on Jane. It had taken all her resolve to wish her sister happy when the engagement had been announced and she had entered into the preparations for the wedding with as much whole-hearted enthusiasm as she could muster. Her sister's doubts worried her.

'Mark is dependable, that's true,' Isabel said. 'But he is almost like another brother.'

'Mark is nothing like a brother.'

'No, of course not. I'm being silly. He's not a bit like Teddy, is he?'

'God forbid! One of Teddy is enough.'

They laughed at this and the tension eased. Jane helped her sister into her day dress and was just brushing her hair and tying it back with a ribbon when they heard the sound of someone arriving. Isabel jumped up and went to the window to see who it might be. 'It's Teddy,' she said. 'My goodness, where did he get that coat? He looks like a bumble bee.'

Jane joined her sister at the window. Their brother, three years younger than Jane and three years older than Isabel, had just descended from the gig he had hired at the Fox and Hounds, where the stage from London had no doubt deposited him not half an hour since. The coat Isabel had commented on was of yellow-and-brown stripes. It had a cutaway skirt and deep revers. His trousers were fawn and his waistcoat yellow with red spots. 'Papa will have something to say about that,' she said.

They were descending the stairs as a servant opened the door to admit him. He flourished a brown beaver topper at them both. 'Jane, Isabel, I hope I find you both well.'

'Very well,' Jane said.

'Where did you get that extraordinary coat?' Isabel demanded.

'Gieves, where else? Do you like it?' He twirled to show it off. 'Where is Papa? I need to talk to him. Is he in a good mood?'

'Oh, Teddy, do not say you have come to wheedle money out of him?' Jane said. 'You know what he said the last time.'

'Well, a fellow can't live decent on what I earn at Halliday's.' Halliday and Son was an eminent firm of lawyers who had a practice in Lincoln's Inn Fields. Teddy had gone to them after leaving university at the behest of his father, who did not believe his son should pass his days in idleness. He was still very junior and could not command the large fees his mentors did.

'Then take a little advice from me, Brother,' Jane went on. 'Change that coat and waistcoat before you see him. It will not help your cause.'

'Wise words, as always, Jane,' he said. 'I'll go up to my room and put on something drab.' He picked up his portmanteau from the floor where he had dropped it and ran up the stairs two at a time.

'He doesn't change, does he?' Isabel said.

'No, unfortunately. I fear we are in for an uncomfortable dinner time.'

* * *

In that she was right. Even though Teddy had changed into a dark grey coat and a white cravat and waistcoat, he had evidently not been successful with their father. He was resentful, Sir Edward was angry and Lady Cavenhurst upset. Jane and Isabel tried to lighten the heavy atmosphere by talking about the wedding and the doings in the village and were only partly successful, not helped by Sophie demanding to know what was the matter with everyone, why the gloomy faces. 'Anyone would think there had been a death in the family,' she said.

'Death of me,' Teddy said morosely, which made his father snort derisively and his mother draw in her breath in distress. But no one commented and they continued to eat their roast beef in a silence broken only when someone asked politely for the sauce boat or the salt cellar.

After the meal ended, the ladies repaired to the withdrawing room, where a maid brought in the tea tray. 'Is Papa very angry with Teddy?' Jane asked their mother as they arranged themselves on sofas.

'He is more disappointed than angry,' her ladyship said. She was still a handsome woman, with an upright figure which belied her forty-nine years. 'Teddy promised him he would limit his extravagance, but it seems not to have happened. But we will not talk of it. No doubt it will be re-solved somehow.' It was typical of their mother to shut her eyes to problems in the firm belief someone else would solve them.

They had not been seated many minutes when Sir Edward and Teddy joined them, but Teddy soon made his excuses to leave. Jane rose and followed him. 'Teddy,' she said, taking his arm. 'Are matters very ill with you?'

'Couldn't be worse. And the old man refuses to stand buff.'

'Oh, dear, what will you do?' They strolled into the book room where there was a comfort-able sofa and sat down side by side.

'I don't know what to do. You can't help me out, can you, Sis?'

'How much do you owe?'

'Well…' He seemed reluctant to go on. 'It's mostly gaming debts and they simply have to be paid.'

'Go on, how much?'

'Five thousand or thereabouts.'

'Five thousand! Oh, Teddy, how did that come about?'

'You know how it is—you win some and you lose some and I kept thinking I would recoup. Luck was against me.'

'Who do you owe the money to?'

'Lord Bolsover holds the biggest of my gambling debts, about three thousand. He's the one making the most noise about it. There are a couple of others. Gieves and Hoby and the vintner can wait.'

'Wait for what? Until you have another winning streak? And I would have thought it was more important to pay your tailor and bootmaker who have a living to make. Gaming debts are not enforceable by law. You should know that, working in a law firm as you do.'

'All the more reason to pay them. It is a question of honour.'

'Honour! Teddy, if you had any honour you would heed poor Papa, who has always done his best for you. He is not made of money, you know.'

'So he told me.' He heaved a sigh. 'He suggests I find myself a rich wife, preferably a widow, old enough and independent enough to curb my excesses.'

Jane could not help laughing and was relieved to see a slight twitch of her brother's lips in response. 'He only said that because he was cross with you.'

'He was in earnest, Jane.'

'You do not like the idea?'

'Oh, I like it well enough, always supposing the wealth came with a pretty face and figure. But where am I going to find such a one who'll have me? Even if I did, it would take time and I haven't got the time. Hector Bolsover wants his blunt.'

'Oh, Teddy, what a mess you are in.'

'I know. Can you help me out?'

'Where do you think I can find so much money?'

'You still have the bequest Aunt Matilda left you, haven't you?'

'That is meant to be my dowry.'

'But, Jane, you are never going to marry, are you?'

Only a brother would be so blunt. It hurt, but she didn't show it. 'Maybe not, but I have other plans for my inheritance.'

'More important than rescuing your only brother from the River Tick?'

She sighed heavily. She had a dream of opening an orphanage for some of the children of men lost in the recent war. The idea had come about when she had been in London the year before. She had seen some ragged, barefoot children running about the streets begging and when she spoke to one of them, to the dismay of her mother who had accompanied her, she was told a tale which made her heart bleed for him. His father had been killed in a battle in far-off Portugal, his mother had been forced into service where children were not welcome and because she was obliged to live in, she had to give up the tenancy of their two tiny rooms. He slept in doorways or under the trees in the park. 'I do well enough,' he told her, holding out his hand for money.

How many more were there like that? she had asked herself, how many children were there without homes, without adequate clothing and enough to eat? 'Surely the government should do something about them,' she had said to her mother, as they left the child clutching a sixpence. 'Their fathers fought for king and country and that is how they are rewarded. It's a disgrace.'

'I do not see what we can do about it.'

'We can speak to Sir Mortimer for a start.' Sir Mortimer Belton was their local Member of Parliament. 'If the problem is put to him, he might bring it up in Parliament. We could make a fuss, bring it to the public's attention. Raise a subscription to provide the children with homes.'

'Oh, dear,' her mother had said. 'That sounds like a crusade.'

And a crusade it had become, but trying to make the government move was like tickling a tortoise. Jane had decided that she must set an example—not on a grand scale, she could not afford that, but she could do something locally. A small boarding school for about a dozen orphans of soldiers in their own vicinity was what she had in mind. It might encourage others to do the same in their own localities. The five thousand pounds she had would not be enough and she had enlisted the help of the Rector, the Reverend Mr Henry Caulder and his wife, to raise funds. They had decided that the best way to do it was to find philanthropic sponsors. To encourage them, she would put her own money into the venture, she had told them. If she gave her inheritance to Teddy, it would put an end to her plans before they had even begun to take shape.

'Can you not ask Lord Bolsover for more time, so that we can think of something?' she queried.

'You don't know his lordship, or you wouldn't even suggest it.'

'If he is such an unpleasant man, why do you associate with him?'

'He is in the group I play with.'

'Teddy, you are a fool and I do not wonder that Papa is angry with you.'

'Do you think you can bring him round? He always listens to you. I will be for ever in your debt.'

She laughed. 'You are in enough debt without adding me to your list, Teddy, but I'll see what I can do with Papa. Not tonight, though. Give him time to calm down. How long will you stay?'

'I cannot show my face back in London until at least Bolsover is satisfied.'

'But what about your position at Halliday's?'

'What position?'

Even the almost-unshockable Jane was taken aback by that. 'Oh, Teddy, don't say you have been dismissed? No wonder Papa is furious.'

'He don't know about that. Daren't tell him. If you can't help me, I will have to go abroad, the Indies or India or something.'

'That will break Mama's heart. And the disgrace will be hard to live down. And there's Isabel's wedding in a month's time. What do you think Mark will say about a scandal like that hanging over the nuptials? Go away, Teddy, go and make yourself useful somewhere and let me think.'

He stood up and left her. Her thinking led her nowhere, except to the realisation that she would have to forfeit her inheritance. The thought of all those orphan children continuing to suffer because of her brother's selfishness was more than she could bear. She had always been tolerant of Teddy's foibles, but this time he had really angered her. If it were not for her mother's distress and her sister's wedding, she would let him stew.

'If it isn't Drew Ashton,' Mark exclaimed when he saw his old friend striding towards him along Piccadilly. 'Where have you sprung from? It's years since I saw you.'

'I've been in India, just arrived back.'

'And looking very prosperous, I must say.'

Mark looked the other man up and down, taking in the perfectly fitting coat of clerical-grey superfine, the embroidered waistcoat, the diamond pin in his precisely tied cravat, the pearl-handled quizzing glass hanging on a chain from his neck, and the gold pocket watch. His trousers were strapped below his polished city shoes. 'You didn't used to be so elegant.'

'I did pretty well out there. You don't look so bad yourself. What have you been up to? How are your lady mother and Lord Wyndham?'

'They are both well. As for me, I've been campaigning with Wellington. Came home after Waterloo and now about to be married. I'm in London to call on my lawyers about the finer points of the marriage settlement and to buy a suit of clothes for the wedding.'

'You've time to join me for a meal at Grillon's, surely.'

'Yes, of course. Glad to.'

Mark turned back the way he had come and they walked a little way down the street to the hotel, where they were soon settled at a table and ordering food and wine.

'Tell me,' Mark said, while they waited for the repast to arrive. 'Why the sudden urge to visit India? I recollect you left Broadacres in somewhat of a hurry. I hope it had nothing to do with Mama's hospitality.'

'No, certainly not. Lady Wyndham's hospitality is of the best. She made me very welcome. It was a family matter that came up suddenly and had to be attended to. I did explain that at the time.'

'So you did. I had forgot. So, what are you going to do now you are back in England?'

'I am thinking of buying a share in a clipper and continuing to trade. It has served me well so far.'

'Trade, Drew?'

'Why not? I am not so top-lofty as to turn my nose up at a good way of making a fortune'. He stopped speaking as a waiter brought their pork chops, succulent and sizzling with fat, together with a large bowl of vegetables. They helped themselves and tucked in.

'A nabob, are you?' Mark queried. His friend certainly gave that impression. It was the only way he could have come by such finery without inherited wealth, which Mark knew he did not have.

'You could say that. I went out with the intention of making a fortune and in that I succeeded. I am no longer the poor relation to be pitied because no young lady of any standing would consider me.'

'I'm sure that isn't true, Drew.'

'Oh, it is, believe me. The young lady I wanted

to marry turned her proud nose up at me. Not good enough, you see.'

Mark detected a note of bitterness in his old friend's tone 'There are plenty more fish in the sea.'

'Indeed, yes, although, unlike you, I am in no hurry to become leg-shackled.'

'I am not in a hurry. We have known each other since childhood.'

'Tell me about her. Is she beautiful? Does she have a pleasing temperament?'

'Yes, to both questions. You have met her, Drew. Her name is Isabel Cavenhurst.'

'Cavenhurst!'

'Yes, you sound surprised.'

'No, no,' Andrew said hastily. 'I do remember the name. Don't the Cavenhursts live close to Broadacres?'

'Yes, on the other side of the village at Greystone Manor. We went there several times while you were staying with us. Surely you remember that?'

'Yes, now you remind me, I do. There were three young ladies, I recall, though the youngest was no more than a child and the middle one, still at her lessons. The elder was seventeen or eighteen. I recall her name was Jane. I misremember the other names.' He spoke nonchalantly, as if it were a matter of indifference to him.

'Isabel is the second daughter. She is by far the most beautiful of the three, but Sophie is young and may grow into her looks. As for Jane, she has some very good qualities I can admire, but good looks is not one of them.'

'So you have taken the pick of the bunch and not the eldest. Isn't that a little unusual?'

'We are not in the Middle Ages, Drew, my parents would never presume to tell me whom I should marry. I was able to please myself. Anyway, Jane would not have welcomed my advances even if I chose to make any. I believe there was some sort of disappointment. I don't know the details, but she withdrew from society and I saw more of Isabel. Then of course I went to Portugal and was away six years. Isabel and I became engaged when I returned.'

'So when is the wedding to be?'

'Next month. The fifteenth.'

'Then I wish you happy.'

'Thank you. You must come down for the wedding.'

'Oh, I don't know about that.'

'Why not? You do not have a prior engagement, do you?'

'No, I am as free as the air until I find my clipper.'

'Then why the reluctance?'

'It is surely up to the bride's family to issue the invitations? They may not wish to include me.'

'That's a feeble excuse if I ever heard one. I can put forward my own guests. Besides, there is something you can do for me…'

'Oh, and what might that be?'

'Jonathan Smythe was to be my groomsman, but he had to go to Scotland to visit an elderly relative who is dying and as his inheritance hangs on his attendance at the death bed, he has abandoned me to go to her. I need someone to stand up with me at the altar.'

'I haven't seen Jonathan since we were at school together. The terrible trio, they called us, do you remember?'

'Yes. Always into mischief, the three of us.'

'My great-aunt and Jonathan's second cousin live in the same area of Strathclyde, both of them dragons.'

'I know, but dragon or not, he has been summoned and I am left without a groomsman.'

'I am flattered, Mark, but why me?'

Mark looked at his friend, his head a little to one side. 'Because I am sure you will do the job admirably and you are one of my oldest friends, so who better? As soon as I saw you coming down the street, I knew my problem was solved. You will do it, Drew, won't you?'

'I'll think about it.'

'Don't think too long. I have to go back to Norfolk the day after tomorrow and before that I have to bespeak me a suit of clothes fit for a bridegroom. Will you help me find it? You can help me choose gifts for my bride and her attendants, too, if you've a mind. It is always good not to do these things alone. A wise counsellor is what I need.'

Andrew laughed. 'From having nothing to occupy me but a good dinner and a game of cards, I suddenly find my time filled with onerous tasks.'

'Helping me buy a wedding outfit is not onerous. I am not short of blunt. I can afford the best and, if it helps, I will undertake to have a hand of cards with you. We can go to White's. Are you a member?'

'No, I haven't been back long enough to join any clubs and without sponsors I am unlikely to be accepted.'

'No matter, I will introduce you. So, do we shake hands on it?' He put down his knife and held out his right hand.

Andrew took it. 'Very well. Tomorrow we go shopping. I make no promises about attending the wedding though.'

Mark grinned. He was satisfied for the moment. He did not doubt that he would be able to persuade his friend to Broadacres and then he might find out the truth about why he had disappeared so suddenly. He did not believe the tale

of family business because, as far as he knew,
Andrew's only family was an elderly spinster
great-aunt who had had no wish to look after the
orphan when his mother and father both died
within weeks of each other. She had put him out
to foster parents until he was old enough to go to
school. From the odd things Drew had told him,
he had been subject to physical abuse and mental torment. Mark had always felt sorry for him
when they were at school, because when all the
boys went home for the holidays, he had been
left behind. He had invited him to Broadacres,
but until Drew was old enough to make his own
decisions he had been forbidden to come on the
grounds it would give him ideas above his sta-
tion. It was when they'd left university that he
had been prevailed upon to spend some time at
Broadacres before looking for a way of earning
a living. Why, if it was family business that had
called him, did he make such haste to go to India?

When they had finished their meal, which Andrew insisted on paying for, they parted, promising to meet again soon. Mark hired a hackney to
take him to Halliday and Son to consult the son,
Mr Cecil Halliday, about the marriage settlement.
Mark was a careful man, but he was not ungen-
erous; he wanted to be sure Isabel had enough
pin money to buy whatever she liked in the way

of gowns and fripperies without having to appeal to him every time. He was not unaware that Sir Edward was struggling—it was obvious by the state of the house and grounds—and he had waived the dowry he had been offered. He knew how much of a sacrifice that would have been for the others—her ladyship, Jane and Sophie—who might suffer as a consequence. It was the last thing he wanted.

He was surprised when he arrived at the lawyer's premises not to encounter Teddy, who was usually scratching away in the outer office. There was another man sitting at his desk.

'Where is Mr Cavenhurst?' he queried after he had been shown into Cecil Halliday's office and they had exchanged greetings and handshakes.

'Mr Cavenhurst is no longer with us.'

'Not working here? Where has he gone?'

The man shrugged. 'I have no idea, back to his lodgings or home to Norfolk, perhaps.'

'What happened?'

'That's not for me to say, sir.'

'I understand your reticence, but he is to be my brother-in-law. Am I to assume you dispensed with his services?'

'You may assume that,' the man said, tight-lipped. 'I shall say nothing.'

'Very well. I'll not embarrass you by asking any more questions. Shall we get down to business?'

* * *

They spent the next hour fine-tuning the agreement and then Mark set off for Teddy's lodgings. The young man had flitted owing rent, he was told by the concierge in aggrieved tones. Mark paid the back rent and returned to his hotel. He had known Teddy all his life, they had played together as children and gone to the same school, although Teddy was four years younger and they'd had very little contact while there. They had not attended the same university and afterwards Mark had joined the army in Portugal and Teddy had subsequently taken up the position of junior clerk to Halliday and Son. It was only recently, because of the wedding, they had seen more of each other.

Mark wanted to like Teddy for Isabel's sake, but he had always found him brash and insensitive, which had come about, he supposed, because he was the longed-for son and heir. Born between Jane and Isabel, he had been thoroughly spoiled by his doting mama. So what had he done to make Halliday give him the bag? Whatever it was would not please Sir Edward.

He was able to make an informed guess later that evening when he and Drew met at White's and were joined by two others in a game of whist. One was Toby Moore, an erstwhile army captain whom Mark had known slightly during the war, and the other was Lord Bolsover. They were not two he would normally have chosen to play with, but all the other men present were already settled at their games and he could hardly refuse a polite request to make up a four.

'You are affianced to one of the Cavenhurst girls, are you not?' Bolsover queried, while they waited for a new pack of cards to be brought to the table. He was a year or two older than Mark, extravagantly dressed. His dark hair was worn short and curled forward over his forehead and ears. His skin was tanned, which was surprising since, as far as Mark was aware, he spent long hours at the gaming tables.

'Yes,' Mark said. 'I have the honour to be engaged to Miss Isabel Cavenhurst.'

'The wedding to be soon, is it?'

'In a little under a month. Why do you ask?'

'Curiosity, my dear fellow. I am well acquainted with Cavenhurst.'

'Sir Edward?'

'No, never met him. I meant the son. We have had a few hands of cards together. I am afraid he is a poor loser. I believe he has run home on a repairing lease. I do hope he recovers quickly, I am not in the habit of waiting for my money.'

Mark could well believe that and wondered

where the conversation was leading. 'No doubt he has gone home for the wedding.'

'So soon? I think not. It is to be hoped his father can come up trumps because at the moment I hold all the cards. I have bought up all the man's debts and they were spread far and wide. I do not think Teddy Cavenhurst ever bought anything with cash.' Everyone knew that creditors who could not make their debtors pay often sold the debts for a fraction of the original figure, in order to be rid of them.

His heart sank, but he hid it with a laugh. 'Sir Edward has always stood buff for his son. Have no fear.'

'I had heard the estate was in a poor way and Sir Edward hard put to come about.' Bolsover spoke nonchalantly as he picked up the pack that had just been put on the table in front of him and broke the seal.

'Where did you hear that? I know nothing of it.'

His lordship gave a cracked laugh. 'Worried that the lady's dowry is at risk, are you?'

'No, of course not. I do not know where you obtained your information, but I suggest you tell whoever it is that they are in error. Now, as we have the cards, shall we play?'

'To be sure.' His lordship finished shuffling the pack and put it on the table. 'Will you cut for trumps, Mr Ashton?'

The subject of Teddy and his debts was dropped, but it worried Mark. From the way Bolsover had spoken about the dowry and the Greystone estate, the amount must be substantial. Surely not enough to ruin Sir Edward? How much was it? He could ask Isabel, or better still Jane. She would be bound to know and also the extent of Sir Edward's problems.

'You are not concentrating,' murmured Drew, during the break between one game and the next as the pile of coins at Bolsover's elbow had grown. 'I had already won that second trick, you did not have to waste a trump on it. That is a beginner's mistake.'

'I'm sorry. It won't happen again.'

'Dreaming about your bride, are you?'

Mark smiled, but did not answer. He picked up the cards Toby Moore had just dealt. This was better; he had a good hand. They played in silence and recouped some of their losses. Drew was a very good player; he seemed to know where all the cards were and by the end of the evening they were in profit.

* * *

'A satisfactory evening,' Drew said, as they strolled to Jermyn Street where he was lodging.

'I think you must be a seasoned gambler,' Mark said. 'Hector Bolsover has a reputation as a sharp, but you made him look clumsy. He won't like that.'

'What do you know of the man?'

'Not a great deal. I believe he is unmarried and spends all his time in the clubs and gaming hells. I have heard he does not always play fair, though no one has seen fit to challenge him. If he has Teddy's vouchers, it could go ill for the Cavenhursts.'

'So that was what you were in a brown study about?'

'It is worrying.'

'Are you concerned about the dowry?'

'Good heavens, no! It is the least of my worries.'

'So, we are still going to look for wedding finery tomorrow?'

'Naturally we are.' They stopped outside Drew's lodgings. 'And you are going to come back to Broadacres with me, aren't you?'

'Have I said that?'

'No, but you will. I want you to meet Isabel again before the wedding. We will invite the Cavenhursts over for supper.'

Drew laughed. 'In the face of such a prospect, how can I refuse?'

Mark went on his way to the Wyndham town house in South Audley Street well satisfied.

Chapter Two

'Papa, can you spare me a minute?' Jane had found her father in the estate office where he worked most mornings. The desk in front of him was scattered with papers. He had evidently been raking his fingers through his greying hair; some of it was standing up on end.

'Oh, it is you, Jane. Come in and sit down. I thought it was that reprobate son of mine and I can hardly be civil to him at the moment.'

Jane advanced further into the room and sat on the chair placed the other side of the desk, a position usually occupied by the estate manager, but she had just seen him leave and knew her father was alone. 'I am sorry to hear that, Papa. It is on his behalf I am come.'

'So, he has descended to sending his sister to plead for him, has he?'

'He feels that you have not fully comprehended

the trouble he is in and that perhaps I can explain it better than he.'

Sir Edward managed a humourless laugh. 'I comprehend it only too well, Jane. What *he* does not comprehend is how impossible it is for me to comply with his outrageous demands without impoverishing the rest of the family.'

Jane gasped. 'Surely it is not as bad as that?'

'It is every bit as bad as that. My investments have failed. Last year's ruined harvest and the demands of my tenants for repairs, not to mention Isabel's wedding, have been the last straw. We are going to have to retrench. I am sorry, but Teddy will have to find his own solution. I warned him the last time he came home that it was the last time. He must learn I meant it.'

'But what is he to do, Papa? He is young and impressionable, it is only natural he wants to spread his wings and keep up with his friends.'

'Then he should choose his friends more wisely.'

'But, Papa...'

'Jane, you will displease me if you continue. You have a soft and gentle heart and it is to your credit, but in this instance you are backing a lost cause. You would do better to put your mind to ways of retrenchment, ways that your mother will accept as reasonable.'

'Very well, Papa.' She rose to go, then turned back. 'Isabel's wedding is not in jeopardy, is it?'

'No, I think we can manage that.'

She left her father, but did not immediately seek out her brother. She needed a little time to herself and she needed to think about the task her father had set her. One thing was very sure: her inheritance was going to have to be sacrificed and the sooner she accepted that the better. She went up to her bedchamber, put on a light shawl and a bonnet and set out for the village.

But for the problems that weighed her down she would have enjoyed the short walk. The sun was shining, the birds were singing and the hedgerows were bright with blossom. Hadlea village, set in the north Norfolk fenland, was not a large one. There was a church, a rectory, a windmill, two inns and several cottages grouped around a triangular village green on which there was a pump and some old stocks, though no one had been put in those in her memory. Side roads from the green led to a farrier and harness-maker who also mended shoes, a butcher and a tiny front-room shop that sold almost anything the village women might need from salt to sugar and soap to candles, working boots to plain cotton tick. For anything like muslin and silk, ribbons and bonnets, they had to make a trip to Norwich or King's

Lynn or wait until the travelling salesman came round, usually at the end of the harvest when his customers had a little money to spend.

Jane made her way to the rectory and was greeted cheerfully by Mrs Caulder. 'Come in, Jane, I will have some tea and cakes brought into the parlour. It's time Henry came out of his study. He has been in there all morning, working on tomorrow's sermon.'

Mrs Caulder was very plump, a testament to a love of her cook's cakes. She fussed around, giving the orders and calling her husband to join them, while Jane sat on one of the chairs and wondered how she was going to explain that the five thousand pounds she had promised for their project would not be forthcoming. She could not divulge the true state of affairs.

'How are you my dear?' Mrs Caulder asked. 'Did you walk here? I did not hear the pony and trap.'

'I walked. It is such a lovely day.' Even as she spoke, she wondered if the pony would have to go, or perhaps the carriage, or the riding horses.

'To be sure it is. Ah, here is Henry.'

The Rector was of medium height, with a shock of grey hair, which he wore long and tied back with a thin black ribbon. He was a jovial man and beamed at Jane. 'What a pleasure to see you, my dear Miss Cavenhurst. I hope I find you well.'

'Very well. But I am afraid I have some disappointing news.'

'Surely not the wedding?' exclaimed his wife, handing Jane a cup of tea.

'Oh, no, nothing like that. It's simply that I cannot give our orphan project the five thousand I promised.' She paused, then resorted to an untruth. 'I find I cannot touch it until either I marry or I reach the age of thirty in three years' time. I have been racking my brains trying to think of a way of going ahead without it.'

'My dear girl, do not look so downbeat, it is not the end of the world,' the Rector said, flinging up the skirt of his coat and seating himself beside his wife to take a cup of tea from her. 'We will contrive somehow without it. We shall have to find a wealthy patron, more than one if need be. I never did feel quite at ease about you giving it in the first place.'

'Oh, I am much relieved,' Jane said. 'I thought it would be the end of all our hopes. You have given me fresh heart.'

'There are orphanages all over the country, some a great deal better run than others. We must ask them how they manage and draw up a list of possible patrons. You, I am sure, could persuade people to donate. It is a good cause and you are so passionate about it.'

Jane laughed at that and the rest of the visit passed cheerfully. She was still smiling as she started out to cross the green on her way home. She had her head down, deep in thought, and did not see the two men until she was almost abreast of them.

'Jane, we are well met,' Mark called out to her.

She looked up, startled, and found herself hurtling back ten years. The man beside Mark was unmistakable. The years had dealt kindly with him. He was tall, broad and muscular and dressed to perfection in a brown coat of Bath cloth and fawn buckskins tucked into shining tasselled Hessians. A gold watch chain hung across his creamy brocade waistcoat and a huge diamond sparkled in his cravat. All this she noted before lifting her eyes to look into his face. It was tanned and the only lines were around his hazel eyes, due either to laughter or squinting in the sun. He was regarding her with a look she interpreted as amusement. Was she a comical figure? To be sure, her dress was plain, but her shawl was pretty and the ribbons on her bonnet were new even if the bonnet was not.

'You remember Miss Cavenhurst, do you not?'

Mark said to him. 'This is Jane, sister to my fiancée.'

'Of course I remember,' Drew said, doffing his hat. 'How do you do, Miss Cavenhurst?'

'I am well. And you?' She had often wondered what it would be like to meet him again and whether the old attraction would still be there. He was an extremely attractive man, to be sure, and a great deal more confident than the man she had sent away, but after ten years, it would have been surprising if she had not found him changed.

'I am in good health, Miss Cavenhurst, and happy to renew acquaintance with you. It has been some time.'

'Ten years,' she murmured and then wished she had not mentioned the time. He would assume she had been counting and dwelling on it, which was the last impression she wished to give him.

'Yes, and every one of them devoted to the goal of returning one day, having made my fortune.'

'And have you?'

'I believe so.'

'He is a nabob,' Mark said, laughing. 'But underneath he is the same Drew Ashton I knew before he went away. He has come to stay with us at Broadacres and be my groomsman.'

'I thought you already had someone,' Jane said, turning towards him. He was almost as tall as Drew, but slimmer and his urbane good looks contrasted sharply with the weathered look of his friend.

'So I did, but he has been called away and when I met Drew in London, the solution to my problem was obvious.'

'How fortuitous for you.' She turned back to Drew. 'So, you came to see how we all go on in Hadlea, Mr Ashton. We are a quiet community, little changes here.'

'Except we all grow older and wiser,' he said.

'That is true, of course.' Was that some reference to their youth ten years before or was he telling her his old passion had died a natural death, as surely hers must have done?

'Jane, I need to have a quiet word with you,' Mark said. 'Perhaps Drew will excuse us for a moment?'

'To be sure,' Drew said. 'I will amuse myself exploring the village.' He bowed to Jane. 'Good day, Miss Cavenhurst. I shall look forward to renewing my acquaintance with the rest of your family while I am here.'

She bowed her head in acknowledgement. 'Good day, Mr Ashton.'

She watched him stride away, then turned back to Mark. 'He is much changed and yet he has not changed at all.'

'Except he is richer,' Mark said with a laugh.

'What is it you wanted to speak to me about?'

She did not want to talk about Andrew Ashton. His sudden arrival was something else she had to deal with. Would he mention the past or would it be a closed book? She hoped the latter. She did not want to be reminded of it.

Mark's smile died and he seemed to be reluctant to go on, which was so unlike him that she wondered what it could be. 'Jane, I met Lord Bolsover while I was in London. Drew and I had a hand of whist with him and a friend of his at White's.'

'Oh, surely you are not a gambling man, Mark? Gambling is an insidious evil.'

'I only play for amusement now and again and never for high stakes. You play yourself of an evening, do you not?'

'Yes, when we have company and then for counters, not money. But do go on.'

'Bolsover is not a man I would normally associate with, but Drew wanted a game.'

'Mark, you are beating about the bush. You are going to tell me Teddy owes him money, aren't you?'

'You know of it?'

'I am the first person my brother comes to when he is in trouble.'

'I believe he owes Lord Bolsover a substantial amount—will you tell me how much?'

'Mark, I know you mean well, but Teddy would

not like me to divulge the figure, not even to you. Why do you want to know?'

'Lord Bolsover is putting it about that Teddy is a welsher and he will have his money by hook or by crook. He even hinted he would have the Manor.'

She gasped. 'It is not so large an amount, Mark. He cannot do that, can he?'

'Not while your papa is alive, but when Teddy inherits, that will be a different matter. Isabel will be with me, of course, but I am concerned for you and your mother and Sophie. Can Sir Edward settle the debts?'

She hesitated. To her shame, she had already told one untruth that day and she did not want to tell another, especially to Mark, but he had truly frightened her with his tale that Lord Bolsover had bought up all Teddy's debts, the full extent of which she did not know.

'Come, Jane, I am soon to be family and would help if I could. I will not repeat what you tell me.'

'Whether Papa can or cannot is not to the point, Mark. He simply refuses.'

'Oh, dear, does he know how deep in Teddy is?'

'I do not know, Teddy may have told him, but if matters are as bad as you say, Papa would have a struggle to settle, I think. Like everyone he has been badly hit by taxes and poor harvests. I shall do what I can for Teddy with my own money and that may hold his lordship off for a time.'

'Jane, you cannot do that. Your money is your dowry.'

She gave him a crooked grin. 'I am never likely to marry, Mark, and we all know it.'

'Nonsense. You would make someone a splendid wife and I know that you love children. I have seen you with them in the village.' He laughed suddenly. 'If I were not already taken, I might offer myself.'

She could not help it, the tears spilled from her eyes. It was so unlike the down-to-earth Jane, he became alarmed. He put his arm about her and pulled her to him, so that her head nestled on his shoulder. 'I didn't think that would make you cry, Jane. I beg forgiveness.'

Angry with herself, she pulled away from him. 'Oh, it wasn't that. It was…' She gulped. 'It was the thought of Teddy's debts bringing us so low.' She dried her eyes and managed a laugh. 'I could cheerfully beat him.'

'So could I.'

'Isabel knows nothing of it, so please do not say anything. We mustn't spoil her wedding. I have no doubt we will come about.'

'I will escort you home.'

'No, please don't. I shall be fine. Go back to Mr Ashton; he is obviously waiting for you.'

She nodded towards Drew, who was idling on the other side of the green.

It was typical of Jane, to be so unselfish, Mark thought as he rejoined Drew. She always thought of others before herself and that blinkered family of hers took her for granted. Even Isabel, while singing her praises, took advantage of her. As for their brother, he was a scapegrace without an ounce of conscience or good sense and to apply to his sister whenever he was in trouble was the outside of enough. He could pay the debt for them, but he was quite sure Sir Edward would be too proud to accept it, though he did not doubt Teddy would take it eagerly and then go on as before. It would be like throwing money into a bottomless pit. Teddy needed to be taught a salutary lesson. But what and how? It needed some thought and he would do nothing until after the wedding.

'If I did not know you better, I would think you were a little too fond of your future sister-in-law,' Drew said as they turned to walk back to Broadacres.

'Nonsense. I am afraid I unintentionally upset her.'

'Didn't look like that to me.'

'Looks can be deceptive and it is none of your business anyway, Drew.'

'True, and neither is it true of those old biddies

standing by that garden gate, but I have no doubt they will make it so.'

Mark glanced in the direction of Drew's nod. Mrs Stangate and her crony, Mrs Finch, were standing at the former's garden gate, watching them. 'Oh, no, the two biggest gossips in the village. They will add two and two and make five.'

'Whatever did you say to her? It must have been something very telling for you to abandon your usual sense of propriety.'

'I expressed the wish to beat her brother.'

Drew laughed. 'Oh, I assume you told her of our meeting with Lord Bolsover.'

'Yes, but she already knew some of what Teddy had been up to but, I suspect, not the whole. It makes me angry the way everyone in that family leans on Jane and expects her to fetch them out of whatever bumblebath they have tumbled into.'

'Is that so?'

'Yes. She has given up everything for them and is now proposing to use her own money to pay off Teddy's debt.'

'Does she know how much that is?'

'I don't think so. Nor do I think she has enough. According to Isabel, their grandmother left each of the girls a little money for a dowry. Isabel has already spent hers on her trousseau, so it cannot have been a great amount.'

'Tell me,' Drew said thoughtfully. 'Why did

you choose Isabel over Jane, when you so clearly have a high regard for her?'

Mark hesitated before replying, trying to find a satisfactory answer. 'A high regard is not love, is it? Jane has much to commend her, but I did not think of her in that way. Everyone, and that includes me, simply accepted that she was not going to marry and it became easy to think of her as Isabel's unmarried sister. Unfair, perhaps, but that is the way of it.' How unfair he was only now beginning to realise.

'And Isabel?'

'Isabel is beautiful and lively and she loves me. What more can a man ask?'

'What indeed,' Drew murmured.

'Have you never been in love?'

'Frequently. I have been in love with every mistress while it lasts, but it never does. They always reveal their true colours in the end.'

'Then you have not been in love at all. Love is meant to last a lifetime.'

'Is that so?'

'Yes. I fear you are too cynical, Drew. What has made you like that? Have you been disappointed?'

'I have just said so. Frequently.'

'I was not talking about mistresses and you know it. I meant a proper young lady.' He paused, remembering something Drew had said. 'Oh, the young lady who turned you down. That hurt, did it not?'

'At the time, yes.'

'So have you come back to try again?'

'No. It happened too long ago, we are both changed.'

'Who is she?'

'That would be telling.'

'Then tell.'

'One day, perhaps. Now can we change the subject? I find it exceedingly boring.'

Mark laughed. 'Very well, keep your secrets. Would you like to ride this afternoon? We could go round the estate and across the common to the fen. I can find you a good mount.'

'An excellent idea.'

They turned in at the wrought-iron gates of Broadacres and made their way up the gravel drive to the house. It was a very large house, testament to the wealth of the Wyndham forebears who had built it. Almost a castle, it had a turret on each of its four corners and a cantilevered flight of stone steps up to a huge oaken front door. Four storeys high and with a crenellated roof decorated with carvings, its long windows reflected the sun and shone like a myriad of mirrors. Mark loved it. It was his inheritance and it was to this home he would bring his bride. It was certainly extensive enough to support two families; he did not need or want to find another home for himself and Isabel.

'What do you think of Broadacres?' he asked his friend. 'Is it as you remember it?'

'Yes. Even better. Lord Wyndham has a good estate manager, methinks.'

'The best, but my father likes to involve himself in the running of it and he always tries to include me in any decisions, so when the time comes—though I pray it is a long time off—I will be able to take over with little or no disruption.'

'You have your life planned out so neatly, Mark, does nothing ever upset your equilibrium?'

'Occasionally, but I try not to let it. To be constantly up in the boughs is not good for one's health.'

Drew laughed. 'Then you and I must differ. I like a little excitement, doing something out of the ordinary just to feel I am alive.'

'Was India not exciting enough?'

'It had its moments.'

'Tell me about it. I promised Isabel we would travel widely for our wedding trip and India might be the place to go.'

'It is an extraordinary continent. There is enormous wealth and abject poverty side by side, and there are always battles of one kind or another between the natives and the East India Company. It is also very beautiful if you can tolerate the heat.

The best place to be in the summer months is up in the mountains. If you really intend to go and I have bought my ship, you could take passage on her. It will be my wedding gift to you both.'

'That is very generous of you, thank you.'

'Not at all. You and your parents have been generous to me. I have not forgotten that.'

'We shall have to find you a bride.'

'If I need a bride, I will find one for myself,' Drew said. 'I abhor matchmakers. Begging your pardon, my friend.'

Mark laughed and they climbed the steps and entered the cool interior of the house.

Jane walked home with her head in a whirl of mixed emotions. The last few days had upset the even tenor of her life. From helping her sister with her wedding, determined to make it the best she possibly could in the hope that it would settle her demons, she had been flung into what she could only call disarray. First there was Teddy and his problems, which were bad enough, then her father's revelation that they were not nearly as comfortable financially as everyone thought and now the sudden arrival of a ghost from the past which unnerved her. Was she as immune to him as she had always hoped she would be if they ever met again? Only time would tell; he had taken her breath away and made her heart beat fast, but what did that signify except surprise? How long did he intend to stay? According to Mark he was down for the wedding, still three weeks away. And to top it all, Mark had seen her cry and had taken her in his arms and the demon that sat on her shoulder had done a little dance of glee. At all costs she must conquer it.

She took the long way home in order to calm herself and put her mind to what was important, so she turned down a quiet lane that led into the ancient wood which shielded the house from the north wind that came down from the Arctic with nothing in its way to stop it.

The woods were quiet, but there were sounds if one took the trouble to listen. The song of the birds, always stronger in spring; the cooing of pigeons; the rustling of small animals in the last of the dead leaves; the sighing of the wind in the tree tops; the distant barking of a dog; her own, almost silent, footsteps. And there were other things to see and note: the buds on the chestnut trees; the unfurling of pale, new bracken stems; bluebells with their gently nodding heads; the odd browned leaf hanging on the bare branch of an oak, not yet in new leaf; a butterfly emerging from its chrysalis and drying its wings in a patch of sunlight filtering through the branches. Spring was a time of new beginnings, of hope. Where was her life going from here? Would she go on as she had been doing for the last ten years, or would it take a different direction? How could she best help her father?

She emerged on to the lane, crossed the narrow road and went through a gate which led to the back of the house. She stood a moment to look at it. It was old, but not as old as Broadacres, having been built just before the Civil War, when it was sequestered by the Parliamentarians and given to her father's ancestors for their service to the cause. They seemed not to have suffered for their allegiance because in the subsequent restoration of the monarchy, they had been allowed to keep the prize. It had all happened a hundred and fifty years before and Sir Edward rarely spoke of it. Jane had deduced he was perhaps a little disappointed that his forebears had not been granted a peerage, which would have set him above the common people. He made up for it with aspirations for his daughters, which was why he had been so against any connection between Jane and Andrew Ashton. Jane, who adored her father and always obeyed him, had sent her suitor away.

It would be untrue to say she had mourned his going ever since. She grieved for a year or so and then pulled herself together to settle into her role as the unmarried daughter and everyone's hopes had turned on Isabel. A marriage between Mark and Isabel had been talked of for years, but he had not formally proposed until he came back from the war. Ever since then everyone's attention had been concentrated on the wedding. But now, it seemed, that was destined to be overshadowed by financial problems. Her father had asked her to think of ways of retrenchment and she had so far done nothing about it. She would do so that very afternoon and draw up a list.

Pulling herself up, she quickened her pace and was soon indoors. Having shed her shawl and bonnet in her room, she went downstairs to the small parlour where she found her mother and Isabel scrutinising the guest list for the wedding. Most of their close friends and neighbours knew about it already, but there were others further afield that Lady Cavenhurst felt ought to be invited. In that they were at loggerheads with Sir Edward.

'Papa says we do not need to invite so many,' Isabel complained when Jane took a seat beside them. 'He says it is all getting out of hand and we must limit the number to fifty, when I had been planning on a hundred and fifty, at least.'

'Do we really know that many people?' Jane asked mildly.

'Of course we do. Papa is being unreasonable.'

'No doubt he has his reasons. Let me look at the list.'

Isabel handed it to her. 'But there is everyone

here you have ever spoken half-a-dozen words to, Issie,' she said, scanning it quickly. 'They would only come to stuff themselves at the banquet and not to wish you well. Would it not be better for it to be a little more intimate, with only close relations and friends who would be happy for you? Mark, I notice, has not asked for a great number to be invited and you do not want his guests to be overwhelmed by yours, do you? It would look like a slight, an effort to diminish him.'

'Would it? I hadn't thought of that. Now you have put a doubt in my mind. Mama, shall we cross some of them off?'

'Perhaps we should take another look at it,' her ladyship said. 'But we really cannot limit our guests to fifty—that would be parsimonious.'

It was evident to Jane that her mother either did not know or was shutting her eyes to the extent of their financial problems and her father had lacked the courage to tell her. Unless she had badly misjudged the situation he would have to do so soon

'There is one that will not be coming, I have discovered. I met Mark in the village and he told me Jonathan Smythe has been called away to a relation's death bed and he has appointed a new groomsman. No doubt he will tell you when he sees you.'

'Which will be tomorrow evening,' Lady

Cavenhurst said. 'We are all invited to Broad-acres for supper.'

'All of us?' Jane queried, her heart sinking.

'Yes, of course. Lady Wyndham would not leave anyone out, would she? Did Mark say who his new groomsman is to be?'

'Yes. Mr Andrew Ashton. He was with Mark when I met him.'

'Ashton!' exclaimed her mother. 'Why on earth did he choose him?'

'He is an old friend of Mark's, Mama, so why not?'

'Andrew Ashton,' Isabel murmured. 'Didn't he come and stay at Broadacres years ago?'

'I believe he did.' Jane said. 'He is much changed, having come back from India after making his fortune there.'

'India! Mark has said we may go there for our wedding trip. I shall enjoy asking Mr Ashton all about it. Mama, what shall we wear for this supper party? Is it to be formal?'

'No, dear, Lady Wyndham says informal on her invitation and there is to be music and cards.'

'Then we must contrive to keep Teddy away from the card table,' Jane said, a remark upon which they all agreed.

The interior of Broadacres was as imposing as the exterior. It had a grand entrance hall where

the cantilevered staircase of the outside was repeated with the addition of a wrought-iron bal-
ustrade. There was a long gallery lined on one
side with paintings, not only of the family, but of
landscapes and seascapes, horses, dogs and cattle. There were long windows on the other side,
which looked out over the sweep of the carriage
drive. Chairs and sofas were placed at intervals
and a long Turkish carpet laid down the centre
covered the stone flags. Off this gallery were
several beautifully furnished reception rooms,
a book room, a formal dining room and at the
far end, occupying the whole of the ground floor
of one wing, a magnificent ball room. Upstairs
the bedchambers were equally spacious and well
equipped.

'To think this will be your home,' Jane whispered to Isabel as they were conducted down the
gallery and along a corridor to the family withdrawing room. Ahead of them marched Sir Edward and Lady Cavenhurst and an unusually
subdued Teddy. 'You will one day be mistress
of it.'

'Oh, don't say that. It terrifies me. I wish we
could have our own place, something smaller and
less grand, but Mark will not hear of it. He says it
is so big we need never come across his parents
if we do not wish to.'

'I am sure you will manage very well.'

The footman who was conducting them opened the door of the withdrawing room and announced them one by one as they entered. As Lady Wyndham came forward to greet Sir Edward and his wife, Jane looked about her. Although it was a grand room, it had a comfortable feel about it, as if real people lived in it and used it, unlike the public rooms at the front of the building which seemed cold and impersonal.

She came out of her reverie when she heard Lady Wyndham introducing Drew to her father and mother and Sir Edward's response. 'I believe we have met, sir.'

'Indeed, you have,' Mark put in. 'Mr Ashton stayed with us for a few weeks when we left Cambridge. That was… How long ago, Drew?'

'I do believe it was all of ten years,' Drew responded. 'So long that I am not at all surprised that Sir Edward has forgot me. I was but a stripling with pockets to let.'

'Now he is a nabob.' Mark laughed. 'As rich as Golden Ball and certainly no stripling.'

'That much is evident,' Sir Edward said. Jane knew he was remembering and wondering if he had come to renew his suit. She had wondered about that herself, but dismissed the idea. Too much water had flowed under the bridge in those years.

Lady Wyndham turned to Jane. 'Do I need to introduce you to our guest, Jane?'

'No, for I remember him very well, but I doubt Isabel and Sophie do.'

'No, I don't,' Sophie said. 'I never met a nabob either. What does a nabob do?' She addressed her last remark to Drew, who was bowing in front of her.

'He trades in India, Miss Sophie,' he said. 'He sends Indian artefacts, spices and jewels back to these islands in fast ships and they return with items of English manufacture, furniture, ornaments, gowns, those sorts of things, and thereby he makes a profit.'

'And have you made a good profit, Mr Ashton?' This came from Isabel, who had been standing beside her sister, staring at Drew in fascination.

He bowed to her. 'Tolerable, Miss Isabel. You see, I do remember you, though you were still at your lessons at the time.'

'Let us sit down until supper is served,' Lady Wyndham said, ushering them towards chairs and sofas.

They arranged themselves about the room and Isabel contrived to be sitting next to Drew. 'Do tell me about India,' she said. 'Mark has promised to take me there after we are married and I would like to learn all I can before we go. Tell me,

is it necessary to speak the language and wear…
What do they call those gowns the natives wear?'

'Saris, Miss Isabel. They are more intricate
than they look, but they are very cool in the heat
and the fabrics are superb. I have known European women take to them when the heat has become too much.'

'Oh, I should dearly like to try one.'

'I am sure you would look charming,' he said.

'And what about the language? Is it difficult
to learn?'

'There are several languages in India, but you
would not need to learn any of them. The native
servants speak a kind of pidgin English and, apart
from visits to the bazaar, you would not need to
communicate with other natives. And you would
never go to the bazaar unless accompanied by
someone familiar with the language and customs.'

Jane watched this exchange with some misgiv-
ing. It was not polite of her sister to monopolise
the gentleman, certainly not at the expense of
Mark, who was standing by the window watching them. On the pretence of looking out at the
terrace and formal gardens beyond it, she went
over to stand beside him.

'She means no harm, Mark,' she whispered.
'She is simply interested because you said you
would take her to India.'

'I know.'

A footman came to tell them supper was served and they made their way into the dining room. They were silent while the servants waited on them, but the conversation began again when they stood aside, this time led by Lord Wyndham and Sir Edward, who began a discussion about the dire state of the nation's economy. The year before had been miserable, with no summer to speak of, the crops failing and labourers and returning soldiers out of work. There was unrest among them everywhere. At the end of the year there had been a mass meeting at Spa Fields, addressed by Henry Hunt, who had a gift for rabble-rousing, and the whole thing had got out of hand and had to be quelled by the militia. Revolutionary plots were being uncovered everywhere, which had led the Government to suspend habeas corpus and outlaw seditious meetings.

'It is a mercy we have escaped here in Hadlea,' his lordship said. 'I have managed to keep all my men employed and even take on one or two more. No doubt it is the same with you, Cavenhurst?'

'Indeed,' Sir Edward said, though he did not elaborate. Jane knew he had not taken on any men for some time, not even when old Crabtree retired at the age of eighty and one of the younger men went off to pastures new.

'At least there is some good news,' Lady Wyndham put in. 'Princess Charlotte is with child again and there are high hopes that she will carry this one to full term.'

'Let us hope so,' Lord Wyndham said. 'A new heir to the throne will divert people from their dislike of the Regent.' An attempt on the Prince Regent's life had been made in January when an unknown assailant fired at his carriage on the way back from opening Parliament, but fortunately he had been unhurt.

'I am concerned for the soldiers' orphans,' Jane said. 'They are living on the streets, learning nothing but to be beggars and thieves. They need homes and a little education to fit them for work when they are old enough.'

'Yes, it is sad,' her mother said. 'But, Jane, I am sure Lord and Lady Wyndham do not want to hear of your project.'

'On the contrary,' Lord Wyndham said. 'I, for one, am interested and should like to hear about it.' He was a very big man, both in height and breadth, with a round red face, but he smiled a lot and was easy to talk to.

Given a ready listener, Jane launched into an explanation of what she hoped to do, while his lordship and the rest of the company listened intently. She was glad of the audience, it gave her the opportunity to test her persuasive skills. 'I intend to start with something small, taking local children,' she said. 'But even a small home will be costly to run properly. We have to find sponsors.'

'Jane!' Her mother was shocked by this talk of money over the supper table.

Lord Wyndham laughed. 'You daughter is undoubtedly passionate about the subject. I like that and you may count on me for a donation, Miss Cavenhurst.'

'Thank you, my lord, I am indeed grateful.'

'I, too, will add to your funds,' Drew said. 'What about you, Mark?'

'Miss Cavendish explained her plans to me some time ago,' Mark said. 'I have already promised my contribution.'

'Everyone is being very free with their blunt,' Teddy murmured to Jane.

'Yes, isn't it wonderful?' she whispered back. 'It's better than gambling it away.'

Annoyed by this barb, he turned away and concentrated on eating.

'Now let us talk of more pleasant matters,' Lady Wyndham said. She was an excellent hostess and had seen, if not heard, the exchange between Jane and her brother. 'How are the wedding plans coming along, Grace?'

Lady Cavenhurst was glad to answer and the meal ended pleasantly and was followed in the drawing room with the girls taking it in turns to play the pianoforte and sing, while a card table was set up for those who wished to play. It was late when the party broke up and Sir Edward's carriage was brought to the door to take them home.

Chapter Three

'Mr Ashton is a fascinating man, don't you think?' Isabel asked Jane. 'He has been everywhere and done everything and is so interesting to talk to.'

It was the day after the supper party and the girls and their mother were sitting in the small parlour. Jane was sewing tiny beads on to the skirt of the wedding gown, while Lady Cavenhurst and Isabel sat at the table, writing the invitations on cards.

'So he may be,' Jane said, 'but I think it ill of you to monopolise him in conversation and ignore poor Mark.'

'Oh, Mark did not mind it. He knows how much I want to travel.' She picked up one of the invitations. 'There, I have made a blot on that one. Pass me another, Mama, please.'

'How many have you crossed off the list?' Jane queried.

'About a quarter. We could not take any more off without giving offence and we don't want Papa to look a pinchcommons, do we?'

'I do not think catering for fifty is mean, Issie. Papa is worried about the cost. You know what he said this morning.'

Earlier that day Sir Edward had come in from going round the estate with his steward and found his wife and daughters in the morning room, talking about the wedding. Seizing the opportunity of finding them all together, he had delivered a homily on the need to economise. It was a word unknown to Lady Cavenhurst and Isabel. Jane had produced the list she had made, beginning with the notion that they could all spend less on clothes, bonnets and shoes, which had raised a cry of protest from Isabel and Sophie. A second suggestion was that they often wasted food and that Cook should be instructed not to buy exotic produce like lemons and pineapples and only to use fruit and vegetables grown in their own kitchen gardens and to cook no more than was needed for the numbers sitting down to eat. Her ladyship had said that Cook would not like that at all and the provisions for the wedding feast had already been ordered.

'Unfortunately, even that will not be enough,' Sir Edward had said. 'I am afraid there will have to be serious retrenchment.'

Jane had consulted her list again. 'Then we could cut down on the number of servants. We do not really need three chambermaids and three parlourmaids, and if we helped in the garden ourselves we would not need so many gardeners. I, for one, would not mind doing that. And we could do without the carriage if we had to.'

'Do without the carriage!' her mother protested. 'How are we to go about without one? Tell me that.'

'We could keep the pony and trap,' Jane said. 'One pony is cheaper to keep than four horses and then we would not need more than one groom; Daniel can manage on his own. If we needed to travel further afield, we could go by stage.'

'Go by stage!' Her mother was affronted. 'Impossible.'

'Perhaps I could take paid employment to help,' Jane went on, ignoring her mother's exclamation. She wondered if her mother really understood the gravity of the situation or was simply shutting her eyes to it.

'Heaven forbid!' her ladyship exclaimed. 'You have not been brought up to work, Jane. And what can you do in any case?'

'I can sew.'

'Like Miss Smith, I suppose.'

'No, not like Miss Smith, though there is nothing wrong with what she does. I meant designing and making high-class gowns. Or I could teach. I think I should find that rewarding.'

'Bless you, Jane,' Sir Edward said. 'I hope it will not come to that.'

'Well, I will not hear of it,' his wife said. 'You will make paupers of us.'

'There is no question of that,' he said, trying to smile. 'But we do have to find ways of making substantial savings and the longer we put off doing so, the harder it will be.'

'What about my wedding?' Isabel had wailed.

'I am not proposing to curtail your wedding, Isabel,' her father told her. 'But please limit the guests to fifty and try not to be extravagant over the banquet.'

'We will postpone any decision about savings until after the wedding,' her ladyship said firmly. 'Once Isabel is married, no doubt Sophie will follow shortly afterwards and our expenses will not be so great. We may come about without all these measures.'

Sir Edward gave up and left them. No one had mentioned Teddy's problems, but he was going to have to mend his ways whether he liked it or not. There was no question in Jane's mind that her inheritance would have to go.

She set the gown aside on a nearby chair. 'Let me look at the list.'

'No,' Isabel said. 'You will cross everyone off

and Mama has approved it. You shall not spoil
my wedding, Jane.'

'Will it spoil it if you have only fifty guests?'

'Of course it will. I want everyone to see me
in my wedding gown, marrying the most eligible
bachelor for miles around.'

'The wedding is not the be-all and end-all of a
marriage, Issie. It is only the beginning.'

'I know that. Do you take me for a fool? And
what do you know of it?'

'Girls, do stop brangling,' her ladyship put in.
'It is not becoming and I cannot see how a hand-
ful of guests can make you so up in the boughs,
Jane dear. It is so unlike you.'

The arrival of a maid to tell them that Mr
Wyndham and Mr Ashton had arrived and were
asking if the ladies were at home put an end to
the conversation and set Isabel in a panic. 'Mark
mustn't see the dress, Jane. It is unlucky before
the day. Put it away quickly.' She jumped up from
her seat and knocked over the ink bottle. Its contents ran across the table and over the chair on
which Jane had put the dress. Isabel's terrible
shriek brought the two gentlemen running into
the room.

'What has happened?' Mark demanded. 'Are
you hurt, Isabel?'

'Go away. Go away,' she shouted in a parox-
ysm of angry tears.

'But, my dear, you are distressed.'

'We have had a little accident with the wedding dress,' Jane told him. She was trying to be calm, but the sight of that black stain on the skirt of the dress had made her heart sink. The beautiful fabric and all those hours of work were ruined. She could have cried herself, but one sobbing woman was enough. 'I will calm my sister, if you will excuse us for a few minutes.'

'Of course, we will go away and come back later.'

'That would be best,' Lady Cavenhurst said, as she put her arm about her younger daughter to comfort her.

As they bowed their way out Jane rang the bell for a maid to come and clean the table, then she spread the gown out to inspect the damage. 'It might wash out if we are quick,' she said.

'No, it is ruined,' Isabel cried. 'How can I go to my wedding in a gown that has been washed? It is a bad omen, a very bad omen.'

'Do not be so melodramatic, Issie,' Jane scolded. 'I will see if there is enough material left over to replace that panel.' She doubted if there was, but she had to console Isabel somehow.

'There,' her ladyship said. 'Jane does not think it is irretrievable. Do dry your eyes and go up to your room to wash your face, while Jane sees what can be done.'

'It was her fault,' Isabel said with an angry pout. 'She should not have been sitting so close to the table where I was writing.'

Jane was taken aback and opened her mouth to protest, then shut it again. Isabel was in no mood to be reasonable.

'I do not know what is the matter with you girls today,' their mother said. 'I have not heard you quarrel so much since you were tiny children. This wedding is setting everyone at odds with each other.'

A servant arrived to clean up the table and the carpet where some of the ink had spilled and her ladyship helped Isabel from the room, leaving Jane to gather up the gown, being careful not to smear the ink on any other part of it. She carried it up to Miss Smith's workroom, to find the left-over material.

There were several small pieces but not one large enough for a whole panel. She would need some ingenuity to refashion the skirt to make use of them. A join could perhaps be disguised with a band of ribbon, but she would have to put it on all the panels to make it look as if it were meant it to be like that. She would have to unpick some of the embroidery and redesign it around the ribbon. It could be done, but what worried her more and had been doing so for some time now, was her sister's attitude to the wedding. She did not seem to be able to look beyond it to what married life would really be like. 'But what do I know about it?' she murmured to herself, as she sat down and began unpicking. 'An old maid with no prospects of ever enjoying the role of wife.'

She had been working there perhaps half an hour when her mother joined her. 'I have given Isabel a tisane and she has gone to sleep,' she said. 'She was a little calmer and is relying on you to rescue the gown.'

'I think I can, but I will need to have a join halfway down the skirt. I thought of disguising it with ribbon. I am unpicking the skirt now.'

'It was very naughty of her to blame you. I am sure she will apologise when she wakes up.'

'It doesn't matter.'

'Jane, are you very unhappy?'

'Unhappy, Mama, what makes you think that?'

'I thought perhaps the arrival of Mr Ashton might have cast you in the suds.'

Jane managed to laugh. 'After ten years, Mama? Certainly not.'

'I am glad. I know he is now wealthy and sure of himself, but his wealth has come from trade; he is still not a gentleman, nor ever can be.'

'Not in the sense you mean it, Mama, but gentlemanly behaviour and good manners can be learned and I doubt Mr Ashton's antecedents, or lack of them, will make him any less popular in the *ton*.'

'So, you do still have feelings for him?'

'No, Mama, I do not. I was simply trying to be fair to him.' She realised suddenly that what she had said was true. It was not Andrew Ashton who disturbed her heart, but someone much closer to home.

'It is so like you to see the good in everyone, Jane. But if it is not Mr Ashton, what is troubling you?'

'It is Isabel. She seems not to be able to look beyond the wedding day itself and I am afraid she is in for a rude awakening.'

'I cannot think why. Mark is the best of men, he can be relied upon to do his best to make her happy. You must not begrudge her her day, just because…' Her ladyship stopped in mid-sentence.

'Because I will never have one of my own, is that what you were going to say, Mama? Do not think it. I do not. I am content with my life as it is.'

'But every young lady dreams of being married.'

'Not every young lady, Mama.' She was firm on that score, as much to convince herself as her mother.

'You are a good daughter and a good sister, Jane. I would not change you for the world. Teddy tells me you are going to help him out of the coil he is in, since his papa will not, in spite of my pleading.'

'I didn't exactly say I would, I said I would think about it. It will take all of Aunt Matilda's bequest and I so wanted to use it for my orphanage.'

'Papa will make it up to you, when he has calmed down, I am sure.' She watched as Jane detached the stained skirt panel and set it aside. 'Now, put that away and come downstairs for nuncheon. I have no doubt the gentlemen will be back later this afternoon and we must offer our excuses for Isabel and make little of this morning's episode.'

Jane had done as she was bid and was back at her sewing in the parlour while her mother finished off the invitations when Mark and Drew returned.

'Forgive me for returning so soon,' Mark said, bowing to her ladyship. 'But I was concerned for Isabel. She was so distraught, I feared she was going to make herself ill.'

'It was the shock of seeing the ink on her lovely wedding gown,' her ladyship told him, beckoning the young men to be seated and instructing the maid to bring refreshments. 'She is calm again now that she knows Jane can put it right.'

'I am working on it now,' Jane said. 'I am hopeful that no one will ever know it has been altered.'

'Dear Jane,' Mark said. 'So dependable, so calm in a crisis. We are indebted to you.'

Jane felt the colour flood her face. 'You are a flatterer, sir. I beg you to desist. I only do what any sister would do.'

'That is for others to judge.' To have calmly said she would rescue the gown after Isabel herself had spoiled it and blamed her for it was unselfish to a degree. Isabel had not bothered to lower her voice and it had carried clearly as they were leaving. Delightful Isabel might be, delightful and beautiful, but she also had a fiery temperament, which took no account of other people's feelings. Yet Jane was always thinking of other people before herself. Why was he comparing them? He had been doing too much of that lately and it did not bode well.

'I had better put this away.' She folded the gown in its tissue and laid it to one side. 'Now we can have tea without fear of another spillage.'

'How did it happen?' Drew spoke for the first time.

'Isabel is convinced that it is unlucky for the bridegroom to see the wedding dress before the bride joins him at the altar. She was in haste to have it out of sight before you were shown in and so managed to overturn the ink bottle.'

'I thought it might be that,' he said. 'I am glad the gown is not ruined, but I brought this for your sister in the hope it might make up a little for her loss.' He picked up the brown paper parcel he had been holding on his knee and handed it to Lady Cavenhurst. 'If you would be so kind as to allow her to accept it?'

'What is it?' her ladyship asked, a little doubtfully.

'It is nothing very much, my lady. A length of silk for a sari. Miss Isabel expressed an interest last evening. If she does not wish to use it as a sari, I believe there is enough material to make a gown. Call it a wedding present.'

'How very kind of you.' Her ladyship unwrapped the parcel to find a length of silk in a deep pink that was very similar to that of the wedding gown. There was yards and yards of it but, because it was so fine, it could be folded into a very small parcel.

'It is beautiful,' Jane said, reaching forward to touch it. 'Isabel will be thrilled with it. Mark, what do you say?'

'Oh, undoubtedly,' he answered.

'I brought it from India,' Drew said. 'Not only that one, but several others. When I knew I was coming here, I put them in my baggage as gifts for the ladies.' He grinned suddenly. 'It is good business, you know. The ladies wear gowns made of the silk and when they are asked where they came by them, they refer to me. I chose that one for Miss Isabel because I noticed the colour of the one that had been spoiled.'

'How thoughtful of you,' murmured Lady Cavenhurst. 'And if Mark has no objection, I will make sure she has it.'

'I have no objection, why should I?' Mark said. 'Drew has already presented my mother with one.'

'Would you care for one, Lady Cavenhurst?' Drew asked.

'That is very kind of you, sir, but I think not. I do not have the figure for such a thing.'

'As you wish.' He turned to Jane. 'What about you, Miss Cavenhurst? Would you like one?'

'As Mama said, it is very kind of you, but I could not possibly accept such a gift. It is enough that you have promised to donate to my orphan charity.' It was the answer expected of an unmarried lady, but she could not help feeling a pang of disappointment. She had never seen or touched so fine a fabric.

Isabel, who had heard and seen the gentlemen arrive from her bedchamber window, had hurriedly renewed her *toilette* and came to join them. Both men stood up and Mark hurried to take both her hands in his. 'Are you feeling better, my dear?'

'Yes, don't fuss, Mark. I was upset because I thought my gown was ruined, but Mama told me Jane can fix it, so all is not lost, after all.' She turned to Drew. 'Good afternoon, Mr Ashton. I am sorry I did not greet you properly earlier. Please forgive me.' This was said with a dazzling smile.

He bowed to her. 'It is understandable, Miss Isabel. Gentlemen sometimes do not understand the importance of a lady's dress.'

She gave a tinkling laugh. 'But you do, is that so?'

Jane was shocked at her sister's offhand treatment of Mark and her obvious attempt to flirt with Drew. 'Sit down, Issie,' she said. 'The gentlemen cannot be seated again until you do.'

Jane was sitting beside her mother on one sofa, so Isabel sat on the other. Mark seated himself beside her and Drew found a chair. It was then Isabel noticed the silk in her mother's lap. 'What have you there, Mama?'

'It is a sari, my love. A wedding present to you from Mr Ashton.'

'A sari! Oh, Mama, may I accept it?'

'Mark has said you may, so I have no objection.'

Isabel was on her feet again and letting the material cascade over her arm in shining ripples. 'It's lovely,' she said, bright-eyed. 'Oh, thank you, Mr Ashton. You are so thoughtful, I am overwhelmed.'

'I thought it could be used for a new wedding gown if the other was ruined.'

'But it is not ruined and I want to keep this as a sari. There are yards and yards of it. How is it worn?'

'I think you will need the help of your maid. There is a knack to it.'

'Bessie would not have any idea. Can you show me?'

'Isabel, I am sure Bessie will manage it when you are in your own room,' her mother said. 'The parlour is hardly the place to dress, especially with gentlemen present.'

'Mr Ashton can show me on himself.'

'Isabel!' Her mother was shocked.

'I am too big and too clumsy,' Drew said, laughing. 'I have printed instructions with illustrations for the benefit of European ladies. I will have a copy sent over for your maid to study.'

'That will serve admirably,' her ladyship said. 'Isabel, I suggest you fold it up and take it to your room before you knock your tea all over it.'

'Anyone would think I was clumsy,' she said.

'No, but you are somewhat excitable,' her mother said. 'I beg you to calm yourself.'

Isabel disappeared with the sari and the others drank their tea in silence for a minute or two. Jane was shocked by her sister's behaviour. She would not blame Mark if he gave her a put down when he managed to find her on her own. What motive did Mr Ashton have for making the gift? Was it simply as he had said, a wish to help over the accident with the gown, or was there more to it? He was evidently attracted to her sister. Was Isabel aware of it? Was Mark? He would never believe ill of Isabel. Or was she herself seeing more than was really there?

'The weather is set fair for the next few days,' Mark said. 'I promised to show Drew more of our county and we plan an excursion to Cromer tomorrow. I wondered if Miss Cavenhurst and Isabel might like to join us, if you and they agree, my lady?'

'I can see no harm in it,' her ladyship said. 'What do you say, Jane? Do you think Isabel would like it?'

'I am sure she would,' Jane answered. She was not so sure about wanting to go herself, but if her sister went then she would have to go, too, or their mother would never allow it.

'That's settled then,' Mark said, rising to leave. 'We will come at ten o'clock tomorrow morning with the carriage.'

The men bowed to the ladies and left.

'When did you think of an outing to Cromer?' Drew asked, as they walked back to Broadacres. 'You did not mention it before we came.'

'I thought the ladies might like it. It might serve to put Isabel in a calmer frame of mind and give Jane a little reward for the hard work she does. You have no objection, have you?'

'None at all.'

Wyndham's carriage was as comfortable as any well-sprung travelling coach could be; there was plenty of room inside for four. Hadlea to Cromer was not above twenty miles and they arrived in a little under two hours, having spent the time in idle chatter, most of it led by Isabel quizzing Drew about India and his travels.

They pulled up at an inn in the lower part of the village near the church, where Jeremy, the coachman, and the horses would be looked after while they strolled along the beach. It had been warm in the coach, but as soon as they were out of it, they felt the cool breeze blowing off the sea. 'I am glad we decided to bring warm shawls,' Jane said, wrapping hers closer about her. Like her sister, she was wearing a muslin gown and a sarsenet pelisse. Hers was striped in two shades of green, Isabel's was white. They both wore straw bonnets firmly tied on with ribbon.

'Would you prefer to stay in the carriage?' Mark asked her. 'Or go to a hotel?'

'Certainly not,' she answered. 'I came for the

bracing sea air and that is what I mean to have. What about you, Issie?'

'Me, too. I am sure the gentlemen do not want to be cooped up indoors and I am not a bit cold. I want to go down on the sand.'

'Then you shall,' Mark said, offering her his arm.

She took it, leaving Jane to walk beside Drew, though she did not take his arm. They strolled down a narrow cobbled road at the end of which they had their first view of the beach and the sea. 'It looks cold,' Jane said.

'It nearly always is,' Mark said, turning to her with a chuckle. 'There is nothing between Cromer and the Arctic, except sea. But at least that is calm today. Would you like to go bathing? It is supposed to be beneficial and there are machines down there if you would like it.' It was early in the summer, though a few brave souls were taking a dip.

'No, I do not think so,' she said. 'I shall be content to watch.'

'It must seem even colder to you, Mr Ashton, after the heat of India,' Isabel said.

'Oh, I am a hardy soul, Miss Isabel. I might take a dip myself. What do you say, Mark?' There were men in the sea a little further along the beach, but the girls would not go near them, for they nearly always took to the water naked, unlike the women who were hampered by voluminous clothing and did not stir far from the bathing machines where they changed.

'I think I should stay with the ladies,' Mark said. 'But do you go if you have a mind to.'

Drew would not go alone and all four made their way down a cliff path on to the sand. The beach was not crowded and they walked towards the water's edge. Jane was more inclined to stride out when they reached the firmer wet sand and Mark kept up with her. Drew, behind them, stooped to pick up a flat round stone and threw it into the sea in such a way it bounced along the waves two or three times before it disappeared.

Isabel clapped her hands. 'Oh, how clever of you, Mr Ashton! Do show me how to do it.'

He picked up another stone and put it into her hand. 'You need to throw it quite hard and keep the trajectory low,' he said. 'Set it spinning flat as it leaves your hand.'

She tried and failed and tried again. 'No, do it like this,' he said, taking her hand and closing her fingers round the stone. Mark and Jane, who had gone a little ahead, turned to see why the other two were not close behind and were greeted with the sight of Drew with his arms about Isabel, trying to direct her aim. And they were both laughing.

'Oh, dear,' Jane said. 'Isabel has no sense of

propriety at all. It is as well there is no one on the beach who knows us.'

'It is not her fault,' Mark said. 'Drew sometimes forgets he is not still in India where no doubt such familiarity is allowed.'

Jane did not know how accurate that statement was, but it was so like Mark to see no harm in his beloved. She hurried back to her sister, followed by Mark.

'Drew has been teaching me how to make a pebble bounce,' Isabel called to them. 'Do come and try it.'

Jane could not rebuke her sister in front of others, but as they walked further along the beach she contrived to draw her out of earshot of the gentlemen. 'I hate to scold, Issie, but really, you should not have allowed Mr Ashton to put his arm round you, nor should you have referred to him by his given name. Surely, you know better that that.'

'Oh, don't be such a fusspot, Jane. There was no harm in him showing me how to spin a pebble and Mark always uses Mr Ashton's given name. It just slipped out.'

'I am sure it did, but do try to be more careful.'

'You are a fine one to talk. You have been seen in the village with Mark's arms about you. Sophie had it off her friend, Maud Finch. Mrs Finch saw you with her own eyes.'

Jane had a vague memory of seeing Mrs Finch

talking to Mrs Stangate when she met Mark and Drew on the village green. 'I stumbled and he prevented me from falling,' she said. 'You may trust Mrs Finch to make a mountain out of a mole-hill and Sophie should not have repeated it.'

'You have quite ruined my day with your scolding.' Isabel pouted. 'I was having such fun.'

But it was not long before she was holding her skirts up in her hand and racing over the sand to the water's edge, laughing as the waves rippled over her kid shoes, which would undoubtedly be thrown out when they arrived home. Jane felt un-happy about the rebuke. It had made her sound a killjoy and she had not meant it to be like that at all. Her concern was for Mark. He had said nothing and even tried to excuse Isabel, but un-derneath he must have been feeling hurt. And if Mrs Finch's gossip reached his ears he would be doubly embarrassed.

Further along the beach they watched some fishing boats unloading their cargo of crabs and Mark bought two for the girls to take home for their cook and then they returned to the prom-enade for refreshments in the Red Lion. A short walk along the cliff top followed when they all used Drew's telescope to scan the beach and the horizon.

'How close everything looks,' Jane said. 'Why,

I can see the sailors on the deck of that ship and its name quite clearly. It's called *Morning Star.*'

'That is the vessel that brought me home from India,' Drew said. 'It is a very good ship, well run and fast. It is something like that I have a mind to purchase.'

'And then Mark and I will go to India on it,' Isabel said. 'Three more weeks to go. I can't wait. Will you be sailing on her, too, Mr Ashton?'

'It depends on what turns up,' he said. 'Perhaps.'

'I think it is time we made our way back to the coach,' Jane said. 'Mama will be wondering what has become of us.'

The coach deposited them back at the Manor at five o'clock. Jane and Isabel said goodbye to their escorts and carried the parcel of crabs into the house. They were tired but happy, ready to regale their mother with what they had seen and done. No one that evening thought about tragedy and Isabel had ceased to moan about bad omens and suchlike fancies.

They had not expected to see Mark again so soon, but he arrived at an unheard-of hour next morning, looking so sorrowful that Jane immediately wondered what was wrong. Sir Edward had gone out to the stables to check on one of the horses that seemed lame, but the ladies were still seated at the breakfast table.

He bowed to them all. 'I am sorry to disturb you so early,' he said. 'But I am afraid I bring dreadful news and I did not want you to hear it from anyone else.' He paused and gulped, then went on. 'My father passed away in his sleep last night.'

Lady Cavenhurst was the first to recover from the shock. 'Oh, you poor man,' she said. 'What a dreadful thing to happen. His lordship seemed so well when we dined with you the other evening.'

'His valet found him when he went to wake him this morning and immediately alerted me,' he said. 'I sent for Dr Trench, though I knew it was too late to do anything for him. His heart just gave out, the doctor told me. As you can imagine, my mother is distraught.'

'Poor Lady Wyndham,' Jane said. 'Is there anything we can do?'

'I do not think so. Later, perhaps, she might appreciate a visit.' He turned to Isabel, who was staring at him as if he were an apparition. 'Isabel, I am so sorry, but the wedding will have to be postponed while I am in mourning.'

'Postponed,' she echoed, then burst into tears.

Jane ran to comfort her. 'Hush, Issie, you must be brave for Mark's sake. He will have a great deal to do in the next few weeks.'

'That is true,' he agreed. 'And I am afraid I must go. I will let you know about the arrangements for the funeral later. Isabel, will you accompany me to the front door? That is if her ladyship agrees.'

'Of course. Go along, Isabel. And please offer my condolences to your mother, my lord.'

He managed a wry smile. 'I suppose I will have to get used to that, but please don't stand on formality, my lady. I was Mark, I remain Mark to you.' He reached out a hand to Isabel. 'Come, my dear, I wish to talk to you.'

Isabel took the hand and together they left the room. Jane and her mother were left looking at each other, not knowing what to say.

'This is dreadful news indeed,' her ladyship said. 'I feel for poor Lady Wyndham. Theirs was a true love match. I wonder how long a period of mourning there will be?'

'A year is usual, Mama.'

'I know. We shall have to help Isabel bear up. And I suppose I had better make a start on cancelling the wedding invitations and ask Cook to cancel the orders for the banquet.' She smiled suddenly. 'At least your father will be spared the expense of it for now.'

Jane supposed someone had to think of the practicalities, but she was more concerned with how Mark and his mother were feeling and her heart went out to them. To lose one so dear so suddenly must be very hard to bear.

Chapter Four

Mark returned to Broadacres, overwhelmed by misery and the weight of responsibility that now rested on his shoulders. There was so much to do and a wedding was the last thing on his mind. Isabel had been upset, which was understandable, he supposed, but he had managed to calm her before he left, telling her the time of mourning would soon pass and then they would have the wedding she dreamed of.

'We might not be able to have the long wedding trip we planned,' he had told her. 'There will be much to do on the estate. But perhaps we will be able to go later when I am settled into my new role. It has come so suddenly, I cannot take it all in.'

'Mama called you "my lord". That really brought home to me what has happened and how your life will change. You might not be the same person at all.'

'Nonsense. I shall not change just because I have inherited a title and an estate. You, of course, will become Lady Wyndham when we marry.'

'And shall I be mistress of Broadacres?'

'Naturally, you will.'

'I am not sure I shall be any good at it. I might let you down.'

'Oh, you silly goose,' he had said, dropping a kiss on her forehead. 'Of course you will not let me down and you will have the mourning period to become used to the idea. Now I must go. I shall see you again when you and your mother call on my mother.'

Lady Wyndham, he was told when he arrived home and enquired for her, had been given a tisane by her maid and was resting in her room. He did not disturb her, but spoke to the steward about matters of the estate, telling him to carry on as usual, then he set about writing letters to everyone who needed to be told of his father's demise. It was sad work and he had to stop frequently to overcome his emotion. His father had been the best of fathers, spending time with him as he grew up, teaching him to shoot, fish and ride, making sure he had a good education, instilling in him a sense of what was right and proper, and showing him by example to care for those around him. 'High and low, we are all human beings,' he had said once. 'We should treat everyone with the dignity they deserve whether they be the poorest labourer or the king of England.' Now he was no more.

Already the news was becoming known in the village and people were going about with long faces. Many of the servants and even the hardy outside staff were openly weeping. Lord Wyndham had been a popular figure, known for his humanity and fairness. Mark prayed he would be able to live up to his father's ideals.

Drew came to him as he was finishing the last of the letters. 'I assume there will be no wedding yet a while,' he said. 'And now is not the time for house guests. I plan to leave for London by tonight's mail.'

'I shall miss you, Drew.'

'And I you. But I will return for the funeral, if you would like me to.'

'Of course. Next Thursday, here in Hadlea.'

'Please convey my gratitude to Lady Wyndham for her generous hospitality. I have written her a note, which I have asked her maid to pass on to her when she is feeling up to receiving it.'

'That is kind of you.'

'And express my good wishes and condolences to Miss Isabel. It is going to be hard for her to have the wedding postponed and cope with a very different life from the one she envisaged. How did she take the news?'

'She is very sad, of course, but took it well enough, all things considered. She has the support of her mother and Jane, for which I am grateful, for I cannot give her the attention I would like just now.'

'I am sure they understand. Now, if you will excuse me, I shall go and pack.'

'There is something you can do for me,' Mark said, as they shook hands. 'Will you make sure my letters go on the mail?'

'Gladly.'

'I've just one more to write. I'll send them to you when they are ready. Jeremy will drive you to the Fox and Hounds.'

Drew left and Mark pulled another sheet of notepaper towards him, dipped his pen in the ink and resumed writing.

An hour later he was free to receive Lady Cavenhurst and her three daughters. All four bent the knee and addressed him as 'my lord', which made him feel thoroughly uncomfortable and he begged them not to change towards him.

'How is your dear mother?' Lady Cavenhurst asked. 'I would not intrude on her grief if she does not wish it.'

Even as she spoke Lady Wyndham entered the

room. She was dressed in unrelieved black, but was dry-eyed and upright. 'Grace, thank you for coming,' she said.

Lady Cavenhurst hurried towards her and took both her hands in her own. 'Helen, I am so very, very sorry. If there is anything we can do for you, you have only to ask.'

'There is nothing that I can think of. Will you be seated?'

They sat in a little circle, not knowing what to say until Jane spoke. 'Lord Wyndham will be sorely missed by everyone who knew him,' she said. 'He was such a good, kind man, always ready to listen and so generous, too.'

'Yes, he was, wasn't he?' Lady Wyndham smiled suddenly. 'I remember when he found Jeremy as a child running about the streets of London and brought him home. He was filthy and verminous, but nothing would do but he should be given a bath and new clothes and fed. He slept in the stables and has been with us ever since.'

'You mean Jeremy, your coachman?' Isabel queried.

'Yes, he has grown into a fine man and would do anything for my husband and for Mark, too.'

'That is why his lordship listened to my tale of wanting to set up a home for war orphans,' Jane said. 'He understood.'

'His promise will be honoured, Jane,' Mark said quietly.

She turned to him and noticed the sparkle of tears in his eyes and her heart went out to him. The pity of it was that she could not tell him so. 'Thank you, Mark, but you have more important matters to deal with, I am sure.'

'Have you decided on the funeral?' Lady Cavenhurst asked him.

'Yes. It is to be in St Peter's in Hadlea next Thursday. The Bishop of Norwich and the Reverend Caulder will officiate. There will, of course, be refreshments here afterwards and the reading of the will.'

'I shall mourn for the rest of my days,' Lady Wyndham said. 'But we will not keep Mark and Isabel waiting too long for their wedding. I want to see grandchildren playing about the place before I leave this world. I think six months will be enough for the official mourning.'

'Thank you,' Isabel said. 'You are very kind.'

'I have no doubt you have much to do,' Lady Cavenhurst said, rising. 'We will take our leave. Please do not hesitate to send for us if there is anything we can do for you.'

As they were leaving they met Drew on the gravel in front of the house. He was about to climb into the gig which was to take him to the Fox and Hounds. He bowed to each of them. 'Ladies, I regret I cannot stop and talk. The mail is due in twenty minutes.'

'Are you leaving?' Isabel asked with something like dismay in her voice.

'Yes, Miss Isabel. I would not intrude on the household grief, but I shall come back for the funeral. Lord Wyndham was very good to me, when I was struggling to make my way.' He bowed again, climbed into the gig and was driven away.

The pony and trap in which Jane had driven them to Broadacres was waiting for them at the door. It was just big enough to seat four comfortably. She was a competent driver and enjoyed bowling about the village in it, though her mother and Isabel much preferred the coach.

'It was considerate of Lady Wyndham to think of you, Issie,' Jane said, skilfully turning the pony towards the entrance gates. 'In the midst of her sorrow, she is still thinking of others. Six months is not so long to wait and the time will soon pass.'

'I knew spilling that ink on my gown and letting Mark see it was a bad omen,' Isabel said. 'And I have been proved right.'

'That is just a silly superstition,' her mother told her. 'Do not think of it.'

'It is not the only one about weddings,' Sophie piped up. 'It is said a postponed wedding never takes place.'

'Sophie, how could you?' Lady Cavenhurst re-

monstrated as Isabel burst into tears. 'There was
no call to repeat such nonsense. You have upset
your sister, for no good reason.'

'Sorry,' she mumbled.

But nothing would comfort Isabel and she continued to weep all the way home.

'Issie, do dry your tears,' Jane said as gently
as she could, though she was fast losing patience
with her sister. 'If Lady Wyndham and Mark can
bear up, so should you. Their loss is the greater.'

'It's all right for you, Jane,' her sister grumbled. 'You have not had your wedding snatched
away from you.'

'Isabel, it has not been snatched away,' her ladyship said. 'It has merely been postponed for six
months. It is to be hoped that by that time you will
have learned how to be more dignified. Think of
the position you will have as Mark's wife. You
will be Lady Wyndham and mistress of Broadacres. Everyone will look to you to set a good
example. Mark does not want a wife who bursts
into tears at the slightest setback.'

Isabel did not answer and Jane pulled up in
front of the stables and they all dismounted, leaving Daniel to unharness the pony and rub him
down. They met Teddy in the hall, as they were
going upstairs to take off their bonnets.

'Teddy, where have you been?' his mother

asked him. 'We have just been over to Broadacres to offer condolences. You should have been
with us.'

'I had business in Norwich. I will go over later.'

He did not elaborate on what the business
might be. Jane had little hope that he had been
looking for a way out of his dilemma. She knew
their father had spoken to him about the need
to make savings, but she had no idea what her
brother's reaction had been. She sighed as she
continued upstairs to her own room. She must
write to the bank manager to ask him to release
her savings. And then what? Would Teddy turn
over a new leaf?

The funeral had been attended by almost the
whole male population of the village and distant
relatives and friends of the Wyndham family
came from far and wide, including Drew. Although it was not usual for ladies to attend funer-
als, but to wait at home for the menfolk to return,
Lady Wyndham had insisted on being present
at the interment of her husband. She had been
dry-eyed throughout and regally upright in her
widow's weeds. She had maintained the stance
throughout the service and even afterwards when
everyone gathered for refreshments in the long
gallery at Broadacres. Helped to a seat by Mark,
she sat accepting condolences and listening to the

mourners recounting tales of what Lord Wyndham had said and done, some of which raised a wry smile. Mark was here, there and everywhere, being the perfect host, but Jane could see the strain in his eyes. To be suddenly catapulted into his inheritance years before he expected it must be a daunting prospect for him.

One by one the mourners began to leave until only the family and servants remained for the reading of the will. Mark caught Jane as she was preparing to leave with the rest of her family. 'Stay, Jane,' he said. The look of dismay on Isabel's face made him add, 'And you, too, Isabel.' He turned to Sir Edward. 'I will see them safely home afterwards, Sir Edward.'

Leaving their parents, Sophie and Teddy to go home in the family coach, the girls took seats near Mark and Lady Wyndham as the lawyer cleared his throat to begin. There was nothing remarkable in the will. There were bequests to all the servants commensurate with their status, small bequests to nephews and nieces, a generous allowance for his widow and three thousand pounds to Jane to use for her orphans. The amount made her gasp. His lordship had promised a donation, but she had never dreamed it would be so much. It made her realise that she would have to go ahead with it; there could be no backing out now. Mark, who had been standing by his mother's chair, bent and whispered in her ear. 'I will match that, Jane. You shall have your orphanage.'

The lawyer was coming to the end. 'Finally, to my beloved son, Mark, I leave the estate of Broad-acres and all its lands and holdings, the London house in South Audley Street, the overseas invest-ments and the residue of monies after all other bequests have been fulfilled.' He looked round at his audience, but, as no one had any comments, he gathered his papers up and prepared to leave.

Some of the relatives, who had come a dis-tance and would be staying at Broadacres over-night, went to their rooms to rest and change for dinner and those living locally took their leave of Lady Wyndham and Mark, leaving only Jane and Isabel.

'Drew, will you be so kind as to escort the la-dies home?' Mark asked. 'I must stay with my mother and my guests.'

'It is not in the least necessary,' Jane said. 'It is a fine day and we can easily walk.'

'Then I shall walk with you,' Drew said. 'I am staying at the Fox and Hounds. The Manor is not so very far out of my way.'

'Oh, thank you, sir,' Isabel said before Jane could protest again. 'I, for one, shall feel more at ease with an escort.'

This was a strange statement from one who

was accustomed to walking about the village with only Jane or Bessie as a companion. Jane looked sharply at her, but did not comment. With Drew between them they set off. No one spoke as they made their way down the drive and out of the huge iron gates on to the road to the village.

'It has been a sad day,' Jane said. 'We were all very fond of Lord Wyndham. Her ladyship stood up to the occasion very well, don't you think, Mr Ashton?'

'Indeed, yes. She showed enviable stoicism, but underneath I am sure she was suffering. They were so devoted, an example of what a marriage should be.'

'Yes, it is a pity all marriages are not like that,' Jane said. 'But I suppose it is down to finding your soulmate, someone you wish to spend the rest of your life with. So often marriage becomes a matter of convenience. Husband and wife lead almost separate lives, each with their own interests and circle of friends.'

'Unfortunately that happens all too often' he said.

'You have never been married?' Isabel queried.

'No.' He laughed. 'I never found my soulmate. I thought I had once, but it was not to be.'

'Why not?'

Jane held her breath for his answer, praying he would not mention her name. He looked at her and smiled. 'We were both too young, too immature and I had yet to make my way in the world.' He laughed suddenly. 'Since then I have been too busy making my fortune to think of marrying.'

'Would you go back to her if you could?'

'Isabel,' Jane remonstrated, 'you should not quiz Mr Ashton in that fashion.'

'Oh, I do not mind it,' he said. 'To answer your question, Miss Isabel, I thought I would. I thought that if we met again and she saw how prosperous I had become, she and her papa might think differently and I would win her. But I have thought better of it since.'

'Why not? Is she not as beautiful as you remembered?'

'Oh, more so. It is not that—'

'Issie, did you notice how strained Mark was looking today?' Jane interrupted the conversation, which was becoming too embarrassing to be borne. 'It is hardly to be wondered at, but I hope he manages to sleep tonight. He will need his strength in the next few weeks.'

'There will be no wedding,' Isabel said, ignoring Jane's attempt to divert her. 'Did you know that, Mr Ashton?'

'I knew it had been postponed, but it will take place later, will it not?'

Isabel sighed. 'I am no longer sure of anything.'

'Isabel, what are you saying?' Jane exclaimed.

'Surely you have not changed your mind about marrying Mark?'

'I don't know. I am so confused. Watching how everyone behaved today, especially Lady Wyndham, I thought I shall be expected to be like her, to direct that huge household and remain calm whatever the crisis and I do not think I can manage it.'

'It has been a trying day,' Jane said, wishing her sister had not voiced her doubts in front of Drew. 'You will think differently when you have had a night's sleep and are more yourself.'

'It's not just today. I have been worried about it for ages.'

'Oh, Issie, I am losing patience with you. This is all because of the ink spilled on your gown and that ill-considered remark of Sophie's.'

'What remark was that?' Drew asked.

'It was nothing,' Jane said. 'A silly superstition our sister picked up from somewhere.'

'Postponed marriages never happen,' Isabel told him.

They had been walking side by side, but now he turned to Isabel. 'I am inclined to agree with Miss Cavenhurst. It is silly.'

'Oh, I would not mind it if I had not already been having doubts,' she said.

'Now is hardly the time to express them, Issie,' Jane remonstrated. 'Think of poor Mark. He has enough to contend with without that.'

'He knows how I feel.'

'And what did he say?'

'That I would have the mourning period to get used to the idea.'

'There you are, then.'

'Jane, I wish you would not try to be a second mother to me. You are always telling me what I should and should not do and I am tired of it. You can know nothing of how I feel. I do not believe you have a heart.'

Jane was hurt as she was often hurt by her sister's thoughtlessness, but she would not show it, certainly not in front of Drew. 'Issie, you knew that if you accepted Mark one day you would be Lady Wyndham and mistress of Broadacres. It is not something new.'

'I didn't think it would be for years and years when we had grown quite old. And now it has happened.'

'But if you truly love Mark, that would not matter in the least. Now, let us speak no more of it. I am sure Mr Ashton does not want to hear it.'

They continued in silence. Jane was appalled at what Isabel had said and in front of Andrew Ashton, too. Did Mark really know how Isabel was feeling? It must have added to his sadness over the loss of his father. The bride he had chosen did not want to become the sort of wife a man in his position needed. Was he expecting

Isabel to become used to the idea or was he really worried about it? The pity of it was, that she, the unmarried sister, could not speak to him on such a private matter. What could she say if she did? Nothing. Her own feelings, locked away in the heart Isabel declared she did not have, could never be brought into the open.

She stole a sideways glance at Drew, wondering if he would pass on what he had heard. He looked sombre as if debating the issue within himself. He turned his head towards her and caught her looking at him. 'Do not worry,' he murmured. 'Your secret is safe with me.'

She looked away in confusion. What secret? Isabel had said Mark knew how she felt, so that was no secret. That she and Isabel had been arguing about it? That was hardly a secret either. Surely he had not guessed how she felt about Mark? That would be too mortifying.

They arrived at the front door of the Manor. Drew declined Isabel's invitation to come in for refreshment, bowed and took his leave. Jane and Isabel went indoors and rejoined their parents and siblings. Nothing was said of the conversation on the road.

Jane had been promised enough money to buy a house for her children's home without the need to use her aunt's bequest, so she had agreed to hand that over to her brother.

'I do it for Papa's sake, not yours,' she told him, a few days later when she caught him coming into the house in the middle of the morning. He looked dishevelled, as if he had been up all night and she wondered if that had been the case. He was rarely at home. 'I have asked the bank to pay it into your account, but it will be the last. Use it wisely and no more gambling.'

'Thank you, Sis.' He grinned. 'I suppose a jobation is a small price to pay for it, but you know you are sounding more and more like Papa.'

'It is because we both worry about you, Teddy. You do not seem to have any sense of responsibility.'

He heaved a melodramatic sigh. 'I am a sore trial to you, I know. How much is it, by the way?'

'Five thousand pounds and I begrudge every penny of it and make no bones about it. If it had been for anything else but gambling...'

'It will pay my way out to India and keep me going until I make my fortune.' He stopped her before she could begin scolding him again.

'India! What are you talking about? No one has mentioned India.'

'Well, it might be the West Indies. I haven't made up my mind.'

'Teddy, that money is meant for you to pay off

Lord Bolsover and your other debts. It was not given to you to fund your travelling.'

'Unfortunately I have no choice. Five thousand is not nearly enough to see me clear and Hector Bolsover, for some reason of his own, has been going round buying up all my debts, not only the gambling debts, but everything else. I don't know what his game is, but it ain't good to have all one's debts in one pot. Spread about a bit they can be managed by paying off a little here and there, robbing Peter to pay Paul, as it were, but as it is I am trumped. There is nothing for it—I must emigrate.'

She was appalled. 'Teddy, have you been gambling since you returned home?'

'I've only been trying to recoup my losses. I thought it would save you having to stand buff for me…'

'Now you are in deeper than ever.' She was exasperated that he never seemed to learn.

'Sorry, Jane.'

'Have you told Papa and Mama you are leaving?'

'I am about to.'

'And when will you go?'

'On tonight's mail. Wish me luck, Jane.'

'Luck! I would sooner box your ears. You have brought disgrace on this family, Teddy, with all this talk of luck. I can only hope that a spell abroad and some real work will bring about a miracle.'

'Oh, Jane, give over your lecture. You will not see me again for some time, let us not part at odds with each other.'

His engaging grin was still evident and she relented enough to hug him and tell him to take care.

The family was all at odds, she reflected as he hurried away. Her brother was a scapegrace and her sister, Isabel, was having serious doubts about a marriage that had been talked about for years and welcomed by both families. Her father was worried to death about his finances and her mother blind to it. So far there was nothing wrong with Sophie except a tendency to speak without thinking. As for her own thoughts and feelings, they were as much in disarray as everyone else's. The best cure for that, she decided, was to occupy herself with something worthwhile.

She was determined to make her orphanage a success and although she had enough to start looking for premises, she would still need a regular income to run it. To find that she must raise more money and the best place to do that was London. Her father would never allow her to go alone and he was too preoccupied to take her. It would need some thought.

* * *

Jane consulted the Rector and Mrs Caulder and though the Reverend said he would enquire about premises, he cautioned her not to consider travelling to London without a male escort. 'Instead you could make a start by writing letters to influential people,' he said.

'Begging letters?' she queried in dismay.

'Well, yes, but in a very good cause. Shall we give the organisation a name so that you are not asking for yourself, but on behalf of everyone connected with the idea? I would ask Lord Wyndham to put his name to it, but it is too soon after his bereavement. I will sound out one or two others.'

They spent some time suggesting and discarding names for the project. Jane did not want the word orphanage to be used. 'It will be a home,' she said. 'A home and a school.' In the end they decided on the Hadlea Children's Home and she would spend a little of the money having headed notepaper printed.

She was walking home, turning the phrases of her letter over in her mind, when Mark caught up with her. 'Jane, I was on my way to visit you.'

Long practice had made her adept at calming herself when she met him. She turned and smiled, taking in his dark suit and black cravat, the bleakness of his countenance, and wished she could comfort him. There was no one to do that, except perhaps his mother, who was too immersed in her own grief to do it. Isabel seemed incapable of it.

'My lord,' she said.

'Oh, for goodness' sake, Jane, let's not have any of that "my lord" nonsense, or I shall become very cross with you.' He fell into step beside her. 'What were you so deep in thought about, that you did not hear me?'

She told him about her plans for the Hadlea Children's Home. 'Thanks to you and your father, we have enough to look for premises, but we need a few wealthy philanthropists to pledge future income,' she said. 'Papa cannot take me to London at present, so I must write letters. If I could mention one or two influential people, it would help.'

'You may use my name, Jane.'

'Oh, I didn't mean… Oh dear, it sounded as if I was asking…' She stopped in confusion because he was laughing.

'Oh, yes, you were, and blatantly too.'

'But you did ask what I was thinking about.'

'I did, that is true, and it is also true I would have offered in any case. I will help in any way I can.'

'But you have so much to do, sorting out the estate and getting used to your new role.'

'It is not that difficult, Jane. My father involved me in the affairs of the estate as soon as I was old enough to understand. He groomed me well for the job and the workers are all good men who know what is expected of them. The difficulty arises because my father is no longer here to advise me and I miss that. Mother looks after the house and the indoor servants, but she has never taken an interest in what is happening on the estate. I am on my own there.'

'You have our support for what it is worth.'

'It is worth a great deal, Jane.'

She felt the colour flood her face. 'You said you were on your way to call on us.'

'Yes. I have to go to London on business and wondered if Sir Edward or Lady Cavenhurst had any little commissions I could do for them while I am there.'

'That is kind of you.' She paused, as an idea came to her. 'You could do something for me, though.'

'Gladly. What is it?'

'Take me with you. I am sure Papa would allow me to go if you were to escort me. I could stay with Lady Cartrose, widow of my mother's brother. She lives in Mount Street. All you need do is take me to her.'

'I am not sure…'

'Please, Mark. I could do my fund-raising so much easier in the capital, make appointments to meet people, have the notepaper printed, that sort of thing. Aunt Emmeline is well up in society and could perhaps introduce me to people. I am sure I could be more persuasive face to face than by correspondence.'

'Oh, I am sure you could,' he said. 'And I would take you willingly if I thought it could be accomplished with propriety.'

'And why would it not? You are to be my brother-in-law, are you not?'

'I am not sure that guarantees anything, Jane,' he said with a wry smile. 'Let us see what Sir Edward thinks, shall we?'

Sir Edward, when he was approached, was dubious. 'My daughter thinks she is mature and independent,' he said. 'And to some extent she is, but we cannot flout convention. It is bad enough that Teddy... No, we will not speak of him.' Teddy had departed in a welter of tears from his mother and anger from his father, who had told him he had washed his hands of him.

'It would be perfectly proper if Isabel were to go, too,' Lady Cavenhurst said. 'Then Jane would be their chaperon.'

'Oh, yes, yes,' Isabel said, eyes shining. 'I should like that very much.'

'Yes, that would serve,' Sir Edward agreed, turning to his wife. 'Do you think your sister-in-law will have them?'

'I am sure she will. She is always asking when we are going to pay her a visit. I will write to her at once. My lord, will you take the letter to the mail office on your way home?'

'Gladly, my lady. There is something you could do for me in return. Would you call and bear my mother company while I am away? She is still feeling very down and I do not like leaving her.'

'Of course I will. When do you go?'

'I was planning to make a start tomorrow, but I will defer it until the day after to give the ladies time to pack. I mean to be on the road betimes, so I will call for them with the coach at half past eight if that is not too early.'

'We will be ready,' Jane said.

He bowed his way out, leaving Isabel jumping up and down in excitement.

The journey was accomplished in two days with frequent changes of horses at the various staging inns along the way and an overnight stay at the halfway point. Isabel spent much of her time looking out of the coach window and exclaiming at what she saw, while Jane and Mark discussed Jane's fund-raising.

'There are several orphanages in London,' he said. 'Some good, some downright bad. You should visit a few of them and find out how they are run and how they raise their money and perhaps learn some of the pitfalls to avoid. They might give you some ideas. Once my business is done I will be happy to escort you. Perhaps to-morrow afternoon.'

'Yes, that will be convenient, thank you,' Jane said. 'It will give me time to prepare some notes in the morning.'

'How boring,' Isabel said.

'You do not have to come, Issie, dear,' Jane said. 'I am sure Aunt Emmeline will find some-thing for you to do more to your taste. You know what a busy social life she leads.'

'But you will be taking Mark from me.'

'I will make it up to you, Isabel,' he said. 'You must allow your sister to have her children's home. After all, you have your wedding to look forward to.' He smiled. 'Already two weeks of the six months have passed.'

'Yes. I am a crosspatch, aren't I?'

'Not at all,' he said. 'Shall you like to visit Bullock's Museum? I believe they are display-ing Napoleon's coach captured at Waterloo. We could all go one afternoon.'

She had been mollified by this idea and had recovered her good humour by the time the coach drew up outside Lady Cartrose's house in Mount Street. Mindful of his escort duties, he bade Jer-emy take the coach on to Wyndham House and entered the town house to hand his charges and their maid over to her ladyship, who had received her sister-in-law's letter and was expecting them. Since Jane had last seen her she had put on a great deal of weight and was now a roly-poly of a woman. She was dressed in a dark-purple gown and wore a white cap on dyed red hair.

'Come in and let me look at you,' she said, as the maid who had conducted them to the drawing room disappeared to fetch refreshments and Bessie was conducted up to their rooms to unpack. 'My, you are quite grown up now and so elegant. I did not know I had such beautiful nieces. Do present your escort.'

'Aunt Emmeline, this is Lord Wyndham,' Jane said.

'And am I right in thinking he is your betrothed?' She turned a round, smiling face to Mark.

Jane was dismayed. 'On, no, Aunt. Lord Wyndham is Isabel's betrothed, not mine.'

'Oh, dear, what a foolish mistake to make. I must have misread you mother's letter. My lord, please forgive me.'

Mark bowed to her. 'My lady, it is of no consequence.'

'Do let us be seated.' She waved her hand in the direction of two sofas and some chairs. 'Then we can have a comfortable coze over some refreshments and you can tell me all about yourselves.' She sat on one of the sofas as a maid brought in the tea tray and another appeared with two plates loaded with cakes and pastries.

It soon transpired that her ladyship was very deaf and they were obliged to repeat almost everything they said in very loud voices, while her ladyship munched her way through two large pastries and several cakes. The girls ate one cake each and Mark felt duty bound to manage more than that in order to please their hostess.

An hour later, when her ladyship had satisfied herself that she had learned all she needed to know about their lives and aspirations, Mark prepared to take his leave. 'I shall be occupied on business affairs during the morning tomorrow,' he told her ladyship. 'But I shall call in the afternoon, if I may. I promised Jane to take her to visit some orphanages.'

'Then you should go to the Foundling Hospital,' she said. 'It is open to the public and has raised considerable sums for its upkeep with artwork and musical evenings.'

'Yes, I have heard of it,' Jane said. 'I should like to do that.'

'In the meantime I will invite as many wealthy acquaintances as I can squeeze into my drawing room for music, cards and refreshments two evenings hence, so that you might be introduced to them and talk to them about your children's home. It will not be easy to extract money from them, however. Everyone is complaining of hard times. The war cost everyone dear in taxes and last year's dismal summer and the poor harvest means their estates and investments are not producing the income they have come to expect.'

'All the more reason for people to think about the poor orphans,' Jane said. 'If times are hard for the wealthy, they are even harder for the poorer people.'

'I am sure that your silver tongue will do the trick,' Mark said. 'Until tomorrow, then.' He bowed and was gone, leaving the ladies to discuss social affairs and exchange gossip.

The Foundling Hospital, set up by the philanthropist Thomas Coram over seventy years before, was much bigger than Jane had imagined it would be. Most of the children were the offspring of unmarried women, though there were some orphans. The children were well clothed and well fed and appeared happy in their way, but Jane could not agree that giving them new names and cutting them off from their real parents, even if there was only one, was the way she would go. It was done, she was told, so that the mother could repent of her sin and make a new life for herself unburdened by children.

'I would rather encourage the children to meet and talk about their kin,' she said as she and Mark returned to Mount Street. 'Especially widowed mothers. Families are important.'

He had been supporting her all the way, standing beside her as she spoke to the Governor of the home and asking pertinent questions she might not have thought of herself. This time alone with him was precious, so precious, that it was difficult to give her mind to the purpose of their visit. Every time her arm had brushed his sleeve or he put his hand under her elbow to help her up a step, she had felt the warmth flood her whole body. She really must make herself concentrate on the conversation and not the fact that they were alone together in his carriage.

'I think you are right,' he said. 'Poor Drew's relations did not want anything to do with him when he was orphaned. They sent him to a good school and believed that was the end of their responsibilities. It is one of the reasons I befriended him and brought him to stay at Broadacres.'

'Yes, I remember him telling me. He has done well for himself since.'

'Yes, and I heard him say he would help with your project. You must keep him up to it.'

'If I see him again.' She paused. 'Mark, do you trust him?'

'Naturally I do. Why do you ask?'

'No reason.' She took a deep breath and changed the subject. 'The Coram has given me other ideas for raising money besides writing letters. We could arrange musical evenings with talented musicians for which the wealthy audience would pay handsomely and we could put on a fair in the village and ask for donations for the stalls and prizes for competitions, charging a small entrance fee.'

'A fair would not attract the wealthy,' he said. 'It would mean a great deal of work for a small reward.'

'I know, but it would give the people of Hadlea the opportunity to become involved. I want the home to be part of the community, not cut off behind hedges and walls. And every little helps. I thought the last Saturday in August would give the best chance of good weather and allow time to arrange it all.'

'Then we could do it on Ten Acre Field on the far side of Broadacres estate.'

'But, Mark, would that be wise? You are so recently bereaved. What will your mother say?'

'I will consult her, but she will say it was what my father would have wished. Your project was close to his heart, as it is to mine.'

'What would I do without you?'

'I am sure you would manage admirably.' He turned to smile at her, making her heart flip. Did Isabel realise how fortunate she was?

They arrived back at Mount Street to hear from Isabel that she and Lady Cartrose had been riding in her ladyship's open carriage in Hyde Park and they had stopped frequently so that she could be introduced to some of her ladyship's many acquaintances. 'I am sure it was more interesting than visiting an orphanage,' she told them. 'And guess who we chanced upon, riding in the Row? Mr Ashton, no less. When he heard you were in town, Mark, he said he would call on you. And Aunt Emmeline has invited him to call tomorrow. There was talk of an outing together.' Her face was alight with enthusiasm and excitement, which filled Jane with a kind of foreboding.

Strangely Mark did not appear to see his danger. He smiled and said he would have called on Drew in any case and he would certainly make time for an outing if that was what the ladies wished. Then he bowed his way out.

Chapter Five

The outing was arranged the next morning when both men arrived at Mount Street at the same time. They would visit Bullock's Museum that afternoon and attend a concert in the Chinese Pavilion at Ranelagh Gardens in the evening, a plan which pleased Isabel. As soon as they had taken their leave she began discussing the dress she would wear.

'My green-and-pink-striped sarsenet,' she said. 'With a pink bonnet and gloves.'

'Issie, you must remember that Mark is in mourning and that you, as his betrothed, should be a little more sombre in what you wear.'

'You mean I should go into mourning, too? We are not married yet. His late lordship was not kin to me. I do not see the necessity.'

'Not mourning, Issie, but something quieter out of respect for Mark's feelings.'

'You are always worrying about Mark's feelings, Jane. I begin to wonder if you are not a little in love with him yourself.'

'Nonsense.' Her reply was sharp, but she turned away so that her sister could not see the consternation on her face. 'Aunt, what do you think?'

'Think about what?' the lady asked vaguely. It was obvious that her deafness had prevented her from following the conversation.

'I was saying that Isabel should not wear bright colours in deference to Mark's state of mourning,' Jane said very loudly.

'You may be right,' her ladyship said. 'But there are some lovely shades of lilac and dove grey to be had.'

'The only thing I have in grey is that plain old carriage dress I wore to come here. You do not expect me to wear that again, do you?'

'It would serve,' Jane said.

'Well, I won't. How can I shine in society in something as drab as that? The gentlemen will not like me in it.'

'Gentlemen?' Jane queried. 'What gentlemen?'

'Why, Mark and Mr Ashton, of course.'

She would not be moved and it was a resplendent Isabel in pink and green who greeted the gentlemen when they arrived. Jane was in a plain lilac trimmed with white lace. Both carried parasols for the day was warm.

Bullock's Museum was housed in the Egyptian Hall in Piccadilly, only a short distance away and they elected to walk. There were strange, often bizarre exhibits in the museum, things like skeletons and animal bones, weapons and armour, uniforms with bullet holes in them, and unusual plants. They wandered round the exhibits, then moved on to inspect the magnificent travelling coach used by Napoleon on his campaigns. He had abandoned it after his defeat at Waterloo and taken to his white riding horse to make his escape. When he knew escape was not possible he had appealed to King George for asylum in England, but this had been refused and since the island of Elba could not hold him, he had been sent to St Helena, way out in the Atlantic. His coach had been bought for the museum and people flocked to see it. Painted blue with gold ornamentation, it was very large and luxuriously appointed, with a folding bed, even a desk with pens, paper and ink, and compartments for maps and telescopes. It had bulletproof doors and blinds on the windows. It obviously needed a team of strong horses to pull it.

'Did the Duke of Wellington ride about in a carriage like this?' Jane asked Mark.

'He had a carriage, though it was nothing like as ostentatious as this,' he answered. 'In any case, he preferred to ride.'

'Did you meet him?'

'Yes, several times, though I do not think he deigned to notice me.'

'I shall write one of my letters to him. He is supposed to be in sympathy with the plight of his men and their families.'

'I don't know how you dare,' Isabel put in.

'Nothing ventured, nothing gained,' she said, laughing.

'Well, I think you are wasting your time,' her sister went on. 'It is a national problem. What can one woman do?'

'If we all thought nothing could be done, nothing would be done,' Mark said.

'I sympathise with the children, of course I do,' Isabel said. 'And I always give a few coppers to beggars, but you are talking about thousands of pounds. You are becoming obsessed with it, Jane, and I, for one, am tired of hearing about it. If you and Mark wish to continue the conversation, Mr Ashton and I will find something else to talk about.' She took Drew's arm. 'Come, Mr Ashton, show me the animals.'

Drew looked towards Mark, who answered with a slight nod and Drew allowed himself to be led away.

'Mark, ought we not to follow them?' Jane asked, staring at their disappearing backs in consternation.

'She is bored, Jane.'

'That is no excuse. I am appalled by her behaviour and can only apologise on her behalf.'

'Dear Jane, there is no need for you to apologise for anything. You are not your sister's keeper.'

His endearment meant nothing to him, but everything to her, but she must guard against letting him know that. 'No, but I am concerned that she is not showing proper regard for your feelings.'

'And do you know what my feelings are, Jane?' he queried with a smile. 'Can you read my mind?'

'No, of course not.' She felt the colour flare in her face and wished to end the conversation. 'But I still think we should follow them for propriety's sake.'

He laughed suddenly and it was the first real laugh she had heard from him since his father died. 'Whose reputation were you thinking of, Jane? Theirs or ours? Who is the pot and who the kettle?'

She was obliged to smile at that. 'Then, for all our sakes, let us rejoin them and endeavour not to discuss the Hadlea Children's Home.'

The stuffed animals were in a separate part of the museum for which they had to pay an extra shilling. The entrance was a narrow corridor made to look like a rocky cave, which opened out into a tropical rainforest where the stuffed animals were set in lifelike poses among the vegetation. Drew and Isabel were not to be found there or in any other part of the building. Worried about what had happened to them, they went outside to find them standing on the walkway. Isabel was clinging on to Drew's arm with both hands and had her head on his shoulder.

'There you are,' Drew said. 'Miss Isabel felt faint and begged me to bring her out in the fresh air. I dared not leave her to fetch you.'

'Oh, dear,' Jane said, gently detaching her sister from Drew's side and putting her arm about her shoulders. 'Do you feel better now?'

'Yes, a little.'

'Do you think you can manage to walk back to Mount Street or shall we ask Mark to find us a hackney?'

Mark turned to a little crossing sweeper, who was waiting anxiously to see if they wished to cross the road, gave him a penny and bade him run for a hackney. He sped off and was soon back with the hire vehicle.

Thus they returned to Mount Street and in the few minutes the journey took, Isabel recovered her spirits. Jane found herself wondering if her sister had truly felt faint or if it had been act put on for Drew's benefit, then upbraided herself for her uncharitable thought.

'Issie,' she said as soon as they were alone, 'you should not have asked Mr Ashton to take you away from us. It was very embarrassing for Mark and it put me to the blush to think you could behave in such a forward manner, and to compound it by hanging on to Mr Ashton's arm in that fashion was the outside of enough. I dread to think what Mark made of it.'

'I nearly fainted and I don't care what Mark thinks. And I will not have you scolding me.'

'Issie!' Jane was lost for words.

'Well, I won't. I wish I had not said I would marry Mark.' And with that she flounced out of the room, leaving Jane's heart and mind in turmoil. It was so difficult to tell if Isabel really meant what she said, or if it was a tantrum that she would regret.

Her sister was more subdued than usual when they sat down to a light meal with their aunt at five o'clock, but she would not hear of postponing the outing to Ranelagh Gardens on account of not feeling well earlier in the day.

'I am perfectly recovered,' she said. 'We are only in town for a few days and heaven knows when we will ever come again if Papa is so determined we must economise, so I intend to make the most of it.'

It was with a heavy heart Jane prepared for

the evening when they would again be escorted by Mark and Mr Ashton. She wished the latter would go away, back to where he came from, but her wish was not to be granted.

Drew and Mark arrived promptly at eight o'clock in Mark's town carriage and all four of them were soon on their way to Chelsea.

The gardens were a popular place where the aristocracy mixed with anyone able to afford the two-shillings-and-sixpence entrance fee. It had a Chinese Pavilion, an ornamental lake and several walks. Outdoor concerts were also staged there. Mark and Drew, with the ladies between them, made their way to the pavilion to listen to the music, which did not finish before it became dark. The area around the pavilion was lit by lanterns strung among the trees, but the surrounding tree-lined walks with their little arbours were in darkness and were therefore a popular place for romantic assignations.

In the crush of people leaving at the end of the concert, Jane became separated from her companions. She wandered round for several minutes trying to find them and was beginning to think her best plan was to make for the exit and wait there for them to find her, when she encountered

Mark. 'Where are Mr Ashton and Isabel?' she asked. 'I have been looking for you all for ages.'

'I don't know. I thought they were with you.'

'No. I lost sight of them soon after everyone started to leave. Where can they have got to? If they have been separated, Issie will be frightened; she never liked the dark.' She did not add that if they were together, it was one more indiscretion on her sister's part.

'Our best course is to go to the carriage lines and see if they have made their way there, before we do anything else.'

'Then I will stay here and continue looking.'

'No, Jane, we stay together. I don't want you to become lost, too.'

They went to where the carriages waited, but Jeremy had not seen Mr Ashton or Miss Isabel. They returned to the gardens, now in darkness because almost everyone had left, and began a systematic search of all the paths, taking one of the lanterns from the pavilion to light their way. 'They must have missed their way trying to find the exit,' Jane said. 'Though how that could be when almost everyone was making their way out and they had only to follow, I do not know.'

They walked down one path after another, with Mark swinging the lantern to and fro and in the process managing to disturb more than one pair of lovers to their dismay or indignation, but there was no sign of Drew and Isabel. They turned back towards the pavilion and here they encountered Drew. He was alone.

'Where is Issie?' Jane's anxiety made her speak sharply.

'I have taken her to the carriage. She is waiting there for you.'

'She wasn't there half an hour ago.'

'No. She fainted and fell among the crowd. I picked her up and carried her back into the pavilion to recover, then I escorted her to the carriage and came looking for you.'

'Then let us make haste and take her home,' Mark said. 'That is twice today she has felt unwell. I do hope she is not sickening for anything.'

They returned to the carriage where Isabel sat waiting for them with Jeremy standing by. Jane rushed to join her. 'Issie, what happened?'

'There was such a crush of people, all pushing and pulling, and I could not move and you all left me and I fainted and would have been trampled underfoot if Drew had not seen what happened and rescued me.'

'Then we are indebted to him,' Mark said, taking his seat opposite her. Drew joined them and they were driven at speed back to Mount Street. The gentlemen did not stay long after delivering the ladies safely into the care of their aunt, who fussed round Isabel and suggested the physician should be called, but Isabel would not hear of it. 'I am perfectly well now,' she said. 'It was the heat and the crush of people made me faint, nothing more than that. I am going to bed. Tomorrow we are going riding in Hyde Park. I would not miss that for the world.'

Jane went to her own bed, but she could not sleep. Her sister had a robust constitution and had never fainted in her life, so what was happening now? Was she deliberately throwing herself into the path of Andrew Ashton? Did she really wish she had not accepted Mark's proposal? It would cause the most dreadful scandal for her to back out now. It would break Mark's heart and he would be tainted by it, too. He was too good a man to be treated in that fashion.

Mark was occupied with his lawyer all the following morning and Jane spent it writing more letters, while Isabel and their aunt went shopping. They did not return until it was almost time for the gentlemen to bring the riding horses to the house. Jane went to her room to change into her riding habit, which was the one she always wore for riding at home. It was plain and serviceable in a dark-green grosgrain. She heard the men arrive as she was slipping into her boots. After fastening a green hat on her dark hair with a hat pin, she went downstairs to greet them.

They were standing in the hall, when Isabel came from her room and down the stairs. She was wearing a new riding habit in mauve velvet, cut in the military style with lines of braiding and gold-fringed epaulettes. Her head was crowned with a tall beaver hat with mauve feathers curling round the brim and touching her cheek. Her feet were encased in kid half-boots. Jane could only stare at her.

'Here I am, gentlemen,' she said cheerfully. 'How do I look?' And she twirled to show off her ensemble, though the very long skirt hampered her.

'Lovely, as always,' Mark said.

'Magnificent,' Drew added.

Jane was silent as they made their way to the front of the house and mounted. The road was busy and they could only ride in single file until they entered Hyde Park, when they walked their horses at a sedate pace along the Row. It was not Jane's idea of going for a ride, but she could not leave Isabel who was intent on seeing and being seen.

They had been riding for perhaps half an hour when another rider coming towards them stopped when he reached them. 'Wyndham, good day,' he said. He was a tall, elegant figure with dark curly hair and almost black eyes, which looked Isabel over appreciatively, then turned towards Jane and then to Drew. 'Ashton, we meet again.'

'Indeed,' Drew said.

'Wyndham, are you not going to present me to the ladies?' the newcomer asked.

Mark seemed reluctant, but he turned to Isabel first. 'Isabel, may I present Lord Bolsover. My lord, Miss Isabel Cavenhurst, my future wife.'

Bolsover swept off his tall beaver to her. 'My felicitations, Miss Cavenhurst. My friend Mark is a fortunate man.'

Isabel replied with a ready smile and a nod. 'My lord.'

Mark turned to Jane. 'And this is Miss Jane Cavenhurst.'

His lordship bowed again, but Jane could not bring herself to smile at him. She inclined her head without speaking.

'Daughters of Sir Edward, I assume,' he said. 'And sisters to Teddy. I am indeed glad to make your acquaintances.'

Isabel, who had never heard of Lord Bolsover in connection with her brother, was inclined to be friendly towards him. 'Oh, are you a friend of Teddy's?'

'I know him well,' he said. 'But I have missed him of late. I do hope he is not ailing.'

'Oh, no, he has gone to India to make his fortune.'

Bolsover laughed aloud. 'So that is where he has hidden himself. No matter, there are other ways of skinning a cat.'

'Isabel, I do not think we should detain Lord Bolsover,' Jane put in quickly. 'And we must be on our way.' She gathered up her reins to move off.

'No doubt we shall meet again,' he said, touching the brim of his hat. 'I have business with Sir Edward.'

'I do not like the sound of that,' Jane said to Mark as they resumed riding. 'It sounded almost like a threat.'

'Don't worry, he can do nothing while Teddy is out of the country.'

'He could threaten Papa.'

'I doubt he plans to leave London to go to Norfolk in the middle of the Season, Jane. He can make a fortune fleecing the young bloods who come to town to enjoy themselves. He would not forgo that.'

'Are you really his friend?'

'Certainly not, no more than he is mine. I detest the man.'

'Why?' Isabel demanded, catching the end of the conversation. 'I found him very civil.'

'He is the one to whom Teddy owes money,' Jane said. 'It is that man who drove our brother to emigrate.'

'It was Teddy's own fault, if you ask me,' Isabel said. 'He did not have to gamble.'

'You are right, of course, but I fear Lord Bolsover has not finished with us yet.'

'What can he do?'

'Nothing,' Mark put in. 'Let us forget him and enjoy the rest of our ride.'

'Yes, let's,' Isabel said and kicked her horse into a trot and then a canter. 'I'll race you to that tree over there.' And she was gone at a crazy gallop.

There was nothing they could do but follow, led by Drew, who was the only one riding his own mount, which gave him the advantage. Jane was a good horsewoman, but on a hired hack could not catch her sister, let alone keep up with the men. She was well behind them when she saw her sister ride under the tree she had pointed out. In an effort to pull up, she was caught by an overhanging branch with such force it threw her to the ground.

Drew was off his horse in an instant and kneeling beside her. He had her head cradled in his arms when Mark and Jane arrived and dismounted. Jane fell to her knees beside them.

Isabel was unconscious, her face paper white. 'I fear she is badly hurt,' Drew said, with an unaccustomed tremor in his voice. 'We must get her back to Mount Street as swiftly as possible and have a doctor fetched.'

He turned from addressing Mark to look down at Isabel and the expression on his face filled Jane with alarm. It was more than just the concern of a gentleman towards an injured lady, more than that of a friend. He loved Isabel. She looked up at Mark to see if he had noticed, but if he had, he betrayed nothing of his feelings as he prepared to remount his horse and go for help.

'Issie, wake up,' Jane said, tears filling her eyes. 'Please, Issie, please wake up.'

Isabel's eyelids fluttered and then she opened her eyes wide. 'Where am I?'

'You came off your horse,' Drew said.

She turned her head towards him. 'Oh, it is you.' Her eyelids fluttered and closed again with a soft sigh.

'Wake up, Issie,' Jane implored her. 'Tell us if you are hurt. Are you in pain?'

'My head aches.'

'It is not to be wondered at,' Drew said. 'You hit your head and there is already the beginning of a lump, but I do not think there are any broken bones. We must get you home and send for a doctor to make sure. Mark has gone to fetch a carriage.'

She struggled to sit up, but he gently pulled her back. 'Lie still or you will make your head worse.'

She subsided, leaving Jane to worry about the inelegant position in which her sister lay and the fact that Andrew Ashton was cradling her in his arms in a most loving way. Did Issie know what was happening? Did Mark?

A hired carriage drew up beside them and Mark jumped out. Drew picked Isabel up and carried her to it. He put her gently on the seat and Jane climbed in beside her.

'We will bring the horses,' Mark said, addressing Jane. 'Do not attempt to leave the carriage until we arrive to help. We will be right behind you.'

'We'll soon be home, Issie,' Jane said when the jolting of the carriage as it moved off made Isabel cry out. 'Put your head in my lap, if it helps.

Isabel did that and Jane sat cradling it, noticing the bump on the side of Issie's head growing and turning purple. If she had had doubts about the genuineness of Issie fainting at the Museum and at Ranelagh Gardens, she had none over this. She would not have fallen from her horse deliberately, even if taking off like that had been meant to cause a stir. *Oh, foolish, foolish Issie,* she thought as she prayed there would be no permanent damage to her lovely sister.

The two men were right behind them when they drew up outside the Mount Street house. Mark dismounted and ran to the carriage to help Isabel from it. She was too unsteady to walk, so he carried her up the steps into the house followed by Jane and Drew. The footman who admitted them ran off to fetch Lady Cartrose, who immediately took in the situation. 'She must go to bed at once,' she said, turning to dispatch a footman to fetch her physician.

Mark had put Isabel on a chair, but picked her up again to carry her to her bedchamber. Bessie was sent to help Jane undress her while Lady Cartrose and the two men waited in the drawing room. Neither felt like leaving until they knew the extent of the injury.

'What happened?' her ladyship asked, indicating that they should take seats. 'How did Isabel come to fall from her horse? I understood you were only going out for a gentle hack in the Park.'

'That was the intention,' Mark said. 'But Isabel's horse bolted with her. Drew and I galloped after her to try to bring it to a halt, but before we could do so, she was hit by the overhanging branch of a tree which knocked her to the ground. It was so sudden no one had a chance to prevent it.'

'She was knocked out of her senses,' Drew put in.

'What made the horse bolt?'

'I really do not know,' Mark said. 'I wish we had been watching more carefully.'

'I wish it, too,' Drew said. 'I sincerely hope

there is no permanent damage. I should never forgive myself.'

The sound of voices in the hall told them the doctor had arrived. Her ladyship rose to conduct him to the patient's room, leaving the two men facing each other in a silence which last several minutes. 'Someone ought to see to the horses,' Mark said in a flat voice. 'We can't leave hired horses on the street.'

'I will do it.' Drew jumped up and left the room, leaving Mark musing on his own. He was sorry Isabel had been hurt and would not for the world have wished it on her, but if she had not spurred her horse in that reckless fashion the accident would never have happened. Why had she done it? Why was he having to make excuses for her and pretend the horse was to blame? Would life with her always be like that? What did that augur for their future happiness together?

Lady Cartrose came back into the room. 'She is comfortable and the doctor has prescribed something for the headache. He said she needed to rest for at least a week, but he did not think her life was in danger.'

'Thank the lord for that,' Mark said.

'Jane is sitting with her. She is blaming herself.'

'Whatever for?'

'I do not know, something about not curbing Isabel's exuberance.'

'Exuberance,' he mused aloud. 'Is that what it's called? I would have called it wilfulness. Isabel set off to gallop and the mare got the bit between her teeth and bolted. It had nothing to do with Jane.'

'You are very fond of Jane, are you not?'

'Indeed I am. I admire her greatly for the way she tries to keep the family together, making sacrifices for them, which they seem to take for granted. She is always making excuses for their bad behaviour. If it isn't Teddy, it's Isabel.'

'You make a good champion of her, Lord Wyndham.'

'There is no one else to do it.'

'Not even Mr Ashton?'

'Drew?' he asked, puzzled. 'No, I do not think so. She always behaves coolly and correctly towards him. What made you think it?'

'He is so often in your company, the four of you together.'

'Why not? Drew is my friend.'

'Oh, I see. I did not quite understand.'

He was not one to analyse his own feelings too closely, but the events of the past few days when he had been more in Jane's company had opened his eyes to the differences between her and her sister and what he saw and felt filled him with doubts. Drew returned before he could ponder that more deeply.

'How is she?' he asked, after bowing to Lady Cartrose.

'Awake and sitting up,' her ladyship answered. 'She will recover, but must have a week in bed.'

'Thank goodness it is no more than that,' he said, taking the chair her ladyship indicated.

'Did you manage the horses?' Mark asked.

'Lord Bolsover turned up just as I was rounding them up and offered his assistance. He said he had seen what happened and was on his way to ask after the invalid.'

'What on earth is the man playing at?'

'I've no idea, but I was glad of his help. Four horses on a busy street are not easy to handle. We each rode one and led another.' He turned to Lady Cartrose. 'When will we be able to visit Miss Isabel?'

'I think perhaps tomorrow Mark may see her, if she feels up to it.' It was plain she did not think it fitting that Drew should see the young lady while she lay in bed.

'Then we will take our leave,' Mark said, rising to bow to her. Drew followed suit.

'I had not intended to stay in town above three or four days,' Mark said, as they walked to South Audley Street. 'And I ought to go back to Hadlea and inform Sir Edward what has happened. No doubt Jane will want to stay with her sister. I can come back for them when Isabel is well enough to travel.'

They separated on the corner of Mount Street and South Audley Street, arranging to meet at White's for supper that evening. Mark went to the mews to order his carriage to be ready to return to Norfolk the next morning and then went into the house to change and deal with some paperwork. But he could not settle to it and found himself pacing backwards and forwards, his mind on Jane and Isabel. The latter was lovely, charming and sensitive in many ways, but in others, completely selfish. Not until recently had he realised that.

As for Jane, she was far from the plain Jane she was purported to be. Her beauty was in her inner self, in her compassion and selflessness which shone through in everything she did. Why had he not seen that before? Was it because everyone else overlooked her and treated her as if she did not matter, was as familiar and static as the furniture? He had been as guilty as anyone. It was not that she lacked confidence; she was more independent than most and able to hold her own in an argument when the subject was something she felt passionate about, especially the orphans. Not everyone needed to be lively and flirtatious—indeed that could sometimes pall. There he was, comparing them again. Did that mean he had made the wrong choice? He stopped his thoughts abruptly before they carried him away where it was best not to go.

On his way to White's he stopped at Mount Street to enquire of the invalid and was told by her aunt that she was comfortable and resting. 'Jane is sitting with her,' the old lady said. 'But the medicine the doctor prescribed has made her sleep and there is nothing we can do but watch over her. What her father will say of my guardianship of his daughters I dread to think. I have written to my sister-in-law and told her Isabel will have the best medical attention available.'

'I must return to Hadlea tomorrow,' he said, 'and will call at the Manor to apprise Sir Edward and Lady Cavenhurst of what happened and reassure them that Isabel is recovering. I assume Jane will stay with her sister? I will return to take them home when Isabel is well enough to travel.'

'Thank you, my lord. I do not know what we would have done without you.'

'I did nothing. Please convey my good wishes to both ladies and tell Isabel I wish her a speedy recovery.' He picked up his hat, bowed and left the house for his rendezvous with Drew.

If he had hoped for a quiet supper and then home to bed, he was thwarted by the arrival of

Lord Bolsover. 'May I join you?' his lordship asked. Not waiting for a reply, he sat down at the table where Mark waited for Drew to arrive. 'I would hear how Miss Cavenhurst goes.'

'She is recovering at the home of her aunt.'

'I am glad to hear it. I was fearful that she had sustained a serious injury. A rather headstrong girl, I believe. Has no one told her that the terrain of the park away from the Row is too uneven for a lady riding side-saddle to attempt to gallop? Most unseemly, but courageous, all the same.' He smiled suddenly, but it was the smile of a tiger. 'Undoubtedly Andrew Ashton thought so, for I could see he was most solicitous of her. I helped him take the horses back to the stables, you know.'

'So I heard. We are indebted to you, my lord.'

'He bears watching, that friend of yours.'

'What do you mean by that?'

'Why, you are in danger of losing your bride, or I miss my guess.'

Mark was furious, but contained his temper with an effort. 'You, sir, are impertinent.'

'I am merely stating a fact. It seems to me all the Cavenhursts are untrustworthy.'

'Why are you so interested in my fiancée, Bolsover?'

'I am interested in all the doings of that family. Her brother has deprived me of a considerable amount of money and I cannot let that go unchallenged.'

'What do you propose to do? Neither Sir Edward nor, come to that, either of the Misses Cavenhurst, is responsible for Teddy's gambling debts.'

'Not in law, perhaps, but I am sure Sir Edward would wish to avoid the scandal of a scapegrace son welshing on his debts.'

'I believe Sir Edward considers a spell in India will set him to rights.'

'Only because he does not have the blunt to pay his son's dues, or so I have heard. It is a pity I did not know that earlier before I acquired all the debts. Now, I shall have to rethink my strategy.'

'I do not know how you came by that piece of tittle tattle, but you have been misinformed.'

'I think not. Ah, here is your friend, Mr Ashton.' He stood up. 'I leave you to make what you will of what I have said, but rest assured, by hedge or by style, I will have my revenge.'

'What did he want?' Drew asked as he sat down and beckoned a waiter.

'He was enquiring of the invalid. I do not think he cares a groat how Isabel is, he was simply trying to garner information about Teddy.'

'You can hardly blame him for that. He's lost a deal of blunt.'

'Then why spend more buying up the rest of

Teddy's debts? I do believe it is Sir Edward he is after and he means to do it through his son or his daughters.'

'I do not see how.'

'Neither do I, but he spoke of revenge, which puzzles me, since I cannot see that he has been harmed by Teddy or anyone else in the family. There is more to it than debt.'

The waiter came to take their order and they left off their discussion while they decided what to eat.

'Would you like me to try to discover what it is, while you are gone to Hadlea?' Drew asked as the waiter disappeared. 'Bolsover may have confided in some of his associates, who might not know my connection with you.'

'Yes, please do that. He appears prodigiously wealthy, which is surprising because the estate he inherited from his father is only a moderate one in Northamptonshire, not enough to support the kind of life he leads.'

They talked about how the information could be achieved and used while they ate. Not once did Mark mention Bolsover's hint that he might lose Isabel. Andrew Ashton was an honourable man, a long-term friend and he would not betray him in that fashion. But all the same, he could not quite dismiss the idea, not least because Isabel herself had been behaving strangely ever since she met him. If only she had not had that accident, they would all be on the way back to Hadlea the next day and out of harm's way.

Chapter Six

Mark called the next day before he left town and was allowed a short visit to the sick room, where Jane sat reading to her sister. Jane put the book down and went over to the window to look out on the busy street and give them a little privacy. She heard him ask Isabel how she was and her sister's low answer, but then the conversation stopped. They were silent for so long, she risked a glance. Mark was sitting on the chair she had been using and Isabel was propped up in bed, with the covers up to her chin. They were simply sitting there with nothing to say, both looking down, both unhappy.

'I am going back to Hadlea immediately,' he said at last. 'Have you a message for your parents?'

'Tell them I am doing well and no harm has been done,' she said. 'Tell them not to worry. Jane is looking after me.'

'Ah, the inestimable Jane.' He turned to her. 'You are looking tired, Jane. Has no one thought about how you feel?'

'I feel fine,' she said. 'Do not worry about me. Tell Mama and Papa I shall stay until Issie is well enough to travel.'

'I will come back and fetch you.' He rose, picked Isabel's hand off of the coverlet and kissed the back of it. 'I'll be off then. Don't do anything rash while I am away.'

Isabel laughed. 'I can't do much stuck here in bed, can I?'

He bowed to Jane and left. He was no sooner gone than Drew arrived, but Lady Cartrose did not think it fitting to allow him into the sickroom. She received him in the drawing room and gave him an account of the patient's progress and he had to be content with that.

Day by day Isabel recovered and though Jane spent some time sitting with her, trying to cheer her up, she was quiet and withdrawn. Drew called regularly to ask after the patient; Isabel did not see him, though Jane did. He was most concerned for the invalid, more than was warranted in Jane's opinion, considering Isabel was engaged else-where. She might not have thought of it if she had not seen the look on his face as he cradled her sister in his arms. She wondered whether to confront him about it, but decided against making an issue of it. Once they returned to Hadlea it would die a natural death.

When she was not sitting with her sister, Jane returned to the matter of raising funds and continued to write letters and invite people to Aunt Emmeline's soirée. Her aunt had wanted to cancel it altogether, but Isabel, feeling guilty about what had happened, insisted it go ahead a week later than planned when she was sure she would have recovered enough to play her part. Jane encouraged her to walk about her room to strengthen her muscles and, on the sixth day, Bessie helped her to dress and she went downstairs for the first time. She was there when Drew arrived on his daily visit.

'I am pleased to see you looking so well,' he said, after bowing to Lady Cartrose and Jane. 'I feared you might have sustained a serious injury.'

Isabel laughed. 'A bump on the head, that was all, and it is quite gone now. I am my old self.'

'Then I am, indeed, relieved.'

'Are you going to come to Aunt Emmeline's soirée tomorrow evening? I think it will be a very grand affair.'

'It is not meant to be a grand affair,' Jane said. 'It is to raise funds for my orphanage.'

'Well, I know that, but Aunt Emmeline has invited a great many wealthy people so it is bound to be grand.'

'Whatever it is I would not miss it,' Drew said. 'If Mark is not back in time, I shall stand in for him.'

After he had left, Isabel went back to her room to rest, but as she no longer needed anyone sitting with her, Jane went to walk in the garden where she rehearsed under her breath the words she would use to persuade people that the soldiers' orphans were a worthy cause for their charity.

It was there Mark found her on his return. 'Jane, how are you?' He took both her hands in his own and leaned back to look at her. 'You are looking pale. Have you not been sleeping?'

'I am perfectly well, thank you.' His touch was sending shivers into the very core of her. Her love for him was something that could never be cured and must never be spoken of, so every tiny touch, every short private conversation, was secretly treasured. 'You should be asking about Isabel, not me.'

'I imagine she is fully recovered,' he said drily. 'Bessie has just informed me she has gone out with Lady Cartrose and Drew.'

'Gone out?' Jane echoed. 'I thought she had gone to rest before changing for dinner. I did not even know Mr Ashton had arrived. I hope it will not exhaust her.'

'Your aunt and Drew will make sure she does not become too tired.'

'Will you wait for them?'

'Of course.'

'Did you see my parents?'

'Yes, I did. They are naturally very concerned about Isabel, but I was able to reassure them. They are looking forward to having you both safely home again.'

'I shall be glad to go home too,' she said. 'But there is the soirée tomorrow evening. I must stay for that.'

'You are going ahead with it, then.'

'Yes, Isabel would not have it cancelled on her account, so we simply informed everyone it would be a week later. I have been rehearsing what I will say to persuade people to part with their money.'

'While we wait, will you tell me what you are planning to say?'

They seated themselves on a bench in an arbour, shaded from the sun. 'I thought I would begin by telling everyone about the little beggar boy that set me thinking and how I felt not enough was being done for the soldiers' families. The men left their homes, wives and children to risk their lives and die for king and country and we should not forget that. The least we can do is remember their sacrifice and help their children. After that I will tell them about the Hadlea Children's Home and how we plan to run it and how much it will cost. I have worked out some expenditure: buying the home, furnishing it, taking on staff, running expenses like food, clothes, heating.'

'Would you like me to check the figures?'

'Would you? That would be a great help, but can you spare the time?'

'For you, Jane, I will always spare time.'

'Oh.' She was taken aback, but pulled herself together to laugh. 'You want to know how your money is being spent?'

'No, of course not. I trust you implicitly.'

'I was only joking.'

'I know, but other contributors might be more demanding and it is as well to have the answers at your fingertips.'

'If I get any other contributors.'

'I am sure you will.'

'Shall we go indoors? My notes are all there.'

They rose and went into the morning room, where Jane had left her papers spread out on the table.

They were absorbed in the calculations when Lady Cartrose and Isabel returned, accompanied by Drew.

'Mark,' Isabel said as he rose to greet them. 'I was not expecting you back so soon.'

'I came in order to attend the soirée tomorrow

evening and to take you home. Your parents are anxious to have you back.'

'I am not sure I am recovered enough.'

'You were well enough to go out,' Jane said.

'We did not go far and we went in the carriage.'

Lady Cartrose summoned a maid to bring refreshments and they sat down to converse until they arrived. 'I wanted some pink ribbon to match my gown for tomorrow,' Isabel went on. 'And Drew bought us ice creams at Gunter's. Then we saw the Regent riding by in his carriage. He deigned to smile and lift a hand in salute to us, but there were others on the road who booed him. He is enormously fat.'

'He is known to eat prodigious quantities,' her ladyship put in, demonstrating her own ability in that area when a maid brought in the tea tray and a plate of cakes.

'And that when half his people are starving,' Jane added, accepting a cup of tea, but declining anything to eat. 'No wonder he is booed.'

'There are rumours he means to divorce his wife,' Lady Cartrose put in. 'He wants an heir, but if Princess Charlotte manages to bring her latest pregnancy to term, we might have one sooner than we think.'

'I have a good mind to write to him and point out the desperate straits of the soldiers' orphans,' Jane said.

'I do not suppose a letter would ever advance beyond a second or third secretary,' Mark said, smiling at her. 'You would do better appealing to others further down the social scale.'

'Like the Duke of Wellington,' Isabel said with a giggle. 'Do you know, Mark, Jane had a reply from his secretary.'

'Did you, Jane?'

'Yes. He said the Duke was cognisant of the problem and would enter into anything the Government might do to alleviate it,' she answered, 'But he did not feel it fair to subscribe to one small charity above others, especially in a part of the country with which he is unfamiliar. His Grace could not give to all and therefore must decline.'

'An evasive answer if ever I heard one,' Mark said.

They finished drinking their tea and the men took their leave, walking swiftly in the direction of South Audley Street. 'You have been a constant visitor to Mount Street, I believe,' Mark said.

'I go to enquire of the invalid and, in your absence, to see if I can be of service to the ladies. Is there anything wrong with that?'

'No, of course not, but I did notice Isabel referred to you as Drew.'

'A slip of the tongue, no doubt. She often hears you call me that. I do not mind it, if you do not.'

'No, we are all friends. Will you come to the soirée tomorrow evening?'

'Indeed I will. I think Miss Cavenhurst will need all the support she can get. I fear she is going to be disappointed—there are too many people, like the good Duke, who think the problem is for others to solve.'

'I doubt His Grace ever saw Jane's letter.'

'You are probably right, but it is not only that. There have been rumours…'

'What rumours?' Mark asked sharply.

'That Miss Cavenhurst is using whatever funds she gathers, not for the benefit of orphans, but to help solve her father's financial difficulties.'

'Good God! Who is spreading such tales? No, let me guess. Hector Bolsover.'

'You are right. He is saying that none of the Cavenhursts can be trusted with money.'

'I was right, was I not? This is not about Teddy and his debts. Have you managed to discover what is behind it?'

'No, but I think Toby Moore might know something, so I am cultivating the gentleman. He is a very poor card player.'

Mark laughed. 'It is more the case that you are an exceptionally good one.'

'However, when he owes me a great deal of blunt I shall magnanimously offer to waive it for information. I have undertaken to play tonight. Do you come?'

'No, I have Jane's figures to check and suggestions to make ready for tomorrow.' He tapped the folder of notes he carried. 'I want to give her the best possible chance, especially in view of what you have told me.'

They parted on the corner of the road. Mark walked half the length of South Audley Street, dwelling, not on Jane's figures, but on Isabel and Drew and wondering if Bolsover, for all his nastiness, had been right in his insinuation. He should have felt angry and jealous, but surprisingly did not, or only in so far as the gossip would harm both families if the engagement were broken. It would be decidedly dishonourable to consider breaking it himself and so he must remain passive and await events. The alternative would be to tackle Drew and call him out. But what would that achieve? The death or injury of one or the other and a great many unhappy people. And maybe he was reading more into it than was actually there. He shrugged his shoulders and entered his house.

The following evening, with wine and refreshments ready in the dining room and the drawing room cleared of most of its furniture and ornaments to make room for people, Jane prepared herself for what she knew would be an ordeal.

Her gown was a pale sea-green silk of a plain design, trimmed with dark green velvet ribbon. Bessie, who dressed her hair, threaded it with more green ribbon and she wore the pearls her father had bought for her on her twenty-first birthday.

Her head was buzzing with the speech she meant to make, which she intended to be brief in favour of circulating among the guests and speaking to them individually. Mark arrived early so that they could take a last look at her figures and the notes she had made. At eight o'clock friends of Lady Cartrose began arriving and, being plied with refreshments, stood about eating, drinking and gossiping. They were followed by others, less well known, and by nine o'clock the room was full. It was then Isabel made her entrance, wearing her sari and causing something of a stir, which, of course, she had known it would. Jane could do nothing about it as her sister drifted over to Drew and asked him if he approved. Neither Mark nor Jane heard his reply.

'Let us make a start,' Mark said, turning away from the sight of his fiancée flirting with his friend. He called for attention and said a little about the reason they were gathered together and introduced Jane. Then he helped her stand on a stool so that she could be seen and heard.

She was shaking with nerves, but was so passionate about her subject, she forgot everything else and was soon in full spate. At first the audience were silent, but as she went on the murmurs grew until she was forced to stop to deal with them. 'You have questions?' she asked. 'I will answer them in due time.'

'Answer them now,' one gentleman called out.

'Very well. Who is to be first?'

'I will,' the same man said. 'How can we be sure the money you collect from us will be used for the purpose you state? I have heard your father is close to bankruptcy and the money will go to settle his debts.'

'That is a monstrous accusation,' Jane retorted angrily. 'Even if my father were bankrupt, which is a downright lie and which, were I a man, I would call you out for, it would have no bearing on the Hadlea Home, whose finances will be kept entirely separate.'

'So you say.'

'Toby Moore,' Drew had left Isabel talking to her aunt and come to Mark's side. 'He has no doubt been sent by Bolsover to disrupt the meeting. Let us throw him out.'

They moved towards the questioner. Seeing them approach, the man backed away and, reaching the door, bolted through it. But the damage had been done. Jane could not finish her speech for the heckling, as one question after another was fired at her, not about the home, which she could have understood, but about her father and brother. She did her best to parry them, but in the end it was Mark who rescued her, helping her down from the stool and climbing on it himself.

'If you will not listen to Miss Cavenhurst, then listen to me,' he shouted above the din. 'Most of you know who I am, but for those who do not, I am Lord Wyndham of Broadacres, close by the village of Hadlea. My family has been in residence there for hundreds of years and is well respected both in Norfolk and in London. I and my late father have both subscribed to the Hadlea Children's Home and I will personally guarantee Miss Cavenhurst's integrity.'

'You have an interest, you are betrothed to her sister,' someone commented in a loud voice.

'So I am, but that is all the more reason to make sure my good name is not brought into disrepute. I will appoint my own man of business to set up a trust and oversee the funds. This home is important for the little children who need it and I think it is shameful that so good a cause should be sullied by innuendo and downright calumny. Now, if you would like to make a donation, Miss Cavenhurst is here to take it. If not, I bid you goodnight.'

He stood and watched as several people made their escape, but one or two came forward to ask Jane more about what she planned to do and she was able to make the points she had been prevented from making earlier.

Only when they had all gone and she had some pledges, though not nearly as many as she had hoped, and a small pile of jewellery to which she had added her own pearls, was she able to breathe freely and thank Mark for his timely assistance.

'You were magnificent,' she said. 'I could not have managed without you.'

'It was my privilege and pleasure.'

'What did that man mean about my father being bankrupt? Where did such rumours start?'

'From Lord Bolsover, I imagine.' He paused. 'Jane, has anyone in your family ever come up against him before?'

'Besides Teddy, you mean?'

'Yes. Perhaps some time ago, something that might explain the grudge he seems to have.'

'Teddy owes him money and has escaped his clutches, is that not grudge enough?'

'I am not sure it has anything to do with Teddy. I think getting his hooks on Teddy was only a means to an end.'

'What end?'

'That I do not know, but I will endeavour to find out.'

'I cannot think of anything. Papa has always

been straight and true. I am sure you must be mistaken.'

'Perhaps.' He paused. 'You are looking tired, Jane. This has all been too much for you after looking after Isabel as well.'

'I am a little tired, but a night's sleep is all I need.' She paused, motioning to the pledges, the money and jewels. 'Will you take charge of these? I do not want to bring any more accusations down on my head if I keep them by me.'

'Yes, of course. If you are agreeable, I shall call tomorrow morning and we will go to Halliday and have a trust set up and open an account at the bank in the name of the trust. That way everyone can see it is all above board.'

'Yes, please.' She picked up a canvas bag, put everything into it and handed it to him. 'I knew something like that would have to be done, but I had not thought it was urgent. This evening has made me see so how naïve I have been. I needed you.'

'My pleasure.' He smiled and touched her hand. 'Away to your bed, Jane. I shall bid goodnight to Isabel and her ladyship and be off.'

When he had gone, she said goodnight to her aunt and sister and went to her room, undressed and tumbled into bed. It had been an eventful and troubling day, but it was over and she had made a start on her big project. She could not have done it

without Mark's help. Those rumours being spread
by Bolsover were worrying, too. They could be
very damaging especially if it became known that
the Cavenhursts were having to economise. As always happened in such cases, every creditor who
had been prepared to wait for his money would
now be knocking at their door.

Mark had said he would try to find out what lay
behind Bolsover's animosity and she could trust
him to do his best, but it was unfair of her to lean
on him so heavily. She should be more self-reli-
ant and that meant tackling Lord Bolsover herself. If only she could make him see reason about
Teddy's debts and retract his calumny, they might
all live in peace and her father's money troubles
need not be made public. It would have to be the
next day because Mark was taking them home the
day after. But how to do it? She did not know his
lordship's direction and, even if she did, it was
certainly not the thing for an unmarried lady to
visit a gentleman in his quarters. He gambled at
White's and probably other clubs, but she certainly could not venture into St James's.

Before she could decide what to do, she had
drifted off to sleep.

Jane woke next morning very early with the
problem still in her mind and it had not been
solved by the time Mark arrived with his tilbury.

She did not think that she needed a chaperon, but her aunt insisted on one and, as she was far too fat to squeeze into a vehicle meant for two, Bessie was told to accompany her.

Even so, it was a tight fit and Jane found herself so close to Mark, his trouser-clad thigh hard against hers, that she could feel its warmth through her dress. It was so unnerving she could think of nothing else and found herself almost lost for words when Mark spoke to her. When they arrived, he jumped down to hand her out and she pulled herself together to precede him into the building.

Going through the front office, where the juniors worked at their desks, Jane was reminded that her brother had once been a junior here and had left under a cloud. Would that make Mr Halliday less inclined to help her? A clerk conducted them up to the younger Mr Halliday's office, where Mark was greeted cordially.

'I have brought Miss Cavenhurst to meet you, Cecil,' Mark said. 'She would do some business with you.'

Jane bobbed, shook the outstretched hand and was offered a chair.

'The Cavenhurst affairs are usually handled by my father,' the lawyer said as he and Mark also seated themselves. 'If it is about Mr Cavenhurst…'

'It is not about Teddy or my father,' she said. 'Lord Wyndham will explain.'

As Mark spoke, the lawyer's initial wariness vanished and he became interested in Jane's project and readily agreed to set up the trust. 'Who had you in mind for trustees?' he asked.

'Miss Cavenhurst, of course,' Mark said.

'It is unusual for an unmarried lady to serve in that way,' Mr Halliday said.

'Yes, but it is Miss Cavenhurst's project, she is its leading light, so I think we should allow it,' Mark said. 'But there must be others who are not connected with the family. Would you be one, Cecil? And perhaps we could ask our bank manager.'

They had gone on to discuss the details and, an hour later, left with everything in hand and without the canvas bag containing the money and jewels. The latter would be auctioned and the proceeds added to the funds and Mr Halliday had undertaken to make the arrangements for that. Mark escorted her out to the carriage and saw her safely in. 'I have a little business of my own with Mr Halliday, Jane. I won't be long.' He went back into the building, leaving Jane sitting beside Bessie.

The street was busy with people hurrying to and fro on the pavement and vehicles of all kinds passing up and down, from gigs to grand carriages, from coster barrows to heavy drays. She was so engrossed in watching a skirmish between a skinny terrier and a spitting ginger cat, she did not see the man who approached the carriage and stopped.

'We meet again, my dear Miss Cavenhurst.'

She looked round to find Lord Bolsover doffing his hat to her. 'My lord.'

'All alone? No stalwart knight to defend you?'

'Lord Wyndham is with me.'

'I do not see him.'

'He has gone back inside for a moment, but I am glad we have met.'

'How flattering!'

'I did not intend to flatter, my lord. I wish to speak to you about the rumour being spread about my father being bankrupt.'

'Rumours? Dear, dear, that is unkind.'

'I believe you perpetrated them to discredit me and prevent me raising money for my orphans.'

'Now, why would I do that, Miss Cavendish? I am as sympathetic as the next man to the orphans' plight, but I doubt you will be able to do anything about it.'

'Why not? Someone has to if the children are not to grow up thieves and beggars. All I want is to give them a chance.'

'The reason is obvious, Miss Cavenhurst— you are a woman trying to get along in a man's world and you will meet resistance at every turn. Women are not built to fight with reason. They fight with their emotions.'

'And what is wrong with that?'

'It inclines then to make wrong decisions. You will find out the truth of that in due course.'

'My lord, that sounds like a threat. I wonder why you have taken such an aversion to me. We have only recently met and until a few weeks ago I had never heard of you.'

'Had you not? That is surprising.'

'If my brother had not been so foolish as to play cards with you, I should still be in ignorance of the kind of man you are.'

'I venture to suggest you are still in ignorance. There are two sides to every argument and you have heard only one.'

'Perhaps, but if you value truth and justice you will let it be known that you were mistaken, my father is not bankrupt and you have no reason to believe I will not conduct the affairs of the Hadlea Children's Home honestly.'

'You are assuming that it was I who started the rumour. You have no proof of it.' He smiled suddenly. 'But if the rumour is true, then I would be a fool to deny it.'

'Of course it is not true.'

'I should ask your father when you get home, Miss Cavendish, or you could go back inside that building and ask Mr Halliday senior, who is the Cavenhurst lawyer, I believe.'

'I will do no such thing!'

'You know,' he said, still smiling, 'you are quite beautiful when you are angry and your eyes flash defiance. I find myself strangely in sympathy with you and that is a weakness I cannot allow myself to indulge in.' He bowed to her, replaced his hat and strolled away.

She watched his departing back in fury and was fighting back angry tears when Mark rejoined her. 'I hope I have not been too long,' he said, climbing in beside her. 'Shall we have an ice cream at Gunter's? It is a warm day and… Jane, are you crying?'

'I am angry.'

'Why, because I left you? I am sorry for that, but I was gone only a few minutes.'

'No, it is not that. I have had an argument with Lord Bolsover. He is an odious man and refuses to admit it was he who spread the rumours about my father and he said my project can never succeed because I am a woman ruled by emotion.' She gave a cracked laugh. 'And here I am, proving it.'

'Oh, Jane, why did speak to him at all? You should have cut him.'

'I wanted to plead with him to stop the rumours.'

'You do not plead with men like Bolsover,

Jane. They would see it as weakness. Now let us go and have that ice cream and forget about him.'

But she found it difficult to do that. The man's words ate into her brain and would not go away. She longed to go home, to the peace of Greystone Manor and the comforting presence of her parents. More than anything she wanted reassurance.

The ice cream was refreshing on a very warm day, but they did not linger long at Gunter's. 'My sister and Aunt Emmeline will be wondering what has happened to us,' she said.

Far from wondering what had happened, the ladies had gone for a carriage ride, they were told by a servant. 'Mr Ashton came and they went with him.'

'Then I will not stay,' Mark said. He drew the pearls from his pocket and put them into her hand. 'These are yours, I believe.'

She stared at them. 'How did you come by them? I left them with everything else to be auctioned.'

'I know you did, but I think it would hurt your father to know you had given them away. Keep them safe, Jane.'

'Other people were giving their jewels.'

'Perhaps, but not those they treasured. Your self-sacrifice does you credit, Jane, but the trust can do without them.'

'Thank you,' she said simply and reached up to kiss his cheek. It was an impulsive gesture of gratitude, no more.

'I will bring the travelling carriage here at nine o'clock tomorrow morning, if that is convenient, Jane, and if you think Isabel is strong enough for a long ride. Otherwise we could start later and go slower. It would mean spending two nights on the road instead of one, but I do not mind that.'

'I shall ask her, of course, but I think Isabel is strong enough and we will not need to prolong the journey. I am anxious to be home again as I am sure you are. We will be ready.'

He left and she went to join Bessie, who had gone up to her room to begin packing. Jane had not brought a great many clothes with her and it was soon folded neatly into the trunk she and Isabel shared. 'I will do Miss Isabel's this afternoon,' Bessie said. 'But I do not know how we shall get it all in, she has bought a great many new clothes.'

'I expect Lady Cartrose will lend her another trunk.'

Lady Cartrose, Isabel and Drew returned soon after this. Drew did not stop, saying he was sorry he had missed Mark because he needed to speak to him before they all left for Hadlea. 'I will go and seek him out,' he said. He bowed to her ladyship, then to Jane and finally Isabel, who looked woebegone. 'Goodbye, Miss Isabel,' he said. 'Have a safe journey and my felicitations on your forthcoming nuptials.' Then he was gone.

'That was a strange thing to say,' Jane said. 'It sounded as if he were not going to be at the wedding.'

'He isn't.' Isabel was openly crying. 'He is going away. I am never to see him again. He said it was for the best.'

Jane was inclined to agree with that, but refrained from saying so in view of Isabel's distress, but she realised her fears had been justified: Isabel imagined herself in love with Andrew Ashton. How deep and how lasting it was, she did not know. The sooner they were home the better. 'Mark is coming for us at nine in the morning,' she said, turning to more practical matters. 'I have done my packing. Bessie is planning to do yours this afternoon, Issie. Aunt, do you think you can lend Isabel a trunk? She has bought so many new clothes they will not all go into the small trunk we brought with us.'

'I am sure there is one in the attic,' her aunt said and went off to ask a footman to fetch it down.

'I don't want to go home,' Isabel burst out, amid her tears.

'Why ever not?'

'Because everyone will be talking about the wedding and I cannot bear it.'

'How can that be? Less than a month ago you were talking of nothing else and looking forward to your big day.'

'Yes, and I collect you saying that a wedding was not the be-all and end-all of a marriage and you were right. I see that now. I just wanted to be a bride and Mark is so handsome and rich, but it was a mistake to say I would marry him.'

'But you did and I am very sorry if anything I said made you have second thoughts. I only meant that the wedding itself was only the beginning and played only a small part in a marriage.'

'I know what you meant, but it set me thinking about being bound to Mark for the rest of our lives and I simply cannot see it. And please do not say it is nerves, for I know it is not. I cannot marry Mark. He is not the love of my life.'

Her sister's words were hurting Jane more than she could bear. Her sister could not envisage a life with Mark whereas she could hardly envisage life without him. 'Issie,' she said slowly. 'Is there anyone else?'

Isabel lifted eyes full of misery to Jane's. 'You have guessed?'

'Is it Mr Ashton?'

'Yes. I have fallen in love with him, Jane. I think about him all the time. My heart lifts when he enters the room and drops again when he leaves it. The touch of his hand sets my body on fire and I want to cling to him and never let him go.'

Jane knew that feeling and felt herself sympathising with her sister, but for Isabel to fling off one suitor in favour of another when the announcement had already been made would cause the most terrible scandal. 'Does Mr Ashton share your feelings, Issie? Has he spoken of them?'

'Not directly, but I know he does. I know by the way he looks at me, the way he speaks. But he is too careful of his friendship with Mark to betray him, he told me that. That is why he is going away. I am so miserable, Jane. If I have to marry Mark, there will be three very unhappy people because I could never make him happy.'

Jane reflected there would be four, but that was her secret. 'I do not know what to say, Issie. Perhaps once we are home again and back into our usual routine, you will forget Mr Ashton and remember why you accepted Mark in the first place.'

'You do not understand.'

'Oh, I do. Believe me, I do.' She stood up. 'Go and help Bessie with your packing and then we will have an early supper and go to bed. We have an early start in the morning.'

Lady Cartrose returned as Jane was staring out

on to the terrace, her mind in a whirl. 'I have had a trunk sent to Isabel's room,' she said. 'Bessie is packing, but Isabel is sitting on her bed weeping.'

'She does not want to go home.'

'I know, but I do not flatter myself it is because she wants to stay with me.'

'You know?'

'I am deaf, Jane, but I am not blind. It has been obvious to anyone with eyes to see what was happening.'

'It is very worrying, especially for Mark.'

'He seems to be bearing up very well.' She paused. 'I do not think you should force her to go ahead with the marriage, Jane. It would be a disaster.'

'It is not up to me, Aunt. I am hoping when we are home again and our parents take a hand in the matter, Issie will come to see that her *tendre* for Mr Ashton is mere infatuation, a fleeting thing she can put behind her.'

'I wonder you can advocate that, Jane, considering your own feelings.'

Jane was startled. 'My own feelings do not come into it, Aunt Emmeline.'

'Then they should. You are making a martyr of yourself by ignoring them.'

Jane did not answer. She had spent more time than usual with Mark of late, which had done nothing but strengthen her feelings for him. Had it become that obvious?

* * *

Mark was busy giving orders about preparing the carriage, packing and shutting the house when Drew found him.

'How did it go with the lawyers this morning?' he asked.

'Very well. The trust has been set up and the jewels will be auctioned.' He paused. 'After our business was concluded, I left Jane in the carriage to go back inside. I wanted to rescue her pearls from the auction. Her father gave her those for her twenty-first birthday and she ought not to have sacrificed them. I bought them back.' He smiled at the memory of that peck on the cheek. 'While I was away, Bolsover turned up and he and Jane had an altercation about the rumours, which had her in tears. Even Jane is persuaded it is more than Teddy's debts with him.'

'Yes, it is. It cost me the forfeit of a thousand pounds and a top-of-the-trees stallion in winnings, but according to our friend Toby Moore, it is a long-standing grievance, something to do with the fact that his forebears once owned Greystone Manor and were cheated out of it by an ancestor of Sir Edward. He has vowed to get his revenge and establish himself once again as Lord of the Manor of Hadlea. He has not only bought up all Teddy's debts, but is doing the same with Sir Edward's. He is almost ready to make his move.'

'It is worse than I thought.'

'I wonder if Sir Edward knows what is happening.'

'I do not think so. I am sure neither Jane nor Isabel know the story or I am sure Jane would have told me. It is going to cause the most dreadful scandal if it gets out…'

'Which it cannot fail to do.'

'Poor Jane, I do not know how her orphan home will survive it.'

'And there is your wedding.'

'Yes. We must endeavour to resolve the situation before then. I am wealthy, but I do not think I can rise to such a vast sum without endangering my own estate. We must think of something else.'

'If it is money you want, then you shall have it, but it is my opinion Bolsover will refuse it. He is prodigious wealthy and is determined on having the Manor.'

'How did he come by his wealth? He seems not to have a large estate.'

'Gambling for the most part, though whether he cheats is a matter for conjecture—no one has ever caught him at it.'

'Perhaps, if we could prove that…'

'By "we", were you including me?'

'Only if you want to be included.'

'I am off on my travels again, Mark. There is nothing for me in this country after all. I came to bid you goodbye.'

'Is it because of Jane?'

'Jane?'

'Yes. It was Jane who drove you away last time, wasn't it?'

'Did she tell you that?'

'No, I guessed. Did you come back to try again?'

'I wasn't sure, but I was intent on letting Sir Edward know I had made good and that he had made a wrong decision in refusing his permission for us to marry.'

'Did Jane share your feelings?'

'I believe she did at the time, but it is certainly no longer true.'

'So you are going away disappointed again.'

'Not over Jane.'

'Who, then?'

'It does not matter because nothing can come of it. I go away for her sake and yours.'

'Isabel!'

'Look after her, Mark, and be happy.' And he turned on his heel and left.

Mark stood for a minute so confused he could not think coherently. When he pulled himself together to go after his friend, the street was empty.

* * *

Somehow the day was got through, with Isabel white-faced and their aunt flitting about trying to be helpful. Jane was glad when all the preparations were complete and she could go to bed. She undressed and crept between the sheets, but sleep eluded her. She was committed to persuading her sister to go ahead with the marriage because not to do so would be unkind to the man she loved and cause him distress. And it would upset her parents. On top of his money worries, it might very well kill her father. Money worries. What was Lord Bolsover playing at? If only Teddy had not gambled so heavily, if only her sister had not flirted with Andrew Ashton, if only she herself did not love Mark quite so much. Dear Mark. He did not deserve to be embroiled in scandal from any direction. How was it all going to end?

Chapter Seven

Throughout that long journey home, Isabel was quiet and withdrawn, Jane was thoughtful and Mark was unusually taciturn. It was evident they all had a great deal on their minds and hardly conversed at all, except to order food and drink at some of the inns where they pulled up for the horses to be changed and to approve the accommodation when they stopped for the night at the White Hart in Scole. The inn was a very old one, which had once provided lodgings for Charles II and Lord Nelson, not to mention sundry highwaymen, standing as it did on the crossroads between Norwich and Ipswich, Bury St Edmunds and the Norfolk coast.

They were offered exceptionally good food while they waited for their rooms to be prepared, but no one was hungry and the conversation was limited to comments about the magnificent fireplaces and the grand staircase, the food and wine, and the time they meant to be on the road the following morning. Jane and Isabel, who shared a room, were too tired to talk and, in any case, had nothing to add to what had already been said. Even so they slept fitfully.

The second day was spent in much the same manner as the first and thanks to Mark's foresight in arranging frequent stops for fresh horses to be harnessed, they made good time and arrived at Greystone Manor in the early evening. They were home, much to Jane's relief; the responsibility for her sister would now devolve on her parents.

Mark stayed only long enough to oversee the unloading of their trunks and pay his respects to Sir Edward and Lady Cavenhurst before carrying on to Broadacres.

'Oh, it is so good to have you home,' their mother said, hugging them both. 'I have delayed supper and you shall tell us all that you have been up to while we eat. Isabel, are you fully recovered from your fall?'

'Yes, Mama, and no harm done.' She turned as Sophie came hurrying along the hall to greet them.

'Oh, I have missed you,' she said. 'It has been quite boring here by myself. I am longing to hear all your news.'

'Go up to your rooms and change out of those

travelling clothes,' her ladyship said to the two older girls. 'Supper will be served as soon as you come down again.'

Sir Edward looked down at the two trunks which had been deposited in the hall. 'As I recall,' he said, 'you only took one trunk with you. Am I to assume you have been shopping?'

'Well, I could not go out and about town with Aunt Emmeline in the shabby gowns I had taken with me,' Isabel said. 'It was different for Jane, she was too busy with her orphans to worry about how she looked.'

'And how did you pay for them?'

'On your account, naturally. I only had pin money.'

He sighed. 'It is evidently useless to tell you to be frugal.'

'A few gowns and fripperies, Papa, will surely not break the bank,' she said.

'You are impertinent, child. Now go and change before I lose my temper with you.'

Isabel was smiling as she went upstairs with her sister. 'Papa has never lost his temper with me,' she said. 'With Teddy, yes, but never with me.'

'But you do try his patience sorely, Issie. He is looking very strained and I wonder how bad things really are.'

'You do not think that odious man at Aunt Emmeline's soirée was telling the truth, do you?'

'No, of course not.'

When she went to her room, Bessie had already unpacked her things and had gone to do the same for Isabel. Jane sat on the edge of her bed, wondering how much, if anything, she should tell her parents about the rumours and Lord Bolsover. It might only serve to upset them. On the other hand, forewarned was forearmed. She would leave the decision until the next day when everyone was less tired and they had settled in at home again.

Supper was a time for catching up, with Sophie telling her sisters what had been going on in the village in their absence, Isabel chattering about all she had seen and done, avoiding any mention of Andrew Ashton, and Jane apprising them of her visit to the Foundling Hospital and the progress she had made with her orphan project. 'Mark was a great help,' she said.

'Yes, he told us about the Foundlings when he called to inform us of Isabel's accident,' her mother said. 'How did that happen? Hacks in the Park are not usually fraught with danger.'

'I ducked to avoid the overhanging branch of a tree,' Isabel said. 'And my saddle slipped and I came off and hit my head.'

'I am surprised Mark did not check the girth before you started out,' Sir Edward said.

'I am sure he did, but it was a hired mount and a hired saddle, which no doubt did not fit properly.'

'And I believe your aunt arranged a soirée for you, Jane. Did you meet any interesting people?'

'Yes, Aunt Emmeline's drawing room was a squeeze. They knew that I would be speaking about the Hadlea Children's Home. I was very nervous at first, but I soon forgot that as I talked.'

'There were all manner of people there and some were very noisy,' Isabel added. 'There was one man who said—'

'Isabel,' Jane put in quickly, 'Mama and Papa do not want to hear that.'

'Hear what?' her mother demanded.

'It was only someone trying to cause trouble,' Jane said. 'Mark and Mr Ashton soon got rid of him.'

'Trouble?' Sir Edward queried. 'What sort of trouble?'

'He doubted my honesty. There are some people who think a woman not capable of handling money and Mark had to explain that the funds for the Hadlea Children's Home would be administered by a trust of which he would be a trustee and that seemed to satisfy most people.'

'That's not all he said.' Isabel ignored the fierce look Jane gave her. 'He said you were nigh on bankrupt, Papa, and the money Jane collected for her orphanage would go to pay your debts.'

'Issie!' Jane admonished her, noting her father's frown and the high spots of colour on his cheeks and her mother's quick intake of breath. 'There was no need to trouble Papa with that. It is of no consequence.'

'It seems to me you have been mixing with a very bad sort of society,' their mother said. 'I am surprised at Emmeline allowing it.'

'Do not blame Aunt Emmeline,' Jane said. 'She was very particular about those to whom she introduced us. The man arrived uninvited.'

'I heard D—Mr Ashton—say he had been sent by Lord Bolsover,' Isabel went on. 'He's the one Teddy owed all that money to. He is evidently angry that Teddy escaped.'

'Well, I am very relieved that you are both home again and away from all that,' their mother said. 'Let us talk of other things. I have been several times over to Broadacres to visit Lady Wyndham. She is bearing up remarkably well and talking cheerfully of the wedding. Jane, you must finish the alterations to the gown now you are home.'

'I will work on it tomorrow, Mama, when I have come back from visiting the Rector and Mrs Caulder. They will wish to know how well I did raising money.'

* * *

The sun was warm as Jane walked to the rectory next morning and she wore a simple gingham gown and a light lace shawl. The parasol she carried was a pale-cream silk with a matching fringe. In her reticule she had a record of all the people who had donated to the fund and the notes she had made after her visit to the Foundling Hospital.

Mrs Caulder was in her garden cutting early rose buds from the bush that climbed the archway of the gate. 'Jane, you are back. How did it go?'

'Well, I think. I made some notes to show you and the Reverend.'

'I believe he is in the church. I was going to take these roses for the altar. Let us go and find him. He has some news for you.'

'News?'

'Yes, I believe he has found suitable premises for the home.'

'Oh, that is good news. I am hoping we can have everything in place and the first children installed before the winter weather.'

The Rector was in the vestry, making entries into the register, but stopped when he saw Jane. 'Allow me a minute or two to finish this,' he said after greeting her. 'Then we can go into the house and talk over tea and cakes.'

While he was doing that Mrs Caulder arranged

the roses in a vase and put them on the altar and Jane idled the time looking round the church. She knew every nook and cranny of it, having been a regular member of the congregation since she was in leading strings. When she was too young to take part in the service she had feasted her eyes on everything about her. She knew the inscriptions on the tablets on the walls and set into the floor, she was familiar with the lovely stained-glass window depicting Jesus surrounded by children, and the carving on the font. Wandering into the churchyard, she began reading the inscriptions on the gravestones. There was her grandfather and grandmother and their parents and several others with the name of Cavenhurst. And there were the Wyndhams, generations of them, and Stangates, Pages and Finches, and there, in a far corner on a moss-covered stone overgrown with grass and brambles and fenced off from the rest of the churchyard, was a name that stopped her short.

Colin Bolsover Paget, beloved son of Lord and Lady Paget, died by his own hand, May 1649, aged twenty-seven years. May God forgive him and allow him eternal rest.

She brushed the moss from the stone to make sure she had read it correctly and then went round all the graves looking for the names Bolsover and Paget. There were one or two Pagets on more recent graves and she knew there was a memorial on a wall inside the church, but no more Bolsovers. Was it significant? Had she been destined by fate to find that grave? She remembered Lord Bolsover saying he would have his revenge and later telling her she did not know him at all. Did he believe that one of her ancestors had wronged the man in the grave? But it was all so long ago.

'Ah, there you are, Jane.' The Rector's hearty voice broke her reverie and she turned to see him and his wife approaching. 'We wondered where you were.'

'I was reading the inscriptions on the graves. Some of them are very moving, especially the children's. And this one, almost hidden.'

'Ah, yes, a suicide which is why it is outside the consecrated ground.'

'Do you know the history behind it?'

'No, I do not. There might be something in the parish records. Let us go indoors and you shall tell me your news and I will tell you mine.'

Jane followed her friends into the rectory and over tea and Mrs Caulder's honey cakes, she put the mystery of Bolsover to the back of her mind while she told them of everything she had done in London to promote the Hadlea Children's Home, although she did not mention the accusations made at her aunt's soirée. 'When I returned home, I found several letters and small donations as a result of my letter-writing,' she said. 'I am optimistic we can go ahead.'

'You have done well,' he said. 'And I have some news, too. I think I have found a suitable house. It is in Witherington and has been empty for some time since its last occupant died. He was an old man, living alone with only one manservant and a housekeeper. When he died, his heirs were difficult to find and the house was left to the ravages of nature. The heirs have recently come forward and put it on the market. It is large, dilapidated and cheap.'

Witherington was a small hamlet about five miles from Hadlea. It was too small to have its own church and was incorporated in the parish of Hadlea. 'I must go and see it as soon as possible. I will ask Lord Wyndham if he will accompany me, since he is one of the trustees and must approve our choice.'

She said goodbye and left them. She was already over halfway between the Manor and Broadacres, so decided she might as well go the rest of the way and speak to Mark.

She found him in the stables, arranging for the last quartet of post horses to be returned and the carriage cleaned. He was in riding breeches and shirt, which showed off his lithe figure and did strange things to her heart and belly. He turned to her with a ready smile. 'Good morning, Jane,' he said, reaching for his coat which hung on a hook by the door. 'Are you recovered from your journey?'

'Oh, it was nothing. I am quite well and a night in my own bed has worked wonders, also the news that the Reverend Caulder has found some premises for our home. I have just come from the Rectory and decided to call to ask if you could spare the time to accompany me on an inspection. The trustees will need to make the final decision as to whether we buy or not.'

'Willingly. Let us go indoors and we can decide on a day and time. I must fit it in with my obligations here and my duty to my mother.'

'If you are very busy…' she began diffidently.

He smiled at her, a special kind of smile she liked to imagine was one for her alone, but which she knew was fantasy on her part. 'Jane, when I took on the trusteeship, I knew what it would entail and I always make a point of fulfilling my obligations, so think no more of it. We will go as soon as maybe. Perhaps Isabel might like to accompany us?'

They did not have to wait to ask her. Lady Cavenhurst and Isabel were sitting in the morning room with Lady Wyndham. The two older ladies were in animated conversation about plans for the wedding, but Isabel was silent and looking glum, which worried Jane. How long before she got over her infatuation for Andrew Ashton? If she went on looking gloomy for much longer, everyone would notice. But she could not altogether condemn her; she knew what it was like to yearn for someone you could not have.

'I did not know you were coming here, Jane,' her mother said. 'You could have driven the trap, you know how I hate driving it. I am always fearful it will turn over and land us all in a ditch. And your papa positively forbade us to have the horses harnessed to the carriage for so short a trip.'

'I went to the rectory, Mama, and decided to come on here afterwards. Reverend Caulder has found a house for the Hadlea Children's Home and I needed to consult Mark about it.'

'Jane dear,' her mother said gently, 'I do think you should refer to his lordship in a more respectful way. You are no longer children.'

'Oh, no,' Mark put in. 'I should hate that. It means I must call Jane Miss Cavenhurst and Isabel, Miss Isabel. It would be too stiff for words. Let us go on as we always have.'

'Honestly, Jane,' Isabel said, 'do you never think of anything else but that project of your 's? I am sure Mark is bored to death with it. I certainly am.'

'I am sorry you think that,' Jane said. 'I was going to ask if you would like to come with us to view the house. It is at Witherington.'

'No, I should not. I have better things to do with my time. I am sure you do not need a chaperon, being too old for courtship, as everyone knows.'

'Dear me,' Lady Wyndham said. 'I fear, Isabel, you are becoming a little nervous. It must be the wedding playing on your mind.'

'Yes, perhaps it is,' she said and lapsed into silence.

Nothing more was said for several seconds while the heated air cooled and then Lady Cavenhurst rose, followed by her daughters.

'I will call at the Manor later,' Mark said, obviously meaning when Isabel had regained her composure. 'We can arrange the outing to Witherington then.'

Jane followed her mother and sister to the trap, feeling nothing but foreboding. If Isabel continued to be difficult, she feared for Mark's happiness. A calamity was unfolding before her and she could do nothing but watch helplessly.

'Isabel, what is the matter with you?' Lady Cavenhurst asked when they arrived home and her younger daughter had said not a word on the short drive. 'What has put you in the dismals?'

'Nothing,' she muttered, looking at the hall floor.

'Come now, I do not believe that. You have been in the suds ever since you returned home. I begin to think you are not glad to be back and would rather have stayed with your aunt.'

Isabel raised eyes swimming with tears. 'It isn't that.'

Jane put her arm about her shoulder. 'Issie, you had better tell Mama the whole.'

'If there is something to tell, then we will go into the parlour and sit comfortably,' their mother said, leading the way.

Isabel shot a glance at her sister. 'Come, too, Jane.'

Lady Cavenhurst sat on a sofa and patted the seat beside her. 'Sit here, Isabel, and let us hear what is making you so unhappy.'

Isabel hesitated. 'Go on,' Jane said.

Her sister took a deep breath. 'I can't marry Mark, Mama.'

'Can't marry him? Why ever not?'

'I do not love him and I cannot see myself as mistress of Broadacres.'

'Nonsense! Whatever has put that idea into your head? You have been destined to marry Mark ever since you were children. You could not wait to be grown up enough to wed him.'

'I know, but I was young and silly.'

Her mother gave her a ghost of a smile. 'You mean you are no longer young and silly? You have grown old and wise in the space of two weeks? I begin to wish I had not suggested you should go to London with Jane. Your head has been turned by the *haut monde*.'

'It is nothing to do with London or the *haut monde*. I felt like that before I went. Jane will tell you that.'

Lady Cavenhurst looked at her eldest daughter. 'Jane?'

'Issie intimated she was nervous of becoming Lady Wyndham and having to run Broadacres, Mama. She did not tell me she did not love Mark.'

'It is only nerves,' her ladyship said. 'You will overcome them.'

'It is *not* nerves, Mama. If I am made to marry Mark, I shall be miserable and so will he.'

'Well, it is too late to back out now. You have been engaged for over a year and it is a solemn undertaking. You will lay yourself open to breach of promise.'

'Mark would never do that,' Jane put in.

'No, perhaps not, but it would be a terrible blow, not only to him but to his mother, who is not strong enough to withstand it, not after losing her husband so suddenly. It is only the thought of the wedding that keeps her going. She told me that herself. It is why she shortened the mourning period.'

'Mama, I can't go through with it, I simply cannot,' Isabel wailed, tears spilling.

'You will think differently when the time comes. Mark is not a monster. You could not wish for a gentler, more considerate husband. It is more important than being in love. There are any number of successful marriages that did not start out with being in love. That will come later.'

'It won't.' Isabel was sobbing now. Jane moved over to sit beside her and put her arm about her, but she had nothing to add to what her mother had said and reiterating it would be hypocritical.

'Go up to your room and wash your face,' Lady Cavenhurst said, decidedly cross. 'I am going to find your father. He will have to know, though he has more than enough problems without you adding to them.' She stood up. 'Jane, see if you can make her see sense—perhaps she will listen to you.'

Jane helped her sister to her room where she sat on the bed, not weeping now, but white-faced and red-eyed. Jane poured some water from the jug on the washstand into a bowl and dipped a cloth into it. She wrung it out and gave it to Isabel. 'Wipe your face, Issie. Crying so much will spoil your looks.'

'I don't care. Perhaps that will turn Mark against me.'

'One thing you can be sure of is that Mark will never break the engagement, whatever you do. He is too honourable and the scandal would ruin both families.'

'You do not understand.'

'I assure you I do and I feel for you. In time, you will get over your infatuation for Mr Ashton and wonder what you ever saw in him.' She paused, wondering whether to go on. 'I did.'

'You?' Isabel was so surprised she left off crying.

'Yes, when he was staying with Mark years ago, just after they left university. Papa would not agree to me marrying him. He said Mr Ashton had no family and no prospects and I could do better. He went to India and I got over it very quickly.'

'I didn't know that.'

'No reason why you should.'

'It could not have been true love.'

'No, it was not, but I did not realise it at the time. Now I know Papa was right, not because of Mr Ashton's lack of status and wealth, but simply that I only thought I was in love. It wasn't real.'

'There you and I differ. For me it is real and will last all my life.'

'You did not tell Mama that.'

'What was the point? Drew has disappeared and I don't know where he has gone, probably back to India. I am going to be an old maid like you.'

'You will break Mark's heart.'

'I doubt it. He spends more time with you than with me.'

'That's only because he is helping me with the Hadlea Children's Home, and you could join us and take an interest if you chose.'

'I do not choose.'

They were interrupted by a knock on the door and Bessie came to tell Isabel that her father was in the book room and she was to go there at once.

Isabel rose. 'Jane?' she queried.

'No, you must go alone,' Jane said. 'He will only want you to repeat what you told Mama.'

Isabel left her and Jane went to her own room and tried to concentrate on sewing beads on the wedding dress. But her attention wandered and the needle slipped from her fingers. What could she do? She wanted to help her sister and shield Mark from scandal, but she had a dreadful feeling that, if Isabel persisted, scandal was inevitable and both families would suffer. On top of Teddy's flight from his debts and the accusations of Lord Bolsover, it would be the last straw from which they might never recover. She heard a door slam downstairs and running footsteps and then silence. Isabel had evidently fled. She did not come upstairs and Jane wondered whether to go and find her, but she really could not go on trying to persuade her sister to go ahead with the marriage when all her own senses were crying out in despair. It was one more sacrifice she was being asked to make and she was beginning to feel a trifle rebellious. In any case Isabel, who nearly always managed to have her own way, would not listen to her.

Mark could not understand Isabel's moods. He had never known her to be irritable. She flared up occasionally, but her sunny nature usually soon reasserted itself, yet now it seemed nothing he could do was right. And he was appalled by her rudeness to Jane. He could see Jane had been hurt, although she did not show it, except by the bleakness in her eyes. He hoped when he arrived at the Manor, Isabel would have made her peace with her sister and be ready to come with them to Witherington. The Hadlea Children's Home project was important to Jane and he wanted to help her, so was Isabel jealous? If she would not go to Witherington with them, then he must make up for it in other ways.

He took the route through the woods, which surrounded the Manor. The sun filtered through the canopy of trees, making dancing streaks of light along the path ahead of him. Overhead a blackbird sitting on a branch let it be known he was encroaching on its territory. There were other sounds, too—the soughing of the wind, rustling, squeaking, the distant barking of a dog—but they were only small sounds and did not impinge on the peacefulness. And then he heard another sound that was not peaceful. Someone was sobbing not far away, someone in dreadful distress. He hurried to find the source of the sound and found Isabel lying on the ground beneath an ancient oak, curled up in a tight ball.

He ran forward. 'Isabel, whatever is the matter?' He knelt down, put his arm about her and helped her to sit up. 'Why are you crying?'

'Oh, it's you.' The voice was watery.

He produced a handkerchief from his coat pocket and handed it to her. 'Did you fall? Are you hurt?'

'I didn't fall and I am not hurt, at least, not in the way you mean.' She sniffed and mopped her eyes.

'Then what is it?'

'Nothing.'

'Nothing?' he queried, tilting up her chin, making her look at him. 'You do not weep for nothing, so you had better tell me. After all, I will soon be your husband, the one to whom you turn regarding whatever is troubling you, the one whose privilege it is to solve all your problems.'

'You *are* the problem,' she burst out and began to cry again.

'Me? What have I done? If I have hurt you, then I beg forgiveness, it was not intentional. Are you cross because I spend so much time on Jane's orphanage? I'll make it up to you, I promise.'

'I do not care how much time you spend with Jane and her orphanage.'

'Go on.'

'I cannot marry you, Mark. I don't want to be Lady Wyndham. I should make you miserable.'

'You must let me be the judge of that.'

'And I should be miserable, too.'

'Ahh. There is more to it. Come, out with it.'

'Mama and Papa say I cannot break off the engagement, it will cause a dreadful scandal.'

'Not half the scandal if I were to break it off.'

'Do you wish to?'

'Isabel, my dear, I would never hold you to an engagement you found abhorrent. You may jilt me if you choose and I will not complain, but I would like to know the reason for it.'

'I do not love you, cannot love you.'

He gave her a wry smile. 'Well, that is a blow to my ego.'

'I am sorry. I am very fond of you. You are like

a big brother and I would hate to be at odds with you, but the truth is—' She stopped suddenly.

'You have fixed your affections elsewhere, is that it?'

She nodded.

He considered this only for a moment before the truth dawned on him. Isabel had flirted with Drew, had been lively and happy in his presence, and had not wanted to come home. And Drew himself had admitted that was why he was going away. How blind he had been! 'It's my friend Drew, isn't it?'

'Yes, but he said he would not betray you. That's why he went away.'

'Oh.'

'Jane says I'll get over him because she did. He had asked Papa for permission to marry her, but Papa would not allow it on account of his lack of a fortune. It is why Jane never married. She says she soon got over him, but I'm not so sure, because I cannot believe no one else asked her, not when she was young and marriageable.'

'Perhaps Jane is right.'

'She is jealous. Drew told me himself that there had been someone else, but he had got over it long ago and was glad of it.'

Mark remembered Drew saying something of the sort, but he had had no idea it had been Jane. He found his emotions churning and it had nothing to do with being rejected by Isabel. He stood up and held out his hand to help her to rise. 'Come, we will go and see your papa and thrash this out.'

She stood beside him, only reaching his shoulder. There were bits of grass and dead leaves clinging to her muslin dress and she brushed them off with impatient hands. 'You needn't come with me.'

'I was coming to see you and Jane about going to Witherington, or had you forgot?'

'Oh, that pesky orphanage. Yes, I had forgot.'

Sir Edward and Lady Cavenhurst were in the drawing room with Jane and it was evident they had been talking about Isabel's extraordinary behaviour, but stopped when they saw that Mark was with her.

'Come in and sit down, my boy,' Sir Edward said, indicating a chair. 'I can see by the look of you that my foolish daughter has told you of this silly notion of hers.'

'I do not consider it silly,' Mark said.

'No, you would not, but rest assured it is only a passing fancy. It is nerves brought about by your father's demise and the prospect of becoming Lady Wyndham and the role she will be expected to fulfil. We will school her in what is expected of her and no doubt your mother will do so, too.'

'I think perhaps it is more than that, Sir Edward, and I would not hold her to an engagement that is abhorrent to her.'

'But the scandal,' her ladyship protested.

'We can end it by mutual consent,' he said. 'It will be Miss Isabel's decision, of course, but I shall accept it gracefully.'

'But why should you?' Sir Edward queried. 'She will get over her reluctance by the time you and your mother are out of mourning. If it had not been for Lord Wyndham's untimely death, you would have been married by now. Less than a month ago she talked of nothing else.'

'That was before she met my friend, Drew Ashton.'

'What?' Sir Edward exploded, turning to Isabel who had seated herself on a chair near the door, almost as if she were prepared to flee again. 'Has that mountebank turned your head just as he did you sister's?'

'He is not a mountebank,' Isabel cried. 'He is an honourable man. I love him and he loves me.'

'I will not listen to this,' her father told her. 'I sent him packing once before and I shall do so again. You need not think I will ever consent to you marrying him.'

'I expect that is why he went away,' she said miserably.

Lady Cavenhurst turned to Mark. 'I am sorry you had to hear this, my lord. Isabel is not usually given to tantrums, as you must know. No doubt she will be in a better frame of mind tomorrow.'

'I came to arrange to go to Witherington,' he said. 'I am free tomorrow afternoon, if that is convenient to Jane?'

'Yes, quite convenient,' Jane said.

'Then I will call at two o'clock.' He rose and took his leave, leaving a silent and morose Cavenhurst family. He had no doubt they would continue to harangue poor Isabel. He did not want a reluctant wife and would happily release her. In truth, he felt nothing but a huge sense of relief. On the other hand, the revelation that Drew and Jane had once wanted to marry had come as a shock to him, but on quiet reflection, he remembered how they had seized every opportunity to be alone when Drew had come to stay at Broadacres. Sometimes his friend had gone riding alone. Had he been off to meet Jane? Was Jane still hankering after him? Was she jealous of her sister? Had they quarrelled over him? Jane had been very quiet while everyone else talked. He wished he had quizzed Drew a little more before he left. Now he did not know where he was.

* * *

He returned home to seek out his mother, who was resting in her boudoir. He ought to tell her what had transpired. It would be a dreadful shock to her and he hated the idea of upsetting her, but if Isabel did call off the wedding, then his mother would have to know and the news would be better coming from him.

She was sitting in a chair by the window, gazing out over the park. A book lay discarded in her lap. He pulled up another chair and sat down beside her. 'Mama, how are you?'

'There is nothing wrong with me, Mark. I am just a little tired. I like to see Grace, she is a great comfort to me, but Isabel's outburst has upset me. She should not have spoken to her sister like that. I cannot think what came over her.'

'She is worried and afraid, Mama. I have just been over to the Manor and learned the reason...' He paused, wondering whether to go on.

'You had better tell me at once.'

'Isabel has told me and the rest of her family that she no longer wishes to marry me.'

'Not want to marry you! What are you saying, Mark?'

'Just that. She has changed her mind. She says she does not love me.' He grinned. 'That was a blow to my pride, but I will get over it.'

'Fustian! She is a foolish girl. She has wanted

to marry you for years, she cannot have suddenly changed.'

'But she has.'

'What are you going to do about it?'

'Nothing, Mama. It is not up to me, is it?'

'You must talk to her, persuade her of the advantages.'

'Oh, I think she knows the advantages. They are apparently outweighed by the disadvantages. She does not love me and because of that is not prepared to countenance being mistress of Broadacres.' He smiled. 'So, Mama, you will remain in your place here as chatelaine a little longer.'

'You mean you are going to allow her to call the whole thing off? You will be a laughing stock.'

'Better that than take an unwilling bride.'

'She will change her mind. There are some weeks to go before the wedding.'

'Mama, I do not think I want her to change her mind. I am content to let her break the engagement. We could go travelling, you and I, when you feel stronger, that is. The gossip will soon die down when the tattlemongers find something else to talk about.'

'Don't you mind?'

'Do you know, Mother, I don't think I do.'

'But you must marry, Mark. It is incumbent upon you.'

'Perhaps I will, one day, when the furore has died down.'

'And that will be difficult to live down. Every young lady you approach will wonder what is wrong with you.'

'I hope not every young lady, Mama.'

She sighed and put a hand over his. 'As long as you do not mind, I am content. I was beginning to change my mind about Miss Isabel Cavenhurst in any case.'

He laughed and bent to kiss her cheek. 'Then we are in accord.'

He left her to rest and busied himself about the estate, then visited the Rector to learn a little more about the house in Witherington.

Chapter Eight

As Isabel had declined to go with them and the weather continued fine and warm, Mark called for Jane in the curricle the following afternoon, driving it himself. She was ready and waiting, dressed in a morning dress of primrose-coloured sarsenet, trimmed with blond lace, and a matching pelisse. On her dark curls she had tied a cottager straw hat.

'I spoke to Henry Caulder yesterday,' Mark told her as they trotted along the country lanes, now in sunshine, now in the shadow of the trees. 'He told me what he knew of Witherington House. He said it was dilapidated, which is why it is so cheap.'

'Yes, he told me that. By all accounts it will mean a deal of work to make it habitable. Perhaps the cost of repairs will outweigh the low purchase price.'

'That we shall have to see.'

'How much land is there with it? I should like the children to have somewhere to play.'

'Very little. Most of it has been sold to local farmers as arable and pasture, but there is an acre of garden. We should not want more than that or we would have to employ gardeners.'

'The boys could help with the gardening. If you remember, the Foundling Hospital told us the children were allotted tasks as they grew old enough to do them. I think it is a good idea to give them a little idea of the world of work. I want to fit them to earn their living, to make begging and thieving a thing of the past.'

'You will need some staff: a matron, teachers, a housekeeper, a maid or two and an odd-job man.'

'I know. We can use local people who are out of work.'

They continued to talk about the Hadlea Children's Home all the way and Jane was glad of that. It was easier than speaking of the events of the day before, still large in her mind and, she suspected, in Mark's mind, too. After he had left them, her parents had flatly refused to listen to any more of Isabel's pleading and told her she would change her mind and not disgrace the family with gossip. It was bad enough that Teddy had embarrassed them and been forced to flee the country, but this would be worse and they would not hear of breaking it off. Isabel had resorted to weeping all over Jane and begging her to intercede on her behalf. Jane could not do it, could not hurt Mark. He had been very understanding, but she wondered how he really felt, particularly about Issie's confession that she believed herself in love with Drew, but of course she could not ask him.

They passed a few scattered cottages, an inn and a small triangular green where two women gossiped at a pump, then turned into an overgrown drive, whose gates were permanently open and trapped in weeds and long grass. A short ride and the house came into view. It was a large square house, not much smaller than Greystone Manor, covered in ivy, which hung over the windows in long strands. There were several slates missing from the roof and one of the chimney stacks had lost its coping. Mark pulled up at the front door and they sat surveying the building in silence before Mark jumped down and came round the vehicle to help her down. He preceded her up a dozen steps to the blackened oak door with its rusty lion's-head knocker and beat a tattoo.

'No one is living here, surely,' she said.

'I am told there is a caretaker.' He rapped again and waited, but no one came. He tried the door, but it was bolted from the inside. 'Let's try the back,' he said.

They found an old man in the yard chopping wood. 'Are you the caretaker?' Mark asked.

'Who wants to know?'

'I do. I am Lord Wyndham and this is Miss Cavenhurst. We have come to view the property.'

The man stuck the axe in the chopping block. 'Best come with me, then, though if you're expecting a palace, you've come to the wrong place. 'Tain't fit to live in.'

'We know that,' Jane said. 'What is your name?'

'Silas Godfrey, miss.'

He led the way into the house through the kitchen. There was a woman standing at the table, cutting up a hare. 'My wife, Dotty,' he said, then to her, 'These folks have come to view the house.'

She gave them a quick bob and continued her work. Silas led them from the kitchen into a narrow hall at the end of which a door led to the front of the house. 'Have you been here long?' Jane asked him, as they crossed a black-and-white-tiled hall and entered what would have been the dining room. It was oak-lined with a deep window looking out on to a terrace. Weeds were growing in the cracks in the paving.

'All me life. Come here as a nipper, I did.'

'Then you will know what the house was like in the old days.'

'That I do. Grand it were. It were well kept, too, with any number of servants. Sir Jasper and her ladyship useta give dinner parties in this room. There were always sumf'n going on. The hoi polloi from Lunnon useta come down to stay.' They followed him to the drawing room, a large room with lofty ceilings and carved cornices and windows on two sides, one of which looked out on to the terrace, the other on to a tangle of long grass, weeds and overgrown rose bushes, which had once been a garden. 'It all stopped when her ladyship took ill,' he went on while Mark inspected everything, stamping on the floorboards and poking his finger into the window frames. 'She were ill a long time and when she died, Sir Jasper let everything go. He would not have anyone here. Cut himself off, he did, and started acting strange.' They moved to another smaller room, which smelled fusty and airless and made Jane wrinkle her nose. It had obviously once been a parlour, but there was a narrow bed set against the wall by the window. An outer door led on to the weed-infested side garden. 'Shut himself in this here room, he did, and never moved out of it day or night. We'll go upstairs now, but watch out, some of the treads are missing and the banister i'n't safe.'

Up the stairs they went. The old man obviously found the climb an effort because he was breathless at the end of it. He recovered quickly and was soon talking again. 'The servants left one by one.

There weren't much point in a-keepin' 'em on. There were only me and Dotty left when he died. The lawyer what come down from Lunnon asked us to stay and keep an eye on the place while he found Sir Jasper's heirs. Seems he didn't have no close family. Place hev got even worse since then. I can't do the work nor can Dotty.' All the time he was speaking he was going from room to room, throwing open doors. The bedrooms were in semi-darkness because of the ivy, which was already encroaching into the rooms through broken windows. At the end of the wide corridor there were more stairs. 'There's another floor,' he said, reluctant to climb.

'We can manage on our own,' Mark said. 'You go down again, we will find you when we are ready to leave.'

He left them and they climbed more stairs to the next floor where the servants would have been housed.

'It is in a parlous state,' Jane said. 'I begin to wonder if it is worth our while to take it on.'

'I think it is solid enough, the brickwork is sound and the damage fairly superficial. A small army of workers would soon have it to rights.'

She laughed. 'Where am I to find an army of workers?'

'Almost anywhere given the unemployment situation. I can set them on and oversee the work, if you wish. If we decided to go ahead at once, we could have everything done by the winter.'

'But, Mark, you already have so much to do. I feel I am taking advantage of you and burdening you with more problems.'

'Nonsense. You have never taken advantage of me, Jane, and if it is a burden, which I dispute, I bear it willingly.'

'I wonder at you being so kind and helpful given the dreadful way you have been treated.'

'Treated, Jane? You mean by Isabel?'

'Yes. I am so sorry. I wish she had never gone to London with us. It all went to her head.'

'I think it is better that she told me now and not after we were married, don't you?'

'But Papa is determined she will go through with the wedding.'

'I hope he will not insist. Isabel can break it off without too much damage being done. I certainly cannot.'

She looked at him in surprise. 'Would you wish to?'

'I do not want an unwilling wife, Jane.'

'Oh.' Did he really mean he wanted an end to the engagement? It was strange if he did, because both families had been talking about it ever since Isabel left the schoolroom. She remembered it especially because she had been suffering herself at the time and it had made her even more miserable. She had been foolish, she knew that now.

He smiled to reassure her. 'I will speak to Sir Edward.'

'Papa won't let her marry Mr Ashton, I know.'

'But Drew is not the man he was ten years ago, Jane.'

'Oh! So you know?'

'Yes. Do you…? Are you—?' He stopped suddenly.

'Am I still in love with him? No, Mark, I never was, not truly. Oh, I pined for a while, but then I came to my senses and was thankful for my escape. He is rich and self-assured and has turned Issie's head. She will doubtless get over it, as I did.'

'Perhaps, perhaps not. Now let us go downstairs again and inspect the outbuildings. And then we shall have a little picnic before we make our way home.' He started to lead the way down the upper flight, talking over his shoulder. 'I asked my housekeeper to make up a little basket of food and a bottle of wine.'

She knew the subject of Isabel and the wedding was closed and he would not refer to it again, but it left her longing to know how he really felt. Was he just being chivalrous or did he mean he no longer wished to marry Isabel? What would happen if, in a couple of months' time, Isabel succumbed to their father's blandishments and agreed to marry Mark after all? She had begun to hope, just a little, but realised how futile that was. Even if he did not marry Isabel, it was no reason to think he would turn to her. There were any number of younger, more beautiful ladies for him to choose from.

She followed him down. His dark hair curled into the nape of his neck in a most enticing way; she felt an inexplicable urge to reach out and pull her fingers through it, to straighten it and watch it spring back when she let it go. Engrossed in that, she did not look where she was going and her foot caught in a broken stair tread. She flung her arms out to save herself, pushing him in the small of the back. He just managed to save himself from falling and in so doing cushioned her fall so she did not go all the way down. He eased her down on to the next step and sat beside her, his arm about her shoulders. 'Jane, are you all right? Have you hurt yourself?'

'My ankle. I think I've twisted it. It was that rotten step.'

He looked down at her foot. The ankle was already swelling. 'Do you think you can get down the rest of the stairs if I support you?'

'I'll try.'

She did try, but winced and uttered a muffled cry when she put her weight on to her foot.

'I'll carry you,' he said. 'Put your arms about my neck.'

'You will stumble with me. I can do it.'

'No, you cannot.' He scooped her into his arms and carried her down to the ground floor and back down the hall to the kitchen. She could feel the hair which had so entranced her, as she clasped her arms about his neck. It was soft and not wiry at all.

Mrs Godfrey had just put the hare into a pot on the stove and was scrubbing the table. She looked up when they entered. 'Mercy me, what happened?'

Mark lowered Jane carefully into a chair. 'Miss Cavenhurst caught her foot in a rotten stair and twisted her ankle. It will need bathing in cold water and binding up.'

'Them stairs will be the death of someone afore long,' the woman said, as she went to a pail and poured water into a bowl which she placed at Jane's feet. 'Here, take your stocking off, miss, and put your foot in that. It'll cool it, while I fetch some binding.'

'I'll wait outside, Jane,' Mark said. 'Mrs Godfrey will call me when it's done and I'll carry you out to the curricle.'

'I feel such a fool,' Jane said when this was accomplished and she was sitting in the curricle ready to be taken home, one ankle heavily bandaged, its shoe on the floor by her feet. 'We were warned the stairs were unsafe, I should have paid more attention to where I was putting my feet. Thank goodness you were there to cushion my fall. Did I hurt you?'

'No, I only wish I had taken more care of you.'

'It wasn't your fault. And we didn't look at the outbuildings after all.'

'I did while Mrs Godfrey was binding you up.' He flicked the reins to start the horse off on the homeward journey. 'There are some stables, a coach house and a shed. Mr Godfrey was in the garden where he had planted a few rows of cabbages and beans and he showed me round. There is a small dower house on the far side of the garden which is included in the sale.'

'Do you think the house is in too bad a state for our purpose?' Her ankle was hurting abominably, but she tried to ignore it.

'Not if the price is right.'

'I have a picture of it, repaired, redecorated and furnished, its windows gleaming and the garden neat and tidy. And children's laughter echoing everywhere. I want the children to be happy.'

'Of course you do, so do I.'

'The first-floor rooms are spacious enough to make dormitories, the upper rooms the servants' quarters and perhaps a small infirmary if any of the children should be unwell. Downstairs could be the refectory and the school rooms.'

'You were thinking all that as we went round, were you not? It's as if it is already yours.'

'Not mine, Mark, the trust's.'

'As you say. Would you like me to negotiate with Mr Halliday for you? I am afraid you are going to have to rest that foot for a little while.'

'Yes, curse it,' she said. 'But please do what you can.' She paused. 'We didn't have our picnic, did we?'

'No, but it is not too late. Are you hungry?'

'A little.'

He turned the curricle off the road into the shelter of some trees where he brought it to a stop. 'Sit there,' he said, jumping down and removing a wicker basket from under the seat. She watched him place it under a tree. He took off his coat and laid it on the grass, then came back for her.

'I can hop down,' she said, placing her good foot on the step and trying to stand.

'I think not.' He scooped her up as if she weighed no more than a feather and carried her to the tree where he gently lowered her on to his coat and sat beside her, so close she could feel his trouser-clad thigh through her thin dress. It was highly improper, but there was no one to see them and Mark himself seemed unaware of the impropriety. She knew she ought to move away, but she stayed where she was, letting her imagination play with a picture of them as a married couple and it was quite in order for him to put his arms about her, carry her, sit so close they touched.

'Comfortable?' he asked.

'Yes, thank you.'

He pulled the basket closer and began unpacking it, bringing out ham and chicken legs, bread and pastries, two plates, a bottle of wine and two glasses. 'This is a feast,' she said.

'Yes, Mrs Blandish lives in fear that I shall starve, so help yourself or I shall be in trouble if I take anything back.' He was pouring wine as he spoke and handed her a glass.

'It's champagne,' she said as the bubbles tickled her nose.

'Yes, perfect for a summer's picnic, don't you think?'

'It's lovely.'

'You deserve the best.'

She looked sharply at him and realised he was looking intently at her, as if studying her face, waiting for a reaction. For a second or two she wondered if he was going to try to seduce her and what she would do, but then dismissed the idea as preposterous. She was perfectly safe with him. And somewhere in the depths of her, where she kept her most secret thoughts, she wished she were not. She tried a light laugh, but it sounded cracked. 'That's the sort of thing you should be saying to Isabel to make her change her mind.'

'But I might not want her to change her mind.'

'You are hurt and who can blame you? She has been very unkind to you.'

'Not unkind, honest, and that I can admire, but if she does not love me, then there is no way I would try to persuade her to marry me if she does not want to. I do not have to beg for a lady's favour, Jane. I have more pride than that. Now drink and eat and let us not talk of Isabel again, I am becoming tired of hearing her name.'

She obeyed and they ate in silence for a few minutes, but the silence was making her conscious of other things: the warmth of the sun filtering through the leaves; the song of a thrush singing its heart out; the sheep, shorn of their winter fleece, cropping the meadow behind them; his nearness; her yearning and, over it all, the ache in her ankle, which was even more swollen and throbbing painfully. She had to distract herself from it.

'What needs doing to Witherington House first?' she asked, surprised at how normal her voice sounded.

'Once we have possession, you mean? I think the roof must be first, to make it weatherproof, then the stairs…'

'Definitely the stairs,' she said, laughing a little.

'Yes, then any alterations to the rooms and painting and decorating. Then finding furniture and taking on staff.'

'Do you really think we can have it all done by the winter?'

'I don't see why not.'

'And will we have enough money?'

'We must continue to raise more.'

'I can write more letters and organise the fair we spoke of.'

'On one leg, Jane?' he queried, raising an eyebrow to her.

'That will soon mend and I will still be able to drive the trap round the village and round up some help.'

He looked down at the limb in question. There was no doubt it was more swollen. 'I think we had better cool that down before we go on.' He knelt to release the bandage, unwinding it carefully. The foot was beginning to turn purple. 'You must see a doctor as soon as we get back. Sit still. I'll go and soak this in water.'

Sit still! She could hardly move. She ate a little of the bread with some ham and washed it down with wine, which seemed to be going to her head.

He came back with the cloth wrung out in a

stream he had found. 'This should help,' he said kneeling to rebandage her foot.

In spite of his care, she could not stop a squeak of pain mixed with pleasure at his touch. Oh, she was a mass of contradictions.

'I'll be as gentle as I can,' he said.

'You are being gentle, Mark, and I am being a coward.'

'You are certainly not that. Now, is that better?'

'Much, thank you.'

'I think we had better get you home. Have you had enough to eat and drink?'

'Yes, thank you. It was delicious.'

He packed the remnants away and put the basket back in the curricle, then came back for her. Putting his hands under her arms he pulled her upright on one foot, then picked her up. 'I'm sorry to be such a nuisance,' she said.

'You are not a nuisance. It is not often I am called upon to carry a beautiful young lady in my arms and for you it is a pleasure and a privilege.'

Beautiful, he had said. She didn't believe it for a minute; she was plain Jane, always had been, always would be, but it was lovely to hear it. In spite of her injury, it had been a wonderful day altogether. To have him to herself in close proximity was a treat to be savoured and remembered in years to come.

Mark drove very carefully, trying to avoid potholes and bumps in the road, but either she had drunk too much champagne or the pain was making her head swim, but try as she might, she could not keep it upright. Her eyes closed and she lolled on his shoulder.

He turned to smile at her and transferred the reins to the other hand so that the movement of his arm did not disturb her. Why he had only recently noticed how lovely she was, he did not know, and it was not simply a lovely face, she had a lovely temperament, quiet, caring of others, often to the detriment of her own needs, and he loved her. He could not tell her so while he was engaged to her sister, Jane herself would never countenance that, but as soon as he was officially free he would have to speak of it. He wanted her, he wanted her so badly he ached.

He could imagine her as Lady Wyndham, managing his household efficiently and without fuss, standing at his side at official functions, being a wonderful mother to their children, loving him. Was it possible? He was annoyed to think that it all depended on the whim of Isabel. It was a pity Sir Edward was so against Drew. Where was Drew?

His musing came to a halt as he pulled up at the front door of Greystone Manor. Gently he touched her hand to wake her. 'Home, Jane.'

She looked startled, as if not sure where she was. 'Have I been asleep?'

'Yes. It probably did you good. Now we have to face your parents and they will undoubtedly give me a jobation for not looking after you.'

'Do not be silly, of course they will not.'

He lifted her down and carried her up the steps. 'Can you reach the knocker?'

The door was opened by Ruby, the downstairs maid. 'Lord a' mercy,' she said. 'What happened?'

'Miss Cavenhurst has had an accident,' Mark said. 'Fetch Lady Cavenhurst, will you?'

The maid scuttled off and Mark put Jane down to stand on one foot, but he kept his arm about her. They were standing like that when Sir Edward and Lady Cavenhurst came hurrying towards them, closely followed by Isabel and Sophie.

'What happened?' her ladyship said, looking at the pair and then down at Jane's foot.

'I caught my foot in a broken stair tread at the house,' she said. 'It is a little swollen and painful, but it will be better by tomorrow.'

'I think Miss Cavenhurst should be taken to her room,' Mark put in. 'She can tell you all about it when she has been made comfortable and the doctor sent for.'

'Yes, yes, of course,' Sir Edward said. 'I'll send for a footman and...'

'No need, I can carry her. Lead the way.' He

bent to scoop Jane up again, evincing a little 'oh' from Jane and a bigger one from Isabel.

'I will send someone for the doctor,' Sir Edward said, turning away, leaving his wife to precede Mark with his burden up the stairs. No one spoke until Jane was safely deposited on her bed and the injured foot put on a cushion.

'Thank you, Mark,' she said. 'I could not have managed without you.'

'With your permission, Lady Cavenhurst, I will call tomorrow to see how the patient fares.'

'Of course, you do not have to ask.'

He bowed and took his leave.

'Well, this is a fine state of affairs,' her ladyship said, sitting on the bed beside her daughter. 'You had better tell me exactly how it happened. And I do believe you have been drinking.'

'We had some wine with our picnic.'

'Picnic? I was given to understand you were going to look at a house for your home.'

'So we did, but Mark had brought a picnic basket. After all, we were going to be gone some time. I believe it was Mrs Blandish's idea. She thought Mark would be hungry.'

'And did you stumble before or after you drank the wine?'

'Mama, what are you saying? Do you think I was drunk? How could you? If you will stop quizzing me for a minute, I will tell you exactly how it happened.'

There was a knock on the door and her sisters came into the room. 'Are you badly hurt, Jane?' Sophie asked. 'What was it like to be carried by a man and a handsome one at that? I bet Issie is jealous.'

'I am not,' Isabel protested.

'If you must know, it was humiliating and embarrassing,' Jane said.

'Then tell us all about it.' Sophie plopped herself on the other side of the bed, making Jane cry out when her leg was disturbed. 'Sorry, Jane.' She moved away.

'Is it very painful?' Isabel asked, hovering at the bedside.

'Yes, it is.'

'I always thought that home orphanage idea was a bad one.'

'It is not and this isn't going to stop me. We have decided to take the house. It can be made good.'

'By "we" you mean you and Mark, I suppose.'

'And Mr Cecil Halliday. He is also a trustee.'

'If it is in such a sorry state that it has broken stair treads, then it is perhaps not a good idea,' their mother put in. 'You might have been killed.'

'But I wasn't, was I? Mark was in front of me and he broke my fall.'

'It seems we have a great deal to thank Mark for.'

'Yes, indeed. He says the house can easily be

put to rights and it will make an ideal home for the children.'

'Mark this, Mark that—do you never tire of saying his name?' Isabel demanded of Jane.

'Hush, Isabel,' their mother said. 'There is no call to be jealous of Jane.'

'I am not jealous, not even faintly, so you can forget that.'

In the silence that followed they heard the front door knocker. Lady Cavenhurst went to greet the doctor and Isabel followed her from the room.

'Don't take any notice of Issie,' Sophie said. 'She has been a terrible crosspatch ever since you came back from London. Not a civil word out of her.'

'She is unhappy, Sophie, she cannot help it.'

'It is just like you to make excuses for everyone, Jane. Sometimes you are too kind and everyone takes advantage of you.'

Jane laughed. 'And you do not, I suppose.'

'I try not to. The trouble with Issie is that she cannot make up her mind, especially when Mama and Papa keep on at her.'

Before Jane could answer, her mother brought the doctor into the room and Sophie slipped out of it.

While the doctor removed the now-dried bandage, Jane mused on what Sophie had said. Was Issie really being persuaded? If so, how genuine was it? It put the euphoria of her happy day with Mark into perspective. It was an interlude, an intermission, a pause in her humdrum life, a memory, no more, and she was left with the pain.

Mark went home, left the horse and curricle with Thompson, one of the grooms, and went indoors by the kitchen door, carrying the picnic basket. Mrs Blandish was there, preparing the evening meal. 'You are back, Master Mark… Oops, I should have said "My lord", shouldn't I? I can't seem to get used to it.'

'It doesn't matter, Mrs Blandish.' He put the basket on the table.

'Did you enjoy the picnic?'

'Very much, though Miss Cavenhurst had a slight accident on the stairs at the house.'

'I am sorry to hear that, sir. I hope she was not badly hurt.'

'A sprained ankle. But she enjoyed the food and desired me to tell you so.'

'Thank you, sir. It is always good to be appreciated. Your mother is in the drawing room.'

He went on his way. It *was* good to be appreciated and Jane had appreciated his help, too, but did everyone appreciate her? She hardly seemed to notice how much everyone relied on her—brother, father, sisters all made demands on her—but perhaps now she could not do so much, they might come to realise it. One thing he was determined on and that was to help her with her orphanage as far as he was able. There would be some hefty expenses and the trust might run out of money, but he could always assist there, not only from his own funds, but by calling on his many wealthy friends.

His mother turned from gazing out of the window to smile at him as he came into the room and dropped a kiss on her forehead. 'How are you, Mama?'

'I am well. How did it go?'

He sat down near her and launched into a recital of all he and Jane had seen and done, and the fact that Jane had been hurt.

'I must call on the Manor tomorrow,' she said.

'I'll drive you over, Mama. I said I would go and see how Jane is and we need to talk again about raising more funds. Jane has suggested holding a fair in the village with stalls and competitions and donated prizes. I have said we could use Ten Acre Field for the venue, if you agree. It is far enough away from the house not to disturb you.'

'Of course, but you are master here, Mark, you do not have to ask me.'

'And you are still its mistress and I would do nothing to discommode you.'

'Is Isabel still persisting in her foolish notion?'

'I believe so. I have not seen her today, she is bored by the whole project and did not come with us.'

'That is a pity. Going out with Jane unaccompanied is bound to cause gossip, however innocent it is.'

'There is going to be a certain amount of gossip in any case if the engagement is cancelled.'

'All the more reason not to invite more.'

'But Jane needs my help.'

'So she may do, but until you receive word from Sir Edward himself that the engagement has officially been broken off, I advise you to be a little more circumspect. You could even try being a little more attentive to Isabel.' She smiled and patted his hand. 'Now, away with you. I am supposed to be resting.'

He left her and went to the library to write to Cecil Halliday, suggesting the trustees make an offer for Witherington House and followed that by making lists of what needed doing in an effort to take his mind off Jane. He had talked to his mother calmly, but he was feeling far from calm. He felt helpless, waiting for something to happen. It was like a storm gathering on the horizon and not knowing exactly where or when it would strike.

Chapter Nine

Jane was reclining on a sofa in the morning room, talking to her mother and Isabel about her proposals for fund-raising when Lady Wyndham arrived with Mark. Isabel immediately rose, curtsied to them both, muttered something about needing to find Sophie and left the room.

'Please do not try to get up,' Lady Wyndham said, putting a hand on Jane's shoulder as she struggled to rise and ignoring Isabel's hurried departure.

The two older ladies kissed each other's cheeks. 'How are you, Helen?' Grace asked, ringing for a servant. 'You look a little better.'

'I am. I do not think I shall ever recover completely from the loss of my dear Richard, but life must go on, you know. We came to see how Jane is. I was sorry to hear of her accident.'

They seated themselves and Mark took a chair

opposite Jane and leaned forward. 'How are you, Jane? Did you manage to sleep?'

'Yes, thank you. Doctor Trench left a sleeping draught for me. I have to keep the limb up for a few days and then walk a little to see how I manage.' She was aware that she sounded stiff and formal, but she felt embarrassed by what had happened the day before: drinking too much champagne; his touch, which set her limbs on fire; the way their bodies melded together as he lifted her on and off the curricle; the conversation which had, at times, been perhaps too personal, especially when talking of Isabel. It made her feel guilty, too, as if she had been disloyal.

The maid returned with a tray containing a teapot, tea caddy and cups and Grace began dispensing tea, while continuing the conversation. 'I question whether a house in such a dilapidated state is fit to make into a home, even for orphans,' she said, addressing Lady Wyndham, as if orphans did not deserve a home such as other people enjoyed.

'I did, too, but Mark assures me it can be put to rights, but it is a great responsibility for an unmarried lady to take on.'

'The responsibility is divided between the trustees, of which I am one,' Mark put in. 'And I have told Jane I will help all I can.'

'I appreciate that,' Jane said quietly. 'I will try not to call on you more than I have to.'

'Call on me as often as you like.'

'I do think it is a pity Isabel does not interest herself in the scheme,' Helen said. 'A man needs a wife who takes an interest in the things he is interested in, otherwise they may as well live separate lives.'

'Oh, then…' Grace stopped and looked at Mark.

'Mother knows,' he told her. 'She is of the opinion Isabel will change her mind.'

'Of course she will,' Lady Cavenhurst said briskly. 'It is only a silly fancy because she is nervous of the responsibilities she will have as Lady Wyndham. I have told her your mother will be there to guide her.'

'Naturally, I will,' her ladyship agreed.

'Thank you,' Grace said. 'You are very understanding.'

'Not at all. I remember how terrified I was when I married Wyndham. It was his mother who helped me.'

Jane stole a glance at Mark who had taken no part in the conversation. His face was wooden. He sipped his tea and looked anywhere but at her. She was glad when the short visit came to an end and she could return to the plans for the fair which she had started. She needed to involve the whole village and the Reverend Caulder was the best one to help her. She would ask him to make a reference to it from the pulpit on Sunday. The swelling in her ankle would have abated by tomorrow and she would be able to hobble out to the trap and drive into the village. There was a crutch somewhere in the outbuildings that Teddy had used when he had broken his leg years before; if it could be found it would help her to walk to and from the trap.

She was driving round to the stables on her return from the village next afternoon when she noticed a carriage in the yard and wondered who the caller could be. Not Mark or his mother—she knew their vehicles; not anyone in the village, it was too grand and was dust-covered enough to have travelled some distance. The coachman was giving the horses buckets of water helped by Daniel. She stopped and used the crutch to support her as she climbed down. Daniel saw her predicament and ran to help her.

'Who is our visitor?' she whispered, as he helped her into the house by the kitchen door. The front steps were beyond her.

'Mr Halliday.'

'Oh.' With the aid of her crutch she hobbled through the house to the drawing room, where she found her mother and sisters.

'There you are, Jane,' her ladyship said. 'We have a visitor.'

'So I perceived.' She sank gratefully on to a sofa beside Sophie and laid the crutch on the floor beside it. Her leg was beginning to ache abominably after her exertions. 'Is it Mr Halliday?'

'Yes. He and your father have been closeted in the book room for hours. We have all been requested to wait in here until they emerge.'

'Do you know why he is here? Did Papa send for him?'

'I do not think so. They were both looking very serious.' She appeared her usual calm self, but Jane could see she was trembling. 'I suspect they are talking about making economies.'

'Ugh, I hate that word,' Isabel said.

'Papa did warn us,' Jane said.

'So he did, but I cannot think he meant it. People like us just do not economise.'

'People like us?' Jane asked, lifting one eyebrow.

'Gentry.'

'Issie, gentry or not, we have to cut our coat according to our cloth.'

'And that is a silly thing to say.'

'How has your morning been, Jane?' her mother asked, changing the subject abruptly. 'How did you manage?'

'I managed very well. Everyone was helpful.

The Reverend Mr Caulder is going to speak about the Hadlea Children's Home after his sermon on Sunday when he makes the usual announcements. He will ask the congregation to offer their services to help run the fair, and for donations for the stalls and the prizes. We have decided to have it on the last Saturday in August on the Ten Acre Field.'

'Are you sure it will not overtax your strength?' her ladyship queried.

'Mama, I am as strong as an ox and my leg will be quite mended by then.'

They heard a door open and close, then their father, followed by the senior Mr Halliday, entered the room. They both looked sombre. Sir Edward invited the lawyer to be seated and then drew up a chair to sit close to his wife. There was silence for a moment while everyone looked towards him expectantly.

He cleared his throat. 'My dear,' he said, addressing his wife, 'the situation is far worse than I thought. I am afraid we have to make changes in our way of life. Big changes.'

'But why?' she queried. 'It is not as if you are a gambler like Teddy.'

'I don't gamble at the card table, it is true, but I gambled on the 'Change. The harvests have been bad for some time, but last year was the worst. The crops failed, the tenant farmers could not afford their rents and the Home Farm has made no profit at all in three years. In truth, it ran at a loss. My capital was dwindling and I thought buying and selling stock might see us through the worst of it. I was ill advised, not by Mr Halliday, but by others.' He sighed heavily and appeared to be on the verge of tears. 'I lost everything and in order to maintain our style of living I borrowed and allowed the debts to mount up. They are being called in and I cannot honour them.'

'What are we to do?' she asked, while their daughters looked from one to the other in shock. 'Must we do as Jane suggested a few weeks ago and get rid of the carriage and horses and dismiss the servants?'

Theodore Halliday interrupted with a gentle cough. 'My lady, I am afraid such economies would not be enough. It is unfortunate that all Sir Edward's debts have passed into the hands of a single person.'

'Lord Bolsover.' Jane had almost been holding her breath and she let it out on the man's name.

'I'm afraid so. He has made no secret of the fact.'

'What has the man against us?' Jane asked. 'Do you know, Mr Halliday?'

'I am afraid I do not.'

'Do you, Papa?'

He shook his head without speaking. His face was white and his hands were shaking.

She turned back to the lawyer. 'Are his lordship's claims valid?'

'I am afraid they are.' He paused. 'Unless it is put out of his reach, he will claim the whole estate.'

'Greystone Manor?' Grace gasped. 'He can't do that, can he?'

'I am afraid he can if your husband makes no effort to recompense him.'

'But it is our home. The Cavenhursts have lived here for generations, ever since the Interregnum.'

'I am inclined to think his motives might go back as far at that,' Jane put in. 'I found a headstone tucked away at the side of the churchyard. It said…' She paused to make sure she had the wording correctly. '"Colin Bolsover Paget, beloved son of Lord and Lady Paget, died by his own hand, May 1649, aged twenty-seven years. May God forgive him and allow him eternal rest." Do you think that might be significant?'

'Perhaps, but whether it is or not will not help the present situation,' the lawyer said.

'What will help?'

'We have to sell the Manor and move to a smaller house where we can live more economically,' Sir Edward put in, speaking in a choked voice. 'We have no alternative.'

'Then Bolsover has won,' Jane said.

'Not quite,' Mr Halliday put in. 'If it is the Manor he wants, then selling it and paying him off with the proceeds will deprive him of it and leave enough for you to live in more modest surroundings.'

'Where?' demanded Isabel. 'We will never be able to hold up our heads in Hadlea ever again.'

'Why not?' their father demanded. 'You are to be married to Mark Wyndham and will be leaving home. Teddy has already left and no doubt Sophie will soon follow you to the altar, so it is easily put about that your mother and I and Jane do not need so large a house.'

'The Manor is Teddy's birthright,' Sophie said.

'Teddy has forfeited that,' her father snapped. 'If he had not got into Bolsover's clutches, the man would not have thought of buying up our debts, too.'

'I think perhaps Teddy was simply a means to an end,' Jane said quietly. 'I believe his lordship is conducting some sort of vendetta. I have a mind to discover what it is.'

'It will not help,' he said, his dejection evident in every word. He was a defeated man and Jane's heart went out to him.

'Then we must make plans for the future,' she said brightly. 'Where do you think you would like to go? Bath is a good place for retirement.'

'Too expensive,' the lawyer put in.

'We must go home to Scotland,' their mother said suddenly. 'There is plenty of room at Cartrose Hall.'

Cartrose Hall was the home of her parents, Viscount and Viscountess Cartrose. It was in a remote spot in the Highlands, which had glorious countryside, thousands of sheep, but few people. The family had made frequent visits there when the children were small, but they had not been so often as they grew up and developed other interests. Besides, the journey took several days and Lady Cavenhurst, who was a bad traveller, had come to dread it.

'But that's the other end of the earth,' Isabel wailed

'But you will not be coming with us, will you?' her mother said. 'You will stay here as Lady Wyndham.'

'Then I will never see you again.' It sounded as if she were coming round to that idea after all and Jane wondered what Mark would make of it.

'Nonsense, Mark will bring you to visit us, I am sure.'

'I shan't be going either,' Jane said quietly. In the last few minutes she had been considering how a move would impact on her. She was committed to the Hadlea Children's Home project, she could not abandon it. 'I shall move into Wither-ington House.'

'On your own, Jane?' Sir Edward queried. 'Out of the question.'

'I shan't be on my own. I shall have a full complement of staff. I have to stay to help run it and keep raising funds.'

'Other people can do that.'

'But it is my project. It is important to me.'

Lady Cavenhurst began to weep and her husband abandoned his altercation with Jane to comfort her. 'Do not cry, my dear. It will not be so bad. Our daughters were bound to marry and leave home at some time and you would have become used to being without them.'

'But not Jane,' she sobbed. 'Not Jane.'

Made uncomfortable by her weeping, Theodore Halliday rose to leave. 'I will put the sale in hand for you, Sir Edward. I do not think we need advertise it widely. I will tell a few select people and the whole thing can be managed discreetly.'

'Yes, do that.' Sir Edward hardly turned from his wife to bid him good day. No one thought about the man's need for accommodation, until Jane mentioned it.

'Oh, yes, you are welcome to stay,' Sir Edward said. 'But we shall be poor company.'

'I thank you, but I have booked a room at the

Fox and Hounds in order to make an early start in the morning.'

Jane rose and went with him to the front door. 'I am sorry to have been the bearer of such ill tidings,' he told her, as she handed him his hat from the table in the hall. 'I am afraid your family is going to need your stalwart good sense in the next few weeks.'

'I know.' A footman who was soon to lose his job opened the door and the lawyer hurried down the steps and climbed into his carriage. She sighed and turned to go back to the rest of the family.

'To think it should come to this,' her mother was saying. 'Me, a Viscount's daughter, reduced to charity.'

'Charity, Mama?' Jane said. 'No one has said you are reduced to that. You are simply moving house for your own convenience.'

'Yes, so I shall say, and for my health's sake, but it will not make me feel any better about it.'

'Lady Wyndham and Mark will have to be told.'

'Oh, no, surely not?'

'They will think it very strange if we do not confide why we are suddenly selling our home, do you not think? Lady Wyndham has been your friend ever since you married and came to live here. It would be discourteous not to tell her.'

'Yes, I suppose you are right. She made me feel welcome when I was new to the area. I shall miss her more than anyone.'

Jane smiled. 'More than me?'

'Oh, you did not really mean you would not come with us, did you?'

'Yes, I did, Mama. I cannot manage Witherington House from Scotland, can I?'

'Let someone else take it on. I need you.'

'But so do the orphans.' She was tired of arguing, tired of going over the same ground again and again, tired of always giving in. 'Shall I drive you over to Broadacres tomorrow?'

Lady Cavenhurst sighed heavily. 'Yes, let us get it over with, though what I shall say to Helen, I have no idea.'

'The truth, Mama. It was you who taught us that untruths will always come back to haunt us.'

'If I could meet this dreadful Lord Bolsover,' her mother said, 'I would certainly have something to say to him.'

'Then I am glad you cannot, Mama, he would undoubtedly laugh at you. He is an odious man.'

'You have met him?' her mother asked in surprise.

'Yes, briefly when we were in London. I did not like him.'

'I hate him!' Isabel declared. 'He has been our ruin.'

'Not unless we let him,' Jane said. 'Now, cheer up, Mama, and let us begin to make plans how the move is to be achieved without loss of face.'

'I do not want to be poor,' Isabel said. 'I won't be poor, I *will* not. I don't want to live counting my pennies and not being able to have a new gown or new shoes when I want them. I would rather marry Mark after all.'

Jane's heart sank like a stone and her bright cheerfulness suddenly lost its edge.

The thought of leaving her childhood home, the place in all the world where she had been most happy, was heartrending for Jane, but she refused to weep as everyone else seemed to be doing. Tears altered nothing and it was better to be positive. When she said that to Isabel the following morning at breakfast, her sister snapped at her, 'It is all right for you, Jane, you are wedded to your children's home. You do not have to worry about husbands and weddings, you are an old maid and must make do with other people's children. I am being forced into marrying a man I do not love because the man I *do* love chose to be chivalrous and leave the field.'

Jane refused to rise to the bait, but she did wonder if there was some truth in what Isabel said. Was she using the children's home to fulfil a void in her own life? She shrugged; if she was, it would also benefit the orphans she meant to help, so what did it matter? She went to the stables to ask Daniel to harness the pony to the trap, so that she could drive her mother to Broadacres.

'Your papa is going to tell the servants today,' her mother said as they bowled out of the drive on to the village road. 'He has agreed I may keep Bessie, if she is prepared to stay with me when we move to Scotland, but the rest are to be given notice.'

'Perhaps the new owner will let them stay?'

'Perhaps, but we do not know who he will be, do we? Your father says they must be given the opportunity to find new positions, in case he does not.'

Would they be able to find new positions? Jane wondered. Everyone was having to tighten their belts nowadays—having more servants than were needed was a thing of the past, unless you were exceedingly rich. Only stubborn men like her father liked to keep up appearances. She would need some help at Witherington House, perhaps she could take some of them on. It might be seen as a downward step by Saunders, the butler, and Mrs Driver, the housekeeper, who had been with them for as long as she could remember, but it was better than being without a job and a home. The trouble was that Witherington House might not be ready when the time came to move.

Mark heard them arrive and came out to meet them. He was dressed for riding, though hatless. 'Good morning, my lady,' he said cheerfully. 'I did not think to have the pleasure of seeing you again so soon.' He handed her down, then turned to help Jane down. 'How are you, Jane?' he asked, searching her face.

His tender look of concern disconcerted her. 'I am well, thank you,' she said, standing on one leg while she fumbled for her crutch. He picked it up and handed it to her with a smile. It was all she could do to return his smile and thank him.

'Is Lady Wyndham at home?' Grace asked.

'Yes, I will take you to her.'

'I will wait here,' Jane said. She did not want to witness what she knew her mother thought of as humiliation, nor did she think her mother would want Mark to be present. 'I need to speak to you, Mark, if you can spare the time.'

'Of course. Can you manage as far as the walled garden? There is a seat in an arbour there.'

'Yes. I am becoming quite adept at using this.' She lifted the crutch.

He ushered Lady Cavenhurst into the house and Jane made her way slowly to the arbour garden and sat down heavily. Walking with a crutch was not as easy as it looked and made her shoulder ache, but that was the least of her problems. There was a honeysuckle climbing the frame of the arbour filling her nostrils with its scent and she breathed deeply, more to calm herself than to smell the flower. How much to tell him, how much to leave out?

She could see him as he came down the path towards her, and could admire his splendidly muscular figure; the way he walked, not stiffly, but upright with an easy grace; the superb cut of his clothes; the way he smiled. Would Isabel marry him? Her sister would not think twice about changing her mind again, if it meant she did not have to go to Scotland. It pained Jane to think that he would be hurt either way. The gossip would be dreadful if she did not. It might be said that he reneged when it was so obvious there would be no dowry and the family were spendthrifts. On the other hand, if she did marry him, could they be happy?

'Now, Jane,' he said, sitting down beside her. 'What can I do for you?'

'My mama is going to tell your mother a piece of news which will have consequences for all of us,' she began. 'And I have been given the task of telling you because Isabel flatly refuses to do so.'

'That sounds ominous.'

'I am afraid it is.'

'Go on.'

'Oh, dear, this is difficult.'

'My dear Jane,' he said, putting his hand over hers and adding to her nerves. 'Nothing can be so bad that you cannot confide in me, surely? What has your sister done now?'

'Oh, Isabel has done nothing. It is my father. He is in financial straits and must sell Greystone Manor. My parents are going to say they no longer need to live in such a big house and are going to Scotland for Mama's health.'

'Good God!' he said. 'I knew Sir Edward was struggling, but I had no idea it was as bad as that. How did it come about?'

She told him what her father had said the previous day, keeping nothing back; she felt he deserved to know the whole. 'Isabel does not want to go to Scotland and neither do I. I shall go to live at Witherington House. Isabel, of course, will keep her promise to marry you. That is, if you will still have her.'

'Leaving you behind?' She noticed he made no comment on her statement that Isabel would still marry him.

'It is my choice.'

'But Witherington House is not habitable.'

'I am hoping it will be, or at least part of it will, by the time the Manor is sold. The home will need a housekeeper, so why not me?'

'Jane, I do not like that idea at all.'

'You do not have to like it. But I would appreciate your help in getting things moving.'

'That goes without saying. I have already written to Cecil Halliday.'

'No doubt he will know our situation. Do you think it will make any difference?'

'I don't see why it should. Your father's affairs are no business of the trust, whose funds are secure.'

'And do you think we could perhaps take on some of the Manor servants if they fail to find positions for themselves?'

'Dear Jane,' he said gently. 'Always thinking of other people and not yourself. This must have been a terrible blow to you.'

She trembled at the endearment. She must not let him see how affected she was by it, she really must not. She forced a smile. 'My path is clear, Mark. I will tread it firmly.'

'Do you think Sir Edward would accept financial help from me?'

'I am sure he would not and I beg you not to mention it. His pride has already been badly bruised. In any case, the debts are all in the hands of one man and selling the Manor to pay him is the only way Papa will have anything left.'

'You cannot mean Lord Bolsover?'

'Yes. He has done exactly what he did to Teddy.'

'The man is evil. I cannot understand his motive.'

'No, but I found something interesting the other day,' she said. 'I believe he has a connection with Hadlea.'

'I have never heard of it.'

'I found a headstone in the graveyard, not in the consecrated area, but just outside it. It commemorated Colin Bolsover Paget, son of Lord and Lady Paget who died by his own hand in 1649. He was only twenty-seven. There were other old Paget memorials, but none with the name of Bolsover that I could see.'

'It was probably his mother's maiden name.'

'But surely it means there is a connection?'

'It could be coincidence.'

'I do not think so. Lord Bolsover talked of the Manor, of revenge, do you remember?'

'Yes.' He paused. 'I doubt it will make any difference, but I am curious enough to want to find out the story behind that suicide. There are old books at Broadacres that my father collected about the history of the area. I will see what I can unearth.'

'Thank you. I do not know what I would do without you.'

'You said that before.'

'I meant it.'

He stood up and held out his hand to help her

rise. 'We had better go back to the house. Lady Cavenhurst will be waiting for you.'

'Did you tell Mark?' her mother said as the little pony took them back to the Manor.

'Yes. He deserved the truth.' She fell silent for a moment, then added, 'What did Lady Wyndham say?'

'She was shocked. We cried together. I shall miss her more than I can say, but she says we are welcome to visit as often as we like. After all, Mark will be our son-in-law.'

Jane contemplated this idea, but it made her so miserable she thrust it from her. She really must stop thinking about him; he was not for her and never would be. If she could cut herself off from him, she would, but they were both so heavily involved in the Hadlea Children's Home project, there was nothing for it but do as she had told him she would: tread her chosen path firmly. But, oh, how her heart ached.

'Helen said she would need a butler and a housekeeper when she moved into the dower house and would be happy to take on Saunders and Mrs Driver. Daniel, too, because she would need a coachman and she did not want to deprive Mark of his menservants.'

'That was kind of her.'

'I wish you were not so stubborn about not

coming with us, Jane. It is not seemly for an un-married lady to live alone.'

'I won't be alone. I'll have staff—perhaps some of the Manor staff will come with me. Besides, I am well past the age of needing a chaperon.'

He ladyship sighed. 'If you must, you must, but at least you will be near Isabel and Mark.'

Jane made no answer to that.

The following days at Greystone Manor were unhappy ones. Everyone was going about with long faces and tear-filled eyes while they began tackling the packing up of those belongings they would be taking with them. Lady Cavenhurst had received a letter from her parents telling her they would all be welcome, that if they preferred a home of their own, one of their tenant farm-ers was moving away and they were welcome to move in to his house.

'It's a barn of a place,' she grumbled. 'With no conveniences at all. And freezing in the win-ter. I am beginning to feel like the poor relation.'

Jane refrained from pointing out the truth of that and instead suggested her mother should de-cide what to take to make it more homely. Her ladyship would have liked to take everything—sofas, pictures, ornaments, crockery, cutlery, linen—but was warned by her husband he did not intend to hire more than one large wagon and she had better make up her mind what was essential and what could be left behind and sold. He was, Jane noted, uncharacteristically sharp with everyone and she knew the strain was telling on him. Sophie was flinging clothes all over her bedroom and bemoaning the fact that she could not take her pony. Isabel, who had quite made up her mind to marry Mark after all, was reviewing her wardrobe, knowing she could buy whatever she liked in clothes when she became Lady Wyndham, but she certainly did not look happy about it.

As for Jane, she discarded the use of the crutch and took the trap over to Witherington House to inspect it more closely and talk to Mr and Mrs Godfrey about the future, telling them what she intended and to ask them to stay on. 'We'll be right pleased to, miss,' Silas said.

'It will be nice to have children about the place again,' Mrs Godfrey added. 'There were always children about in the old days, laughin' and gettin' into mischief. Sir Jasper let them have the run o' the place and Lady Paget always indulged them with treats.'

'Paget?' Jane queried. 'Did you say Paget?'

'Yes, that wor their name. Didn' yew know that?'

'No, when you spoke of Sir Jasper, you did not mention his family name.'

'I thought ever'one knew it.'

'You said there were children. I understood
Sir Jasper had no close kin and that was why the
lawyers had such a problem finding his heirs.'

'They were the children of cousins. They grew
up and moved away. Stopped comin'.'

'Why?'

'I don' know, do I? Not my business and it were
a long time ago.'

'Have you heard the name Bolsover in connection with the family?'

'Can't say I hev. Why?'

'Oh, no reason.' She strolled away from them,
intending to take the measurements of the first-
floor rooms and make a note of how many beds
each could accommodate, but she could not keep
her mind on what she was doing. She gave up and
went out to inspect the outbuildings she had not
seen before. Silas was giving Bonny some oats.
'He's a sturdy little fellow,' he said.

'Yes, and very easy to drive.'

'We used to hev half-a-dozen hosses here, one
time,' he went on. 'And carriages and the like. I
useta help look after them. Sir Jasper got rid o'
most on 'em, when her ladyship died, but he kept
a couple of mares to hitch to an old chaise, but
when he took to his bed, they were got rid of, too.'

Jane was beginning to feel sorry for old Sir
Jasper, alone and unhappy in his declining years,
but did he have a connection with Lord Bolsover?

Would it make a difference to her plans? She could not wait to tell Mark, forgetting her decision not to call on him any more than she could help.

Mark was sitting in the library with his head in his hands. On the desk in front of him were several old books he had taken from the shelves which he had been perusing when a footman had come to tell him Miss Cavenhurst had arrived and asked for him. She was waiting in the drawing room. Thinking it was Jane, he had hurried to go to her, a smile on his face. She would be interested in what he had discovered.

But it wasn't Jane, it was Isabel. He kept the smile, though it was a little fixed as he bowed to her. 'Isabel, do sit down. I wasn't expecting you. How did you arrive? Have you seen my mother? Have refreshments been ordered?'

'Good morning, Mark.' She sat on one of the sofas and smoothed the skirt of her green-silk dress with gloved hands. 'I walked and, no, I have not seen your mother and I do not need refreshments. We have done nothing but drink tea at home all morning. One would think it was the cure for all ills.'

'I am deeply sorry for what has happened, Isabel. If I can help in any way, you know I will.'

'Thank you.' She turned an appealing smile

on him. 'I have been very silly, for which I beg your pardon.'

'I am sure there is no need for that.'

'But there is. You see, I told you that I no longer wished to marry you and you were so gallant as to tell me you would not hold me to it.'

'Yes, I did.'

'But as I said, I was foolish, blinded by false sentiment, and on reflection I wish to retract—'

'You mean you no longer wish to break off our engagement?' His gut was churning with a mixture of disappointment, fury and helplessness. If he could have told her that he would not accept her change of mind and that as far as he was concerned the engagement was off and had been off ever since she had first mentioned it, he would have. But such a course was not acceptable. A lady might, with small loss to her reputation, break off a betrothal, but a gentleman could never do so. It would lay him open to the condemnation and disgust of everyone in the *haut monde* and he would be shunned. He was as bound to honour his proposal as if he had said his wedding vows.

'Yes. I am sorry. I should have thought about it more carefully before speaking.'

'What about Drew?'

'What about him? He left me to you, didn't he?'

'But your feelings for him? Were they not sincere?'

'Not sincere enough for me to face penury on his account.'

He laughed without humour. 'You have certainly put me in my place.'

'I am sorry, I didn't mean to do that. I am very fond of you, Mark. We grew up together, I am sure we will deal well together and you will not hold my lapse against me.'

'No, of course not.' What else could he say? He pulled the bell rope beside the fireplace. When a servant arrived, he bade her inform Lady Wyndham that Miss Isabel Cavenhurst was here and would she like to see her.

Two minutes later his mother bustled into the room. 'Isabel, how nice to see you. I did not know you were here or I would have come sooner. Is your mother not with you?'

'No, my lady. I am alone. I needed to speak to Mark.'

'Without a chaperon? Dear, dear.'

'I did not think of it. Jane never bothers.'

'We do not count Jane.' Her ladyship smiled. 'But never mind, you are still engaged to my son, are you not?'

'Yes, Lady Wyndham, I am.'

Mark could bear it no longer. He made his excuses and returned to the library, where he flung himself into a chair and, moaning, put his head in his hands. His mother's words burned in his brain. 'We do not count Jane.' How could they be so disparaging? How could they take everything from her and give nothing in return? He loved her, he loved her quiet nature, her unselfishness, the way she cared for everyone, sacrificing her own happiness to do so, for her lovely expressive eyes when she looked at him, her sweet smile, her down-to-earth honesty, her courage. Whoever married her would be marrying a treasure and he wished it could be him.

He heard his mother taking leave of Isabel, then a footman escorting Isabel down the long gallery to the front door and then his mother came looking for him. 'You left us rather hurriedly, Mark.'

'I couldn't bear to hear you speak of Jane in that off-hand way, Mother. She does count.'

'Oh.' She was thoughtful as she sat down beside him. 'So it's Jane. Oh, dear.'

'Mother, you know I was relieved when Isabel said she wanted to break off the engagement, I told you so.'

'Yes, but you did not mention Jane and I thought you were just putting a brave face on it.'

'No, I meant it, but I could hardly jump from one engagement to another, could I? Jane would never have agreed in any case. I needed time. And now it seems I am not to be given time.'

'Does Jane know?'

'Of course she does not.'

'Best she never does. You cannot get away from the fact that you are betrothed to her sister. Perhaps it would be better if you did not see Jane so frequently.'

'That will look odd, considering we are both trustees of the Hadlea Children's Home and have already been working on it for some time. It will look as if we have had a falling-out over it.'

'So, you will go on torturing yourself when you should be making plans for your wedding. Isabel tells me she wants it before her parents leave for Scotland and I have said it would be best. I don't know the date the move is planned, but these things take time and I do not suppose it will be before the six months of mourning is over.'

'Isabel is a selfish little madam. She is only doing this because she doesn't want to go to Scotland with her parents. She has no love for me, only what I can give her—she as good as said so.'

'Oh, dear, I wish you had confided in me earlier, Mark.'

'Why? What could you have done?'

'I could have accepted the situation instead of agreeing with Grace that Isabel would change her mind and assuming she would. Isabel might then have realised there was no going back.'

'Too late, Mama, and I doubt it would have made any difference.'

'Perhaps not.' She rose to leave him. 'What are you doing with those?' she asked, noticing the dusty books on the desk.

'Some research into the Paget family. Halliday has told me Sir Jasper Paget was the previous owner of Witherington House and I thought I had come across the name somewhere.'

'No doubt you have. There are graves in the churchyard and a tablet on the wall inside the church. You must have seen it dozens of times. It is over the pew next to ours.'

'What do you know about them?'

'Nothing at all. The graves are very old. Does it matter?'

'Not at all.'

'Then put them away and walk with me in the garden. It is a lovely day and I have a mind to pick some roses.'

Chapter Ten

Jane stopped at the crossroads in the village, intending to turn towards Broadacres when she saw Isabel walking from that direction. She pulled up and waited for her.

Isabel climbed in beside her. 'I'm glad you came along, Jane,' she said. 'My new shoes are pinching like the devil.'

Jane flicked the reins and the pony trotted on towards home. Telling Mark about Sir Jasper would have to wait. 'Are they the ones you bought in London?'

'Yes. They are fine when I am riding in a carriage, but not when I am walking.'

'Where have you been?'

'To Broadacres.'

'Without Mama?'

'Yes. I needed to speak to Mark.'

'Oh. And did you?'

'Yes. We have come to an understanding.'

Even though she was half-prepared for it, Isabel's words put an end to any hope Jane might have had. More fool her for even entertaining it, she told herself fiercely. 'By that, I suppose you mean the engagement is on again.'

'Yes, it is.'

'And what did Mark say?'

'He was delighted, of course, and forgave me for my doubts.'

'And now you have no doubts?'

'None. We are to be married before Mama and Papa leave for Scotland, so do you think you can set aside your fascination with your orphanage project for a while and finish my wedding dress?'

'Of course. There is little to be done to it in any case.'

They had barely entered the house when Sir Edward hurried towards them. 'Jane where have you been? I have been looking everywhere for you.'

'I have been to Witherington, Papa. Has something happened?'

'There are people coming to view the house this afternoon and your mama refuses to meet them. You will have to take her place.' He turned to his younger daughter. 'Isabel, go and keep your mother company. She is in her boudoir. Sophie is out riding.'

Isabel left them and he turned to Jane again. 'They will be here in less than half an hour.'

'Then I must go and change out of these clothes and have Bessie do my hair. Witherington House is so dusty it is impossible not to get it on one's clothes. I will be as quick as I can.'

Half an hour later she returned to the drawing room, seeing it with a stranger's eyes and realising it would not give a good impression. The furnishings were shabby and there were dark patches on the wallpaper where her mother had had paintings removed. Papa had said she could not take them, but she had not had them put back. They were on the floor, leaning against the wall. The shelves in the cabinet where there had once been a display of china figurines were empty and forlorn looking. And flowers in the vase in the hearth were drooping. She picked it up and put it outside the window on to the terrace, just as they heard the front door knocker.

Mr and Mrs Somerton were undoubtedly *nouveau riche*. He was portly and dressed in a dark-green coat, yellow waistcoat, whose buttons strained across his stomach, and cream trousers, strapped under his shoes. She was even fatter, in puce taffeta and loaded with jewels. She and Jane curtsied to each other while Sir Edward explained he had asked his daughter to receive them because of his wife's poor health. 'It is why we are leaving here,' he said. 'We have already started to gather together our belongings, as you can see.'

'We expected it to be furnished,' Mr Somerton said, looking round in distaste.

The rest of the house, apart from her ladyship's boudoir, were viewed with the same reaction and the couple departed, making it very clear they would not be buying.

It was the same with the next two people Mr Halliday sent to them. Having steeled themselves to losing their home, they now found that no one wanted to buy it. Lady Cavenhurst, Isabel and Sophie were secretly pleased, though Jane was more realistic and Sir Edward was in despair because he knew he could not hold Lord Bolsover off much longer.

Then the dreadful man himself arrived. He bowled up in an extravagant chaise drawn by four superb horses, and banged on the front door with his cane.

Jane was upstairs on the first-floor gallery, having just come from the sewing room where she had been putting the finishing touches to Isabel's wedding gown, when she saw Saunders, on his dignity as usual, admit him and request his name.

'Go and tell your master Lord Bolsover is here to view the property.'

Jane was taken aback. Why did the man want to view the property? Surely Mr Halliday had not sent him? She walked downstairs in as stately and calm a manner as she could manage, though inside she was quaking. He saw her and stood watching her descend. Not until she reached the bottom did she speak. 'Lord Bolsover, good afternoon.'

He bowed. 'Miss Cavenhurst, I hope I see you well?'

'Very well, thank you. Why are you here?'

'I will tell your father that when he deigns to put in an appearance.'

'I expect someone has gone to fetch him. He may be on the estate somewhere. Will you come into the withdrawing room to wait for him?'

'Very well, but I hope he won't be long.'

She led the way and offered him a chair. 'If you had warned us you were coming, we would have been expecting you.'

He laughed suddenly. 'I doubt it. You would all have gone into hiding.'

'We have nothing to hide, Lord Bolsover.'

'No? The fact that Greystone Manor was up for sale? That was an underhand thing to do.'

'What did you expect my father to do? He has debts to pay as you very well know.'

'I doubt the sale will cover them. How much is he asking? Ten thousand, I believe. It is overpriced by at least three thousand.'

'How do you know the figure?'

He smiled. 'I have my sources. I know Sir Edward's debts to the last penny, I know your brother's debts and I know how much Sir Edward hopes to obtain from the sale. Unless my arithmetic is faulty, the figures do not add up.'

She pretended indifference, but could not quell the feeling of despair that overwhelmed her. Was he right?

Her father arrived and saved her from having to answer. 'Papa,' she said, 'this is Lord Bolsover. My lord, Sir Edward Cavenhurst.'

Her father ignored Bolsover's outstretched hand and stood facing him. 'What do you want?' he demanded. 'Why are you here? My wife is unwell and your presence will upset her. Please leave.'

'I will when I'm done. I wish to see over the premises.'

'Why?' Jane demanded. 'You are surely not thinking of buying?'

'I do not need to, do I?' He was addressing Sir Edward. 'Your debt to me easily covers the price you have put on the estate, which I am told is far above its true market value. You haven't been able to sell, have you?'

'There is plenty of time.'

'No, Sir Edward, there is no time at all. I am calling in the debt immediately.'

Jane gasped and her father turned deathly pale. 'Why? Why are you doing this to us? We have done nothing to harm you.'

'Ah, but there you are wrong.' He smiled suddenly, a smile that sent a chill into Jane's veins. 'I need a home and I think Greystone Manor will serve me very well, but I need to look round to see if it covers the eight thousand pounds owed to me.'

'I do not owe anything like that much,' Sir Edward said.

'You do if you add your son's debts to yours and there is the interest being added every day at ten per cent. So, will you show me round, or shall I wander about on my own?'

'Jane will accompany you. I must go to my wife.' He scuttled away, leaving Jane facing Lord Bolsover.

'Shall we go?' she said, leading the way.

She took him from room to room, downstairs and upstairs, avoiding her mother's boudoir where the murmur of voices could be heard through the closed door. Then they returned downstairs and she led him through the kitchen to the stable yard and the outbuildings, which he inspected. 'That's the house and immediate outbuildings,' she said when that was done. 'There is a park of three hundred acres, some woodland, three farms with farmhouses and the usual buildings, and some farm cottages. If you want to see those, I suggest you hire a hack and ride round on your own, but I trust you have seen enough.'

'I was right,' he said, laughing at her sharp tone. 'You are the only one of the family with any fire. I like that.'

'I wish I knew why you were so intent on ruining us.'

'Soon, if all goes well, I shall tell you. Now I wish to speak to Sir Edward again.'

She preceded him back to the drawing room where she left him while she went in search of her father. He was with her mother and Isabel.

'Has he gone?' her mother asked.

'No, Mama, he wants to see Papa.'

Sir Edward heaved himself out of his chair and left them.

'What does that man want?' Isabel asked.

'He says he is calling in Papa's debts forthwith and wanted to be sure the estate covered them.'

'You mean he is not even going to give us time to sell?' her mother queried.

'Not unless Papa can talk him out of it. He has added Teddy's debts to Papa's and is charging ten per cent interest.'

'But that's outrageous!'

'Yes, it is,' Jane agreed. 'I think it is a means to an end. He wants Greystone Manor and is determined to have it and when Teddy got into his debt he saw a way of obtaining it.'

'But why?'

'I asked him that and he refused to say.'

'What are we going to do?' wailed Isabel. 'What about my wedding? What will Mark say? And Lady Wyndham? She can be very intimidating.'

'I am sure it will make no difference to Mark,' Jane said.

'But where will I live until the wedding? I expected to be married from here.'

'Your papa will think of a solution,' her ladyship said with a simple faith in her husband that Jane thought ill founded. 'He will not see us turned out.'

There was a knock at the door which, in their heightened state of nerves, made them all jump, but it was only Bessie with a message for Jane. 'Sir Edward said to rejoin them,' she said. 'They are in the book room.'

Reluctantly Jane went. Sir Edward was seated at his desk, with papers that looked very much like deeds spread out in front of him. Lord Bolsover was standing at the window with his back to the room. He turned as Jane entered.

'Jane, my dear,' her father began and there was

a distinct tremble in his voice. 'His lordship has suggested a way out of our dilemma and it concerns you. I want you to listen very carefully to what he has to say.' He stood up to leave. 'You may not agree and I shall not hold it against you if you do not, but I beg of you to think of your poor dear mama and your sisters.' And with that he scuttled away, closing the door behind him, leaving Jane facing Lord Bolsover.

'Shall we sit down? he suggested pleasantly and, taking her hand, led her to the sofa, where they sat side by side.

Bewildered, she pulled her hand from his and said nothing. Her father's words had eaten into her brain and could only have one meaning. She waited.

'I do not wish to see your family beggared,' he began.

'Then you have a strange way of showing it.'

'I have had my eye on Greystone Manor for a number of years—all my life, in truth. I have always considered it my birthright.'

'Why? The Cavenhursts have lived here for generations.'

'I know. Ever since 1649.'

The date echoed in her head. The date on the headstone. 'Colin Bolsover Paget,' she murmured.

'Ah, so you have found it.'

'Yes, but I do not know the reason for it.'

'Colin Bolsover Paget was so foolish as to fall in love with the daughter of a Roundhead. The Pagets were Royalist to the core. They refused to allow Colin to marry his Gabrielle, but he defied them and changed sides. He found himself opposing his Paget and Bolsover cousins in battle. Gabrielle tried to come between them and in consequence lost her life. Colin survived the battle, but he was cut off from his family and his Roundhead in-laws blamed him for their daughter's death and made his life such a misery, he put an end to it. The Roundheads claimed the Paget home.'

'Greystone Manor.'

'Yes. The last Paget lived out his life at Witherington House, which I believe you have discovered.'

'Where do you come into all this?'

'Colin's mother was a Bolsover, daughter to my father's ancestor, the first Lord Bolsover. I heard the tale at my father's knee as every generation has. Each of us has been sworn to vengeance, but none has managed it until now.'

'I have never heard this story.'

'No reason why you should. It is not something of which the Cavenhursts can be proud, is it? The Pagets that were left hoped their property would be returned to them with the restoration of the monarchy, but it was not to be. Colin Paget was not the only one to change sides.'

'And you think this Banbury tale will make me look more favourably on you?'

'I hope it will because I have a proposal to make.'

'Proposal?' she echoed.

'Yes. You must have guessed.'

'Never!' She was almost shouting and lowered her voice. 'Never in a thousand years. I cannot think why you ever thought of it.'

He laughed lightly. 'It came upon me when I met you in London. You attracted me at once. My widowed mother is anxious to see me settled before she departs this life and insists I marry and set up my own establishment. I need a home and a wife and I think I have found both here.'

'What on earth makes you think I would agree to that?'

'Sir Edward asked you to hear me out and it is only courteous to do so.'

She did not see why she should be courteous to him, but for her father's sake she said nothing, allowing him to go on.

'Your father's and brother's debts together amount to nearly nine thousand pounds, considerably more than the value of the estate, so selling it and paying me off would leave him still in debt.' He paused. 'Ah, that shocks you, I see. But

I am prepared to count only what I paid for the debts, which is naturally a great deal less than their face value, and will allow the lower figure to be set against the value of Greystone Manor. There will, if the agreement is reached quickly, be enough left for your parents to leave here with a little cash in hand and their dignity intact, which is something your father sets great store by. You, of course, will continue to live here as my bride.'

'No.'

'No? Did your father not ask you to think about it carefully? Surely you can see the advantages for everyone? I will have a home and a delightful wife, whom I shall treat with courtesy and respect, my mother will be satisfied, your parents will have a little money to live out their lives in modest comfort, your brother can return to the bosom of his family and you, my dear, will be able to continue your work for the orphans. I might even help you with it.'

She did not answer. Everything he said was driving a nail into her heart and almost stopping it. The whole idea was repugnant to her and the worst of it was her father expected her to agree. How could he? How could he ask this of her? Did he think she was so anxious to be married she would accept this…this…? A suitable epithet failed her.

'I have shocked you into silence,' he added,

'but I will give you a week to make up your mind. In that time I hope you will consider carefully the consequences of refusing. Your family will be paupers and I shall still possess the Manor. And just in case you were thinking of moving everyone to Witherington, I could stop that sale, too.'

She rose and ran out of the room, determined he would not see her tears. She paused in the hallway. In any other circumstances she would have sought comfort and solace from her father and mother, but she could not do that; this time they were the source of her distress. There was no one to turn to, not even Mark, who would undoubtedly try to comfort her, but he was betrothed to her sister and she had vowed not to call on him more than she could help for Isabel's sake.

She ran out of the front door and round the side of the house with no destination in mind. How she ended up in the stables, she did not know, but she found herself sobbing on the neck of Bonny. He was warm and he had never let her down, never made demands on her; his bright eyes seemed to tell her he understood. Still crying, she found harness and saddle and put them on him, even though he was a draught pony and unused to a saddle. She used an old milking stool to mount and galloped out of the yard, ignoring Daniel's shout.

She did not know where she was going. Did not care. She was not even aware of other vehi-

cles on the road, nor that a carriage had to pull
to one side to allow her to pass. She galloped on,
past the Fox and Hounds, over the crossroads,
ignoring the turning to Witherington and was
at the gates of Broadacres and turning up the
drive before she suddenly came to her senses. She
should not be here! 'Whoa there,' she called out
and pulled sharply on the reins, bringing Bonny
to a skittering stop. He reared at being so ill used
and threw her.

At that moment, Mark turned into the drive in
his curricle and only by skilful driving managed
to stop before running her over. Horses, pony and
curricle were in a tangled heap. He extricated
himself and ran to her. Jane was unconscious and
deathly pale and dressed in an afternoon gown,
not a habit. She wore no hat, which might have
offered a little protection for her head. Something
dreadful must have happened to bring her out
like that.

'Oh, my God!' He fell to his knees beside her.
'Jane! Jane, wake up. Wake up, please.' He re-
sisted the impulse to shake her awake and felt
all over her face and head. His hand came away
covered in blood. 'Please God, don't let her die,'
he prayed aloud. 'Let her live. I need her...' She
did not stir. Ought he to pick her up and carry her
into the house? Or should he leave her lying in the
road until a litter could be brought to carry her?

He looked about him. There was no one about to send for one. He stood up, stooped to pick her up and walked the rest of the way up the drive to the house.

He was met by Thompson, who had heard the sound of the crash and the neighing of the horses and was on his way to investigate. Mark told him swiftly what had happened and sent him to take care of the curricle and the horses, then he carried Jane into the house and sent for his mother.

'Mark, whatever has happened?' she said, looking at his burden.

'She was riding up the drive and came off. I almost ran her over. Send for Dr Trench, will you, please.'

'Yes, of course I will. And Lady Cavenhurst, too.' She turned to a footman to give him instructions. Then to Mark, 'If she was riding, why is she dressed like that?'

'I don't know, Mama, but something dreadful must have happened at the Manor. Perhaps she was coming to us for help.'

'Grace will tell us when she arrives. Take her up to the blue room. I'll send Janet up to you.' Janet was his old nurse, who was long past retirement age, but she had nowhere else to go and continued to live at Broadacres, making herself useful in so many ways, especially when anyone in the household was ill.

In the bedchamber, always referred to as the blue room on account of its curtains and bedcover being the colour of a summer sky, he put Jane gently on the bed. She was still deeply unconscious and he was afraid for her life. If she died, he didn't know what he would do. It was his fault; he should not have turned into the drive so fast. He fell to his knees beside the bed and stroked her paper-white face. 'Jane, you must live,' he murmured. 'I love you. Without you, I am nothing. Please, my darling, wake up.' He reached over and gently kissed her cheek. She did not stir and gave no hint that she had heard. His heart was beating too fast and then almost stopping, before thumping on again. He took a deep breath to calm himself and took her hand.

He had been a fool, letting convention dictate what he did. Why had he not seen Jane's worth before he proposed to Isabel? Why had he accepted everyone else's idea that she was plain Jane and not to be considered? She was far from plain, she was beautiful. She had a depth of beauty that Isabel had never had; it came from inside her and shone out in everything she did. 'Jane doesn't count.' The words seared into his brain. She counted for him, more than anything else, more than life, more than riches, certainly more than the opinion of the *haut monde*. The trouble was that Jane herself would never accept him, even if he persuaded her to admit she loved him, too. She would never betray her sister, just as Drew would never betray him. Where was Drew?

His mother bustled into the room accompanied by Dr Trench and Janet. 'Has she come to?'

'No.' He rose from his knees and reluctantly left the room.

Jane's eyes fluttered open, shut again, then opened fully. Where was she? She was in a bed, but it was not her own bed. She turned her head to see Mark sitting in a chair beside her. He looked tired and drawn, but his smile was wide. 'You are awake at last.'

'Where am I?'

'At Broadacres. You came off your horse in the drive, do you remember?'

'No. What was I doing?'

'I think you were coming to see me.'

'Was I?' She struggled to sit up, but was surprised at how weak she felt and her head felt funny. She put a hand up and touched a thick bandage. 'What about?'

'I was hoping you would tell me.'

'Sir Jasper,' she murmured. 'I found out he was a Paget and related to the man in the graveyard.'

'I know. I don't think it was that. You would

not have left home in such a hurry without even changing into a habit just to tell me that.'

'Did I?'

'Yes.'

'Does Mama know I'm here?'

'Yes, she has been every day.'

'Every day?' she echoed. 'How long have I been here?'

'A week.'

'A week!'

He smiled. 'Yes, seven days and in a delirium most of it.'

She was alarmed. 'What did I say?'

'Nothing that made any sense. The only words I managed to decipher were Papa, Roundhead, Royalist, wedding and something that sounded like Bolsover. We had the devil of a job to stop you thrashing about and re-opening your wound.'

'Oh. Who's we?'

'Me, my mother, Janet and your own mother when she came. She was distressed as we all were, but Dr Trench said he expected you to make a full recovery, given time.'

'Time!' she cried, as memory flooded back. 'I do not have time. I have to go home.'

'No, you do not.' He pressed her gently back on to the pillow. 'You are not moving from here until I am satisfied you are well enough. You are safer here.'

'Safer?'

'Lord Bolsover cannot touch you while you are here, can he?' It was said with a smile.

'You know?'

'Your mother told us. The whole idea is preposterous.' He had found references in his own library to the Civil War and to the second Baron Paget who had lived at Greystone Manor. He had been a staunch Royalist in an area of East Anglia that was largely on the side of Parliament. When the Royalists had finally been defeated he had lost his Manor to an early Cavenhurst. A second search of the church records had revealed the story of the suicide. Colin Paget's mother was a Bolsover, a family based in Northamptonshire. That might explain Bolsover's determination to regain the Manor, but not the reason he had offered for Jane. It was not love, he was certain of it.

'I have no choice.'

'The longer you are here, out of the man's reach, the longer we have to think of a solution.'

'There is no solution, Mark. Please do not raise false hopes in me. My duty is plain.'

'Duty! Why must you always be the dutiful daughter?' he said almost angrily. 'Why can you not think of what you want sometimes?'

She sighed. 'Mark, I love my family too much to see them brought low if I can prevent it.'

'What about me?'

'What about you? You are my dear friend, my confidant, partner in my charitable endeavours— I cannot imagine losing all that. I hope very much that will continue.'

'Of course it will, whatever happens, but I—'

'Please, no more, Mark. Will you send someone to help me dress? I wish to go home.'

She had to be strong and resolute because it would be all too easy to lie back on the pillows and play the invalid, letting Mark sit beside her and hold her hand when he should not be doing anything of the sort, and hoping Lord Bolsover would give up and go away. It was a forlorn hope and dwelling on Mark's kindness and concern for her only made her want to cry.

'Very well.' He put the back of the hand he had been holding to his lips and left the room.

She rubbed at her hand contemplatively. He had seemed genuinely distressed by her plight and the way he had searched her face and held her hand made her wonder… Had she dreamed he said he loved her? The voice had been far away, like a distant echo, penetrating her unconscious mind. No, she must not think of it, must not strain to make it real. It was not to be. Isabel would marry him in a few weeks' time and he would become her brother-in-law. She shut her eyes, but a tear escaped from under the lid and slid down her cheek.

* * *

'Jane is determined on dressing and going home,' Mark told his mother when he found her in the parlour doing the household accounts. They were easily wealthy enough not to worry about the cost of food and candles and things like that which could easily have been left to Mrs Blandish, but she insisted on doing them herself. 'My mother always did hers and her mother before her,' she had told him long ago when he had remonstrated with her. 'And your father approves.' His father was no longer there to approve or disapprove, but he let her carry on.

'Surely not? She is not strong enough yet and Grace asked us to keep her here in any case, to buy them a little time.'

'I know. I tried to tell her that, but she will not listen.'

'Poor Mark,' she said.

'It is not poor Mark, it is poor Jane. See if you can persuade her, Mama. I have a mind to speak to Bolsover.'

'No, Mark, you must not. He will make a game of you. You will end up fighting him and who will gain by that? Besides, there is enough gossip going the rounds already and you will only add to it. Squabbling over a woman when you are engaged to another just will not do.'

'I must do something. If only I had known the

true state of affairs at the Manor earlier, I might have been able to do something, lent Sir Edward some money to discharge them.'

'You could not, Mark. By the time your poor dear father passed away and you came into your inheritance it was already too late.'

He knew she was right, not only about the money, but about confronting Bolsover. What he found so difficult to understand was why a man like Hector Bolsover, who enjoyed the life of the capital and spent most of his time at card tables, would want to come and live in a rural spot like Hadlea. It did not make sense.

'Will you go to Jane? I will drive over to Greystone's to tell them Jane has recovered consciousness. I'll bring her ladyship back with me. She will, no doubt, want to see her daughter.'

The damage to the curricle had not been great and had soon been mended and both his own horse and Bonny had not suffered any harm. In no time at all he was bowling along the village street towards the Manor. As he passed the church he saw the Rector by the lych gate, who waved to him to stop.

'How is the invalid?' he asked him, coming to stand with his hand on the side of the curricle.

'Making good progress, I think. She has regained consciousness and is able to speak. I am going over to tell Lady Cavenhurst the good news.'

'That is a great relief to us all. She will soon be back to her old self, then?'

'It is to be hoped so.'

'I heard she was to be married to the gentleman staying at the Fox and Hounds. The people in the village are very excited about it. They say Miss Cavenhurst deserves her happiness.'

'Indeed she does,' Mark said, through gritted teeth.

'I found Lord Bolsover wandering round the churchyard. He made himself known to me and desired me to have the grave of Colin Paget cleared of weeds and the headstone cleaned. He is an ancestor of his, I believe.'

'So I have heard.'

'Perhaps there will be a double wedding. His lordship seemed amused by the idea, but he did not say he did not like it.'

'I'm sorry,' Mark said, anxious to end the conversation. 'I must be on my way to fetch Lady Cavenhurst.'

'Of course. I must not detain you.' He stepped back. 'Please tell Miss Cavenhurst that I am thinking of her and wish her well. Tell her I have recruited some volunteers to help clean up Witherington House when she is ready.'

'I will, but we do not need to wait until Miss

Cavenhurst is out and about again, we can make a start on the house. I think it will please her.'

'Yes, that is a good idea.'

'I will speak to you about it when I have more time.'

So that's what his mother meant about rumours, Mark mused, as he continued on his way. Even if they had not been perpetrated by Bolsover, which seemed likely, he had certainly not denied them. There was an almighty scandal brewing and he did not know how to prevent it.

Lady Cavenhurst seemed unaware of the rumours when he was shown into the drawing room at the Manor and delivered the news that Jane was awake and her mental state had not suffered because of the injury to her head. 'She is wishful of coming home,' he said.

'Much as I would like her home, she must not do that,' her ladyship said. 'Lord Bolsover has called every day and is as determined as ever. He has practically accused her of pretending to be ill in order to delay speaking to him. I had to ask Dr Trench to confirm that she was deeply unconscious and incapable of making a decision. I even hinted that she might have lost some of her mental faculties in the hope he would withdraw his suit, but Sir Edward was quite angry with me.

He says Jane is our only hope, so we must not tell Lord Bolsover she has come round.'

'Then Jane must stay where she is. Would you like to come back with me and talk to her?'

'Yes, please. I will go and put on my hat.' She left the room and he wandered round, waiting for her. He had not realised until now how shabby everything looked, especially with the pictures down and the shelves emptied.

'Oh, it's you, Mark.' He whirled round to face Isabel. 'I thought I heard a visitor arrive. How is Jane?'

'She woke up about an hour ago. She is very weak, but otherwise none the worse.'

'I am so glad. It is dreadful here without her, everyone going about with Friday faces. I will be glad when she comes home.'

'But then she will have to give Lord Bolsover his answer.'

'Why not? She will have to give in, in the end.'

He was angry. 'Isabel, you surely would not condemn your sister to marrying that dreadful man?'

'He isn't that dreadful, not when you come to know him better, he can be very charming and he is our only hope. She is lucky to find a husband at all at her age and he is very rich.'

He was so annoyed he was speechless, but

luckily Lady Cavenhurst returned, wearing her hat and gloves, and he escorted her to the curricle.

He was still seething and wondered if her ladyship had heard and if she agreed with her daughter. Isabel was totally self-centred. He could not marry her, he simply could not. But how could he get out of it with any honour?

Chapter Eleven

Between them, the two ladies and Mark, with the connivance of Dr Trench, persuaded Jane that she ought to stay where she was for another week at least. Jane herself was convinced of the need for it when she attempted to leave her bed unaided and fell to the floor. Mark was passing in the corridor and heard her sharp cry. He rushed in and helped her up, trying not to notice that she wore only a flimsy nightgown that did nothing to hide her curves, nor the soft swelling of her breasts rising and falling with her breathing. He stood, holding her against him, savouring the feel of her in his arms, her body fitting so neatly into his and his hunger for her became almost unbearable.

True, he had held her before, once on the village green when Drew had been with him. *'If I did not know you better, I would think you were a little too fond of your future sister-in-law,'* his friend had said, which was perceptive of him, considering he had not realised it himself at the time. Then when she twisted her ankle on the broken stair, and latterly when she came off her horse in his drive, but she had always been fully dressed. Even when she had been so ill and he lay watching her hour after hour, she had been well covered, Janet had seen to that.

He turned her in his arms and tipped her chin up so that he could look into her face. 'It seems I am destined to be always picking you up off the floor,' he said, attempting humour. And then he kissed her.

It was only meant to be a gentle kiss, a fond kiss to let her know he was on her side, to try to convey he knew not what, but it deepened into something much more and she stood cradled in his arms and let it happen. There was no cry of protest as his lips found hers, no pushing him away in outraged fury. She melted into him and he knew, he knew then, that he could never marry anyone else, no matter what.

'Jane?' he murmured, leaving off kissing her, but continuing to hold her, knowing she would crumple if he did not. Besides, he wanted to. 'Oh, Jane, what are we going to do? I cannot let you go.'

'No, for I should fall down again.'

'I didn't mean that.'

'Neither did I.'

'I love you.'

'It cannot be,' she said, as a tear slipped down her cheek. Telling her that when it was all too late was the greatest torment of all.

'It is a fact.' He kissed the tear away.

'Mark, don't, please don't.'

'Why? Are you going to tell me you do not love me?'

'I…' She stopped in confusion.

'Be honest with me, Jane.'

'I am always honest with you.'

'Well then?'

'Whatever my feelings may be, it still cannot be,' she murmured. 'There's Isabel and…and Lord Bolsover.' She shivered.

'Damn Bolsover.' He picked her up, kissed her again and put her back on the bed, pulled the covers over her and sat down on the edge, holding her hand. 'We could run away and marry secretly.'

'Mark, you are joking, you must be. Think of the scandal, think of your mother, your friends and the villagers, who look up to you and respect you. Would you forfeit that? And there's Isabel. Would you break her heart?'

He was tempted to say 'Damn Isabel', but refrained. Instead he said, 'I do not think it would break her heart, Jane. She broke the engagement off once, she might do so again.'

'Not with Papa's bankruptcy hovering over us

and Lord Bolsover laying down the law. We must do what is right for everyone.'

'Why can't we do what is right for us?'

She gave him a wan smile. 'Mark, I do not feel strong enough to argue with you, please say no more. What happened here this afternoon is our secret, never to be divulged to a soul, though I shall always remember it and think of it in years to come as a time when I knew that I was once loved.' She attempted a smile.

It was all too much. He fled the room before she could see his unmanly tears.

Jane knew she had done the right thing, but, oh, how hard it had been to send him away. He must have realised the rightness of it, too, because he did not come to see her every morning as he had been doing, popping in for a few minutes to see how she was and asking if she needed anything. She missed his cheery smile and the feeling he gave her that she was important. Well, she would just have to live without that. Her head ached and she felt weak as a newborn kitten, but unless she wanted to spend the rest of her life in bed she would have to do something about it. It was time to make a move.

Every day she left her bed and tottered round the room, hanging on to furniture. Round and round she went, stopping when she came to the window to gaze out at the gardeners tending the borders, hoping for a glimpse of Mark. Then on she went again, until she was exhausted. Day by day her legs strengthened until she could walk without support. The bandage was removed from her head, leaving a little bare patch where her hair had been cut away, but the scar had nearly healed and the hair would grow again. Janet had devised a style that used the length of her hair to disguise it.

The next step was to dress and go downstairs to sit in the parlour, sometimes alone, sometimes with Lady Wyndham, either sewing or reading or talking quietly. She began taking her meals in the dining room, which meant she saw and spoke to Mark, but his mother and the servants were always present and they had done little but exchange pleasantries. Even so, she felt the tension in the atmosphere, the constraints that prevented them even looking at each other properly. It was a kind of exquisite torture.

Her mother came frequently to see her, bringing her clothes, and so did Isabel and Sophie. Isabel's moods of cheerfulness alternated with gloominess and Sophie's bright chatter exhausted her.

'Lord Bolsover has gone to Northamptonshire to tell his mother the good news,' Isabel informed her on one visit. 'And he was also going to see his lawyer about the transfer of the deeds and to draw up a marriage contract.'

'But I have not agreed to marry him.'

'He is assuming you will and so is Papa. You cannot turn him down, Jane, you really cannot. Everything depends upon it. He has even promised to pay for my wedding breakfast and we can invite as many as we please.'

'Do you know how long he intends to be gone?'

Her sister shrugged. 'How long does it take to do something like that? I did hear Papa tell Mama that he had withheld some documents about manorial rights and without those his lordship cannot proceed. But he will send for them, no doubt, so it is only putting off the inevitable.'

Jane had decided to go home the next day and was prepared to walk, but Mark would not hear of it and insisted on taking her in his curricle. It was the first time they had been alone together since the day he had picked her up off the floor and kissed her. She sat silently beside him, watching his capable hands on the reins and occasionally glancing up at him, but he kept his gaze firmly on the back of the horse. Instead of going down the main village street when he came to the crossroads, he turned off on to the road to Witherington.

'Why are you going this way?' she asked, breaking the long silence.

He turned to her with a gentle smile. 'So that I may have a little longer alone with you.'

'Oh.'

'And also because I have something to show you.'

'At Witherington?' That he wanted to have time with her both pleased and worried her at the same time. But if she kept her mind firmly on the Hadlea Children's Home and remained businesslike she might just manage to keep her composure.

'Yes.'

'The sale went through, then? I wondered if Lord Bolsover might try to delay it.'

'He was only one of the beneficiaries and the others were all keen to sell. He is not as powerful as he would have us think, Jane.'

'Powerful enough.'

'We will not speak of him. Now, what do you see?' He had turned into the gates of Witherington House, which had been replaced on their hinges and were standing open to reveal a drive cleared of weeds. The house itself had been divested of its festoons of ivy. 'Mark, what a transformation! There's new glass in the broken windows and they have all been painted.'

'There are fresh tiles on the roof, too.'

'However did you manage it?'

'I didn't do anything except point out what needed to be done. It was the people of Hadlea. They love and respect you, Jane, and when they heard from the Rector what you wanted to do with the place, every able-bodied man and some of the women and children came forward and spent their spare time here. I simply bought the paint, glass and tools.'

'They must be paid.'

'They said they didn't want payment, but I insisted on giving them something.' He drove round the side of the house and drew up in the yard where Mrs Godfrey was feeding chickens. These were new, too. 'I thought the home ought to be as self-sufficient as possible,' he said, jumping down and helping Jane to alight. 'Good morning, Mrs Godfrey. Where is Silas?'

'He is in the garden somewhere with some of the folks from Witherington. They decided they wouldn't be bested by Hadlea and came to help. Shall I fetch him?'

'No, let him be. I just want to show Miss Cavenhurst what we have done.'

'Made a transformation, that's what,' she said, then to Jane, 'Miss Cavenhurst, I heard you'd had another accident. I hope you have recovered.'

'Yes, thank you. It was entirely my own fault. I am quite well now.'

'I'll make tea, shall I?'

'When we have finished looking round, we will welcome tea, thank you,' Mark said, leading the way indoors.

The interior had also been cleaned and painted in cream and light green and, with the ivy gone, the rooms were light and airy. 'Oh, Mark, to think all this was done while I was idling at Broadacres.'

'You have friends, Jane, a great many friends,' he said softly. 'Not just me.'

She was tempted to say he was more than a friend, but decided it would be unwise. She went from room to room—everywhere was the same. 'It is ready to furnish,' she said, as they made their way up the repaired stairs. 'Do we have enough money?'

'I think so, but we must continue to raise more. There is the fair, of course. And my mother has said she will open the house and grounds and give a musical recital for her friends. I am sure they can be persuaded to give freely.'

'That is very kind of Lady Wyndham, but she is still in mourning, Mark.'

'She says she will wait until the six months is up, but she is sure that is what my father would have wished. He was all in favour of your idea, as you know. In the meantime we can go ahead with the fair.'

They were standing at the window of the largest bedroom, looking out at a group of people clearing the overgrown garden and piling the rubbish into a heap for a bonfire. She was right; concentrating on the home was making her personal unhappiness almost bearable, but she wondered what all these good people would say if they knew the truth.

They had finished their tour and talked about furnishings and the fair while they sat in the kitchen drinking tea, then set off back to Hadlea.

'I can't thank you enough, Mark,' she said. 'You have made a dream possible.'

'There is another dream I would like to make possible…'

'Don't, Mark. Please don't.'

They were passing the place where they had had their picnic and he pulled up, just as he had before. 'Let us walk a little.'

He helped her down and they walked into the field, where a footpath ran round the perimeter. There was wheat growing in it, almost ripe enough to harvest, but even Jane, who was no farmer, could see it would not be abundant and unlikely to be good enough for making bread. But it was not the state of the harvest which occupied her now, but the fact that Mark had hold of her hand and was drawing her into his arms.

'Mark, you mustn't.'

'Yes, I must.' He bent to kiss her. He kissed her lips, her eyelids, her neck, the round softness at the top of her breasts, peeping above the scooped neck of the striped-gingham dress she wore. It sent a ripple of sensation right through her body and into her groin. She clung to him, not wanting him to stop. It was he who pulled away, breathing heavily.

'I'm sorry, Jane, my love, my dearest love, I have not made it easy for you, have I?'

'No, you have not, but don't be sorry, unless you regret it.'

'Regret it! Oh, my love. How could I?' He went to draw her to him again, but she stepped backwards.

'No, Mark. No more. Take me home before we both do something we regret.'

'Very well.' He put his hand under her elbow to guide her back to the carriage. 'There has to be a way out of this mess, there just has to be and I will find it, I promise you.'

Everyone was pleased to have her home, telling her how well she looked and that the rest had done her good. 'Now, you are not to go dashing about as you have been doing,' her mother said, sitting beside Jane on her bed while Bessie unpacked the few clothes that had been taken to Broadacres. 'It is why you have these accidents. Do take more care in future.'

'Mama, I cannot be idle. It leaves me too much time to think.'

'Ah, I understand. You know Lord Bolsover has left the village?'

'Isabel told me. I suppose it is too much to hope he has given up and won't be back.'

'I am afraid it is.'

'And you still think I should marry him?'

'If it was left to me, I would say no, let him do his worst, but it is not up to me.' She laid a hand on Jane's arm. 'Your papa can see no other way out of our predicament. And there are Isabel and Sophie to consider. Sophie will never find a suitable husband if we are poor. And there's Teddy. I want him home, Jane, I want my son home.'

'I know.' She sighed, then added, falsely bright, 'I intend to enjoy my last days of freedom.'

'Good.'

'Did you know the villagers have been working at Witherington House?'

'Yes, everyone is talking about it. It is good that Lord Bolsover has said you may continue with it, Jane.'

'It will certainly be a condition of my acceptance.' Even as she spoke she wondered if she would be in a position to insist on conditions.

* * *

There was still much to be done. In the following days, she formed a committee in the village to organise the fair and wrote more letters asking for prizes and donations, and perused dozens of catalogues, looking for serviceable furniture for her orphans. Mr Halliday junior had written to her, asking when she intended to admit her first orphans. Her reply was that she knew a brother and sister in Hadlea whose father had been lost in the war and whose mother was finding it difficult having to go to work and look after her children. There were others in the neighbourhood she would approach. They would be the first to be offered homes. As for the rest, she would simply visit nearby towns and keep her eyes and ears open.

Her days were full and for a little while she was able to set aside the prospect of marrying Lord Bolsover, but it was different at night. Tired as she was from her daytime activities, she was never tired enough to sleep soundly.

She had nightmares, which involved Lord Bolsover chasing her, sometimes over flat grassland which suddenly became boggy, sucking at her feet and slowing her down, sometimes through woods at night with strange shapes looming out of the darkness, at other times along high cliffs with the sea crashing on the rocks below them. That was worst—with the menace behind her and the menace in front, she didn't know which way to turn. She always woke just as Lord Bolsover reached out to grab her. At other times she dreamed she was wearing Isabel's wedding gown and her sister was trying to tear it off her, shouting, 'It's mine! It's mine!' That made her feel worst of all and she woke with tears streaming down her face and her bedclothes in a tangle.

She had not seen Mark for some time. She had no idea if he had resigned himself to marrying Isabel, but she assumed he had. Isabel herself talked about it all the time: her gown, her trousseau, what had been ordered for the wedding breakfast, how she would reorganise Broadacres once Lady Wyndham had moved into the dower house. It was as if she dared not stop talking.

'Issie, are you sure you want to marry Mark?' Jane asked her one day when they were alone in the morning room. 'Not so long ago, you declared you could not bear the prospect. You said you did not love him.'

'No more I do, but plenty of marriages have survived without love, especially if there are compensations: a handsome husband, wealth and standing. You should think about that yourself.' She paused. 'Don't you dare tell Mark I said that.'

'I won't.'

The London Season was well and truly over and all the big families had repaired to their estates in the country, where the harvest was being gathered in. All agreed it was a poor one and the price of bread would go up again. The harvest on Broadacres's farms was better than most, but nothing like as good as it ought to have been. Mark had waved the rents of his tenant farmers for the winter term. It was a gesture they appreciated and rewarded him with genuine loyalty, promising to help the fair in any way they could.

But Mark was not in London to sell his grain, but to try to find a way out of his more pressing dilemma. His first call was on Cecil Halliday, who was working on a court case involving the theft of a silk shawl, but left it to greet Mark. 'I wasn't expecting you today, my lord,' he said as they shook hands. 'There is nothing wrong at Broadacres, I trust.'

'No, nothing. My visit concerns Greystone Manor and Lord Bolsover.'

'My father is dealing with that, my lord. I know little of it.'

'Perhaps you could ask your father to join us.'

He disappeared and returned in few minutes with Theodore, who bowed in the old-fashioned way. 'My lord, my son tells me you are interested in Greystone Manor. Are you considering buying it?'

'No, Mr Halliday, I am not. I need to find out

all I can about Lord Bolsover. Are you quite sure
his claims are just and fair?'

The old man smiled. 'Just and fair? Hardly.
But if you are asking me if they are legal, then I
must tell you that as far as I can see they are. Do
you have information to the contrary?'

'No, I hoped you might have. Did you know
he has bullied Sir Edward into allowing him to
propose to Miss Cavenhurst—Miss Jane Cavenhurst, I mean—and his lordship intends to take
her and the Manor in lieu of the debt?'

'No. I did not know. That is indeed troubling
news.'

'I think Sir Edward believes Bolsover has your
support. And Jane—Miss Cavenhurst—is convinced she has no choice but to agree.'

'Good God!'

'Do you know anything at all that might discredit his lordship?'

'Only that he is a gambler and plays deep, but
if he chooses to live in that way, it is his affair.'

'I would like you to dig a little, see what you
can unearth.'

'My lord,' Theodore said with some pompos-
ity, 'Sir Edward Cavenhurst is my client. I cannot
do anything without his permission.'

Mark turned to the younger man. 'Then what
about you, Cecil? Will you take my instructions?'

'I would,' he said doubtfully. 'If I knew why you were asking.'

'I am soon to be married into the family and would not have them brought low if I can help it. I would pay off Sir Edward's debt myself, even though it would have a damaging effect on my own resources, but Sir Edward is too proud to accept. Besides, if Lord Bolsover is crooked, I want him brought to justice, not to pay him off.'

'I'll see what I can do,' Cecil said.

'Then you must do it in your own time,' his father said. 'I do not doubt we will have trouble getting Sir Edward to settle his account as it is. I am not inclined to spend any more time on his behalf.'

Mark left, annoyed that even Sir Edward's own lawyer was turning against him. Cecil's enquiries might take some time and he was too impatient to wait. His next call was at White's, where he hoped to find Toby Moore, but Toby like the rest of London society had decamped to the country. The man did not have a country estate, but was no doubt going the round of friends. Frustrated, Mark went to Horse Guards where he met his old battalion commander. 'Can you tell me anything about Lord Hector Bolsover and Captain Tobias Moore?' he asked him when they had finished clapping each other on the back and Colonel Bagshott had congratulated him on his elevation while commiserating with him on the demise of his father. 'What regiment were they in?'

'I have no idea. I believe they served in the Peninsula, if not at Waterloo. Toby Moore calls himself "Captain". I met him once just before the battle of Cuidad Rodrigo. Never saw him again after that.'

'It will take me a little time searching the records. How long are you in town?'

'Only today and tomorrow. I must return to Hadlea the day after.'

'Let's meet tomorrow evening for supper. Stephen's at eight o'clock suit you?'

'Yes, I will be there.'

Mark went back to South Audley Street to spend an evening at home. He could have gone to his club but he did not feel like being sociable. He had too much on his mind. If he could only find something to discredit Bolsover, he might save Jane from being forced into marrying him. It would please Jane and her parents, but it was not enough. It did not release him from his engagement to Isabel. That was something else entirely.

The following evening he met Colonel Bagshott as arranged. They spent a frustrating hour and a half, talking about old times and old comrades and reliving old battles, before the subject of Hector Bolsover was broached.

'As far as I can tell Lord Bolsover was never in the army,' the Colonel said. 'I believe he went out to the Peninsula as a civilian, though why I do not know.'

'He is a gambler,' Mark said. 'No doubt he was fleecing the troops. What about Toby Moore?'

'He was cashiered for cowardice after the Battle of Cuidad Rodrigo. He has no right to call himself a captain.' He paused. 'Are you going to tell me what this is all about?'

Mark told him the same story he had told the lawyers. 'I was hoping to discredit Bolsover enough to make him leave the field,' he said, 'but so far have discovered nothing except that he is a mountebank of the first order.'

'I am sorry I could not help you further. If I learn anything else, I will certainly let you know.'

Mark had to be satisfied with that and they moved on to other topics, which diverted him for a time, but the reality was that he had made very little progress. So much for his promise to Jane that he would find a solution.

All the arrangements for the fair had been completed. Mark had sent his men to mow the field, mark out the lines for the races and set up some of the stalls the day before. An archway festooned with bunting had been constructed at the gate where Mrs Caulder would sit at a table to take the entrance money. Others would be manning stalls of produce and overseeing the competitions. Mark had donated a pig as a prize for a skittles competition and others had donated prizes for various races and feats of strength. There would be bowls and apple bobbing and later in the evening dancing to the music of a fiddle and a lute. Lady Wyndham had agreed to open proceedings. All they needed was good weather.

On the day, Jane was woken early by Bessie drawing back the curtains. Sunshine streamed into the room. She rose and went to the window. The sky was an overall azure, not a cloud to be seen. 'A good omen, we have been blessed with fine weather,' she said to Bessie. 'I'll dress and have my breakfast in the kitchen, then I'll drive over to Ten Acre Field.'

'It is still very early, Miss Jane.'

'I know, but there is still much to do. The pale-blue muslin, I think, and the matching pelisse.'

She was not the first to arrive. The villagers were all used to rising early, especially in summer, and were already going about their allotted tasks. Mark was there, in his shirt sleeves, busily helping to erect a dais for the opening ceremony and the prize giving. His coat and cravat hung on a nearby post. He smiled at her, a little sadly, but it was a smile. 'Have you prepared your speech?' he queried.

'Me? Oh, no, Mark, I am not going to make a speech,' she protested, trying vainly to take her eyes from the sight of his bare chest under the open neck of his shirt.

'But it's your project. Without you it would never have happened.'

'It is just as much yours, Mark. You make the speech.'

She moved on, checking this, checking that, speaking to everyone, her spirits rising a little as she went. If nothing else was right in her life, this project was. Mrs Caulder arrived and sat at the entrance to the field, a jar for the money on a table in front of her. 'Henry will be here in good time to conduct the prayers,' she told Jane, who was becoming anxious in case no one arrived.

One by one they came, paid their sixpences and wandered round to see what was on offer. It was not only the Hadlea and Witherington residents, but people from further afield who arrived in an assortment of carriages. Jane had not thought about what to do with all the vehicles, but Mark, as ever, came to her rescue by suggesting they line up alongside the drive at Broadacres and his stable boys would see to the horses, for a small fee to be added to the funds. 'I'll go and tell the lads and bring my mother back,' he told

Jane, hanging his cravat loosely about his neck and slipping his arms into his coat.

While he was gone her father, mother and sisters arrived. In spite of the dreadful cloud hanging over them, they were determined to put a good face on it for Jane's sake and the ladies were elegantly dressed and carrying parasols for the sun was warm. 'Lord Bolsover is back,' Sophie whispered to her. 'We saw him arriving at the Fox and Hounds. We stopped so that Papa could get down and speak to him. I think they argued. Papa looked very flushed and his lordship angry.'

'Where is Mark?' Isabel demanded. 'I expect him to escort me.'

'He has gone to fetch his mother,' Jane said, wishing Sophie had not told her about Lord Bolsover and hoping he would not decide to patronise the fair. 'He will be back soon.'

She left her family to make sure everything was ready on the dais for her ladyship. The Rector was there, sitting on one of the chairs provided. 'We shall do well out of this, Jane,' he said. 'Mrs Caulder has already taken three pounds at the gate, though I fear some of the boys have managed to squeeze through the hedge without paying.'

'Never mind. They will need to pay if they want to enter the competitions.'

Mark's curricle drew up and he helped his

mother from it and up on to the dais, where she stood, in unrelieved black, looking about her at the colourful throng, regal but not distant. Mark helped her to a seat and then stepped forward, nodding to a boy at the side of the platform who was holding a brass bell by its clapper. The boy began ringing it, watching in glee as people stopped what they were doing and turned towards him. 'Enough,' Mark commanded, as everyone gathered round the platform. The sound stopped on a last echo.

'Ladies and gentlemen,' Mark began, 'we are here to enjoy ourselves, but also to remember the soldiers and sailors lost in the recent war and think of the children they left behind. All the money raised will go towards the maintenance of Witherington House as a home for some of those children. We would not be here today, if it were not for Miss Jane Cavenhurst, whose idea it was and who has worked tirelessly towards it.' He paused and looked round while everyone applauded. 'Miss Cavenhurst.' He beckoned Jane to mount the rostrum.

She was taken aback and wanted to sink into the ground, but he was holding out his hand to her and the people nearest to her were urging her on. Reluctantly she stepped up beside Mark. 'You will pay for that trick, Mark Wyndham,' she whispered.

'The credit is yours,' he whispered back. 'Tell them about the urchin you met in London, touch their heart-strings.'

She began unsteadily, but as her fervour for the cause took over, her voice strengthened and she saw more than one tear wiped away. 'We are fortunate that the late Lord Wyndham gave a very generous donation to start us off,' she finished. 'And others have also donated. The home has already been purchased, as many of you know, but we still need funds to furnish it and maintain it, so please, buy the produce, enter the games and enjoy the day.'

The Rector stood and led them in a prayer and then Mark called on his mother to declare the fair up and running. It was while she was standing beside her ladyship, looking over the heads of the crowd, that Jane saw Lord Bolsover coming towards her. She looked round for a way of escape, but soon realised she could not flee without creating a scene and she did not want to spoil the happy atmosphere of the afternoon.

Mark had seen him, too. 'Courage, my love,' he whispered. 'Don't agree to anything.'

She was shaking as she stepped down from the dais to face the man she held so much in aversion. He smiled and doffed his hat in an exaggerated bow. 'Miss Cavenhurst. You are recovered, I see, and quite the Lady of the Manor. I chose my bride well, methinks.'

She did not deign to answer that. Instead she said, 'What are you doing here?''

'Why, my dear, I have come for my answer. You have kept me waiting long enough. Let us take a stroll.' He picked up her hand and tucked it beneath his elbow. 'There, that is better, now we may act the happy couple. Do smile, my dear. You will have everyone think our coming union is not to your liking.'

'I do not feel like smiling, Lord Bolsover.'

'Now that is to be regretted, but we shall blame it on your accident, shall we? Not quite yourself yet.'

'I wish you would go away and leave my family alone.'

'Now, my dear, you know I cannot do that. Nor would your father wish me to even though he withheld an important document. Very foolish of him. It did nothing more than cause me the inconvenience of coming back for it. My lawyer refused to proceed without it and I would not trust anyone but myself to fetch it. What your papa seems not to have considered is that every day's delay adds to the interest, which is not inconsiderable. I beg you point that out to him when you tell him you have accepted my proposal.'

'I have not accepted it.'

'Oh, but you will, do not doubt it. Shall we get that boy with the bell to give it a go and announce our betrothal to the whole crowd? I am sure they will all be overjoyed for you.'

'No, please don't.' She hated to beg, but she could see Mark marching purposely towards them with a furious expression on his face and she feared a public quarrel. 'It is too soon. I need more time.'

'You have had over a month.'

'I could not help being ill.'

'But you are well now.'

'After my sister's wedding in three weeks' time,' she said, groping at straws. 'I will give you an answer then.'

Mark was almost upon them when Mrs Caulder came hurrying up to Jane. 'I beg your pardon, my lord,' she said, addressing Lord Bolsover, 'but I must speak to Miss Cavenhurst. It is urgent.'

Jane's relief at the interruption was palpable. She turned to Mrs Caulder with a smile which left her face when she saw how distressed the lady was. 'What has happened?'

'Someone has stolen the gate money. I only turned my back a minute to listen to the speeches and when I turned back it was gone.'

Lord Bolsover laughed aloud. 'I will leave you to sort it out, my dear, but it is only a few pounds.

I can easily make it up for you.' And with that, he strolled away, smiling to himself.

Jane's shoulders sagged as the tension she had been enduring seeped away from her. Her hands were shaking and her knees felt boneless.

'I am mortified,' Mrs Caulder went on. 'I really am sorry, but if his lordship is prepared to make it up, we shall not lose by it.'

'That is not the point.' Mark put in. 'It is theft and we must discover who is responsible. We cannot have people thinking it pays to steal.'

'No, I suppose you are right, but I have no idea who it was.'

'Did they take only the money or the jar with it?' Mark asked

'The jar. Everything. There was a five-pound donation from Sir Mortimer Belton, as well.'

Jane had not seen the Member of Parliament arrive. 'That was generous of him.'

'Yes, but now it is lost. Some people gave more than sixpence to come in, too. They said it was for a worthy cause. There must have been nigh on ten pounds altogether.'

'Did you see anyone loitering nearby?' Mark asked.

'Not that I can recall.'

'Leave it to me,' Mark said. 'We will keep it to ourselves for now. We don't want to cause a stir.'

'I won't say a word. Thank you, my lord.' She hurried away, leaving Mark facing Jane.

'What did he have to say?' he asked.

'Who?'

'Bolsover. What did he say?'

'Nothing he has not said before. I begged him to give me more time. I said I would give him his answer after your wedding.'

'My wedding! Did he agree?'

'He neither agreed nor disagreed. Mrs Caulder interrupted us.'

He laughed. 'Oh, well done, Mrs Caulder.'

'It is not funny, Mark.'

'No, but if she has afforded us more time…'

'Us, Mark?'

'Yes, us. You do not think I am going to let you marry that scoundrel, do you? I have tried to find something to discredit him, but though he is not at all liked, no one seems to know anything against him. There are rumours of sharp practices, but nothing to substantiate the rumours. I shall keep trying.'

'Mark, please do not raise my hopes, if they are to be dashed. I don't think I could bear it. Really, you should be escorting Isabel round the fair and buying her trinkets, not talking to me. I can see her over there and she is looking at us. Go to her, please.'

* * *

'You have been neglecting me,' Isabel complained as soon as he joined her. 'People are beginning to notice.'

'I am sorry, Isabel, but I have had much to do with the organisation of this event and seeing that everything is running smoothly and I had to escort my mother back to the house; she finds events like this tiring. Now something else has happened that demands my immediate attention, so I am obliged to leave you again.'

'A fine marriage we shall have if you are forever going off and leaving me.'

'If you wish to change your mind about that again, please say so.'

'No, no, I didn't mean anything,' she said quickly. 'Go and do whatever it is you have to do. But I hope it will not take too long. Papa has said we may stay for the dancing, so I shall expect you to stand up with me.'

He had bowed and left her to watch the races with her parents while he spent the next hour and a half going round all the stalls, asking if anyone had been spending unusually freely, but no one had. Perhaps the thief was no longer on the field, perhaps had never been any further than the gate. If that were so, it was going to be doubly difficult to apprehend him. Or her.

He went to the gate to ask Mrs Caulder if anyone had approached and not entered, but the good lady must have decided that there would be no more arrivals and had left her post. He turned away and it was then he saw the woman out of the corner of his eye. She was carrying a jar close to her chest, which looked very like the one Mrs Caulder had been using. He dodged behind the hedge and watched her. She approached the deserted table and, looking furtively about her, set the jar on the table. Mark left his hiding place and confronted her.

'It is Mrs Butler, is it not?'

'Yes.'

'What were you doing with this?' He picked up the jar. It was heavy with coins.

'Putting it back.'

'What were you doing with it in the first place?'

'Nothing. Putting it back, I told you. I found it.'

'Oh, come, madam, you do not expect me to believe that, do you? Shall I tell you what I think? I think your boy took it.'

She gasped. 'He didn't mean no 'arm, sir. He's only a little lad and he wanted to 'elp me. I lost me ol' man to the war, yer see, and now I've lost me job, on account of staying at home to look after Lizzie, who was sick. You in't a-goin' to turn 'im in, are you?'

'No, I do not think so. We have the money safe. Go home and see to your family.'

'Thank you, m'lord. God bless you.' She bobbed a curtsy and fled.

He took the jar back to Jane. 'It is all here,' he said. 'No harm's done.'

'Oh, thank goodness. I didn't want the day marred by something so unpleasant. Who took it?'

He told her what had happened. 'Did you not say you were thinking of offering the Butler children a home?' he asked.

'Yes. I haven't mentioned it to Mrs Butler yet, but I will do so soon. She may not want to part with him.'

'I think she might. She has just lost her job and her chances of finding another while she has two children to care for are slim.'

'She could work at Witherington House, then they could all be together. I need to recruit staff.'

'Good idea. Shall we join your parents and sisters?'

Jane looked round and spied them watching the skittles competition. Lord Bolsover was with them. 'No, I do not think I will. I'll go and see Mrs Butler. You go.'

But he did not want to join them either and went in search of the parson's wife to give her the good news and return the pot to her after emptying its contents into a canvas bag Jane had stowed under the dais for just that purpose. There was money being taken on all the stalls and it occurred to him that it might be a good idea to take temptation out of the way and collect it. He would take it up to the house and put it in the safe until it could be paid into the Hadlea Children's Home account. By the time he had finished the bag was heavy. They had done well, but he would not count it— that was a pleasure he would leave for Jane.

Mark was almost home when he saw a familiar figure coming towards him, a slightly plump figure dressed in a blue military-style frockcoat, embellished with silver braid. 'Jonathan Smythe, you old dog,' Mark said, smiling with pleasure. 'Where have you sprung from?' They clapped each other on the back.

'Scotland, where else? I've been up to the house and your mother told me where to find you.'

'I will be going back there after I have put this in a safe place.' He held up the bag. 'Come with me.'

Jonathan turned and they walked side by side. 'I was sorry to hear of your father's demise, Mark.'

'Thank you.'

'My mother's cousin died, too. I've inherited a

pile of stones, as cold as charity, but it comes with a sizeable fortune so I must not grumble. I assume your mourning has delayed your wedding?'

'Yes. Much has happened since you left.'

'If you still want me to be your groomsman, I am yours to command.'

Mark could think of nothing to say to that except to thank him again.

'You'll never guess whom I met while I was up north. Drew Ashton. I hadn't seen him since we were at school together. He's come up in the world by all accounts.'

'Drew is in Scotland?'

'Yes. He was visiting his great-aunt. I must say I was surprised by that. She never bothered with him when he was a boy and he don't need her blunt now. I reckon it was a convenient bolt hole. He was havey-cavey when I asked.'

'He always played his cards close to his chest. You don't happen to have his direction, do you?'

'I think I have it in my trunk. I left it at Broadacres, by the way. I assumed you would invite me to stay, what with the wedding and all.'

'Of course, stay as long as you like. There's a fair on the Ten Acre Field that I've been helping to organise, which is why I am carrying a bag of small change. I have to go back as soon as I've put it in the safe. There's to be a country dance this evening which I am obliged to attend. Come if you like.'

It was incredible how cheerful he suddenly felt. At last he could see a way out of his dilemma.

Chapter Twelve

The field was lit by lanterns on poles for the dance in the evening. Everyone joined in, including the children, and it proved to be the most fun of the whole day, if only because it was impossible to dance properly on grass. Jane and Mark partnered each other in an eightsome, which meant occasionally holding hands in full view of everyone. She was acutely aware that she must in no way betray how she felt about him, but the slight squeeze he gave her fingers every time they met and circled together told her he was aware of it, too. He seemed unusually light-hearted, smiling and joking with everyone. Afterwards she sat with her parents, watching him dance with Isabel while his friend, Mr Smythe, danced with Sophie.

She was quietly congratulating herself on the success of the venture and enjoying the spectacle of everyone amusing themselves when Lord Bolsover stood over her to claim a dance. She pleaded

tiredness, but he would not take no for an answer
and led her into the throng.

He was clumsy and stumbled more than once.
'I can't get the way of this,' he said, giving up
after only a few minutes. 'If this is what you call
dancing...'

'It is meant to be fun,' she said. 'This isn't a
London ballroom. If that is what you want, I suggest you return to the capital.'

'Not without my answer.'

'I have told you when I will give you that.'

'And I shall hold you to that, never fear. My
mother is become impatient to have a grandson.'
Still smiling, he bowed and strolled away. Jane
let out a long breath of relief.

The result of the fair was forty pounds to add
to the funds, which was far more than Jane had
dared to hope for. She and Mark spent Sunday
morning at Broadacres, counting the pennies
and sixpences and the occasional gold sovereign.
'People have been so generous,' Jane said. 'I can
buy enough beds and bedroom furniture to fill
the dormitories at Witherington. I will ask the
Rector to announce the result in church.'

The announcement after evensong had brought
gasps of delight and it was suggested it should be
an annual event, which had pleased her. There

was so little to please her nowadays; she was becoming hopelessly resigned to marrying Lord Bolsover. He was staying at the Fox and Hounds, but was constantly at Greystone, seemingly unaware of how unwelcome he was. He would talk of the alterations he meant to make, the refurbishment, the parties he would host, smiling all the while with that oily smile of his, which sickened Jane, if no one else. The only way she could avoid him was to spend as much time as possible at Witherington House where she could immerse herself in what was going on there and for a little while, forget her coming fate.

Gradually the furniture arrived and was put in place until it began to look like a real home. She was helped by Mrs Butler, who had accepted her offer and moved in with ten-year-old Robert and two-year-old Lizzie, who had been conceived when her husband came home in 1814. He had only come home to die of his wounds within weeks, unaware that his wife was carrying another child. The family had lived on poor relief until Mrs Butler had found a job working in the fields. It was piece work and the poor woman was so exhausted she was unable to earn more than a pittance. Jane heard the tale little by little as they worked together.

Jane and Mark together interviewed several local people for positions and took on a married couple to be master and housekeeper. They came from a school and would have to give notice to their present employers and would not arrive until the end of September. Mrs Godfrey remained as cook and old Silas looked after the outside. Already what they were doing was becoming known and men and women were turning up asking for employment. They would need more staff when more children were taken in, so she took their names and said she would let them know when the time came.

One was a Portuguese man who said his name was Paolo Estaban. He told her he had been a servant of a British officer in the late war and had returned to England with him. The officer had not paid him for several weeks and he needed employment. He was used to looking after horses and he had seen her pony and trap outside. She was about to say they were not hers and did not belong to the home, but then realised she might well need such a conveyance to get about as she had been doing. She would ask Mark if the funds would stretch to buying it from her father. She told the man to come back the following week.

News of what she was doing had spread and she was also approached by several charities asking for places for children. Three of the most needy had already arrived. Harry, Tom and Emma had been begging in Norwich when they had been picked up by a local parson who had heard about her venture and come to see her. The result was the children had been put on a carrier's wagon and arrived filthy, half-starved and dressed in an assortment of rags. They were also very wary of her and their new surroundings and not at all keen to be put into a bath, brought into the kitchen for the purpose. She asked Robert and Lizzie to make them feel at home and this worked better than anything the adults could do. Bathed, with their tangled hair washed and brushed, and dressed in new clothes, they were different children. She began looking for a teacher because they would need to be schooled.

The whole project was keeping Jane so busy she did not have time to dwell on the fact that the six months of mourning at Broadacres was coming to a close, that half the contents of Greystone Manor had been packed up ready for the move as soon as the wedding was over, not only Isabel's wedding to Mark, but her own to Lord Bolsover. She refused to make any preparation for that, praying as she had never prayed before that something would happen to prevent it.

Mark had said he would think of something, but he had not mentioned it again. After the fair he had seemed more cheerful, making jokes with the children and flattering Mrs Godfrey outrageously. She did not ask him how he was dealing with Isabel, but assumed all was well between them. She tried desperately to forget he had ever said he loved her. It seemed he had done so, for he stopped coming to Witherington. She told herself that was as it should be; she could not continue to rely on him for help. He had other matters nearer home to attend to. She must endure the heartache as best she could.

Mark had certainly not forgotten. He was in a state bordering on panic. There were only two weeks to go to the wedding he wanted so much to avoid and Drew had not answered his letter. Supposing he had moved on and the letter never reached him, what then? He would have to do something himself, something drastic like eloping with Jane. He knew she would never agree to that. Could he abduct her? That would be dishonourable and illegal. And whatever he did would have to be done with the consent of Isabel. He could not see her giving it. The euphoria he had felt when Jonathan arrived had long ago evaporated.

He paced the house, watched by his worried mother, went riding with Jonathan, covering mile after mile, exhausting his mounts until, one morning very early, they came to a halt at the edge of the fen. There was a landing stage there and a lopsided dwelling where the ferryman lived. The meadows on either were only dry in summer and were used for grazing cattle, which grew fat on the lush grass. There was a small rise in the ground on the right, not really big enough to call a hill, and on top of it an old hovel which had many years before been a fenman's dwelling. It was a place Mark knew well, for he had often wandered about here as a child, frequently in the company of Teddy and his two older sisters, picking wild flowers, watching for frogs and toads, having imaginary battles in which the hovel was a fort. Happy times in which the future was unknown.

'What in God's name is the matter with you, Mark?' Jonathan said, as they dismounted. 'You are certainly not acting like the happy bridegroom. I am forced to the conclusion you do not want this wedding.'

'No, I do not.'

'Are you going to tell me why?'

Mark sighed and put his head into his horse's neck. 'I suppose I must.' He paused, wondering where to begin. 'I suppose it started when I offered to help Jane with her orphan project.'

'Jane?'

'Yes, Jane.' He went on to apprise his friend of all that had transpired since Jonathan left for Scotland.

'My, you are in a coil,' his friend said when he finished.

'I have done my best to discredit Bolsover and

sorely neglected Isabel in order to help Jane, in the vain hope she would tire of me and call the whole thing off, but she seems not to mind. Jane is not a rival in her mind. If you have any idea how I can come about, I shall be glad to hear it.'

'Short of kidnap and leaving your bride at the altar, you mean.'

'I can't do that.'

'No, I can see you can't. You could try throwing yourself on the mercy of Miss Isabel.'

'I thought of that, too, but it will not do. I would be seen as a bigger scoundrel than Bolsover, Isabel could sue for breach of promise and I would never dare show my face in Hadlea again.' He did not add that, worst of all, Jane would hate him for it and would certainly not agree to marry him. Bolsover would win. It was a bitter pill to swallow.

'Come, let us go back,' Jonathan said. 'There are still two weeks to go. Something might turn up.'

They mounted again and walked their exhausted horses back to the stables, approaching the house from the rear. Mark stopped to look at it, taking in the mellow Tudor bricks, the twisted chimneys, the mullioned windows, the stable block with its ornate clock which hadn't told the time in years. He loved his home, every inch of it, outside and in. He loved his mother and owed her his allegiance and he had responsibilities in the village. His honour was at stake and that counted for everything. There was no alternative but to go through with the wedding. *'Jane, forgive me.'* His lips moved on her name, but he made no sound.

With hunched shoulders and head bowed, he rode on, left his horse with Thompson, ordered the curricle to be readied and entered the house. He neither knew nor cared whether Jonathan followed him. He had to change and find Jane. She must be told and told at once while he still had the courage.

Harry and Tom had disappeared. Jane had no idea where they had gone. Neither Robert nor Emma could tell her anything, except they had been whispering together that morning. She searched every inch of the house before going outside to look in the outhouses and stables. Surely they had not run away? Where would they go? Would they try to go back to Norwich?

Silas was coming towards her; the old man was almost running in his agitation to impart some news to her. 'Miss Cavenhurst,' he said between gasps for breath. 'Someone's stole yer trap. I went to tek Bonny some oats and it were gone, Bonny with it.'

Jane could hardly believe it. Could the boys have taken it? Did they know how to harness

Bonny? Could they drive it? The answer was yes, they probably could. They hated to be indoors and, ever since coming to Witherington, had spent most of their time outside, following Silas about. They would have watched him with the pony and seen how the old man harnessed him. He had even taken them on short jaunts to pick up supplies for her. 'Have you seen Tom and Harry?' she asked him.

'They were down the garden with me early on, but disappeared after a bit. Don' know where they went.'

'Do you think they could have taken the trap?'

'Why would they do that, miss?'

'For a lark, perhaps.'

'I dunno. It in't hard to drive and Bonny is a placid old thing. I s'pose they could.'

As far as she was aware no one had come to the house that morning, certainly no one who would have reason to go to the stables. It had to be the boys. But where had they gone? And without the trap how could she go after them?

'I am going to fetch help,' she told him. 'If they come back, grab them and don't let them out of your sight.'

Without even stopping to put on a bonnet, she set off on foot for Broadacres. This was an emergency and she needed Mark's help. At every step she castigated herself. Whatever had given her the idea she was fit to look after children, especially children damaged by the life they had been forced to lead? She had been a conceited fool to think urchins living as they had been doing on city streets would settle down to a placid life in the country. She ought to have taken on a teacher to give them something positive to do instead of waiting until she had a full class. If her negligence became common knowledge, the gossip alone would ensure she did not take in any more children.

She was almost running, stumbling in her haste. What would Mark say? What would anyone say? She had been too wrapped up in her own misery to look after the children properly, that's what. 'Let him be at home,' she prayed.

She struck out across the fields to cut off a corner and sped across Broadacres park towards the side of the house. Jeremy was in the yard, harnessing the curricle. Almost too out of breath to speak, she stopped in front of him.

'Miss Cavenhurst, whatever's afoot?'

'Fetch Lord Wyndham, please, it's urgent.'

The man disappeared while she stood with her hand at her aching side, slowly recovering her breath. Mark joined her almost at once. 'Tom and Harry have run away and they have taken Bonny and the trap. We've got to find them.'

He was admirably calm as he helped her into

the curricle, climbed up beside her and set the horses off at a fast trot. 'I don't know what possessed them to do it,' she said. 'They have never given the slightest hint they were unhappy.'

'All boys like mischief,' he said. 'I doubt they will have gone far. We'll go back to Witherington House first. They might have returned.'

At the crossroads he was forced to slow down. There was a flurry of activity at the Fox and Hounds as a stage coach turned in to change horses, set down passengers and take others up. The inn's gig was standing by, ready to take incomers to their final destination. As soon as the road was clear he drove on and turned on to the lane to Witherington.

'I am so thankful you were at home.'

'We'll find them, stop worrying.'

'I cannot help it. It is all my fault. I should have taken more care of them. I should have taken on that teacher we spoke of. I shall never forgive myself if anything bad has happened to them. They could have overturned in a ditch and be lying there, unable to move. They could even be...' She could not say it.

'Jane, stop it, stop it at once. You are not to blame and they are how old?'

'Harry is ten and Tom is nine.'

'I was driving a gig all over the estate at that age. They are old for their years, Jane. Do not think of them as children, they are very small, very wily adults, used to fending for themselves.'

She managed a smile. 'Let us hope you are right.'

They were almost at Witherington House when they saw the trap turn out of a narrow lane in front of them. The boys were in it, but it was being driven by a man. 'Don't call out,' Mark said as he pulled in a little way behind them, matching his horse's gait to that of Bonny. 'We do not want to frighten the fellow into galloping. When they leave the lane for the high road, I'll look for an opportunity to overtake and stop them. I can't do it here, the road is too narrow.'

But they didn't take the high road, the trap turned into the gates of Witherington House and continued up the drive, closely followed by the curricle. As soon as both came to a stop, Jane scrambled out and ran to the boys, intending to confront the man. He jumped down and bowed to her. '*Senhora*, I believe these belong to you.'

'Mr Estaban!' she exclaimed.

Mark was beside her. 'You know this man, Jane?'

'Yes, he came to me for a job.'

Everyone started to talk at once—Jane expressing her gratitude, the boys excitedly telling of their adventures and Mark accusing the man of abducting the children and stealing the pony and trap.

'I beg your pardon, *senhor*,' Paolo said. 'I deny that. I found the young gentlemen trying to turn the vehicle in a field gate. A wheel had become stuck against the gate post. I recognised the pony and helped them to free it, then persuaded them to allow me to bring them back.'

'Is that the truth?' Mark asked Harry.

'Yes,' he said, shame-faced. 'We only wanted to try driving.'

'Then you had all better come inside and tell us about it,' Mark said, ushering them through the kitchen door.

'Here they are,' Jane told Mrs Godfrey and Mrs Butler, who were sitting at the kitchen table discussing the situation. 'Safe and sound. I am sure they are hungry and thirsty, so could you find us all something to eat and drink and bring it to the little parlour?' The room, which had once been old Sir Jasper's bedroom, had been thoroughly cleaned and was now a comfortable sitting room, which Jane liked to think of as her office.

It did not take long to establish the truth of what Mr Estaban had said and to hear the boys' account of their adventure. They had intended to go the nearest town just to look round, they said, but realised they had taken a wrong turn when the road ended in a vast expanse of water. In trying to turn round they had become stuck. The gentleman had helped them out.

'I explained to them the worry they would cause you,' Mr Estaban said. 'You are a woman alone in a household of women with only one elderly male servant. It is not good. You need a man.'

Jane looked at Mark and felt the colour flood her cheeks.

'Mr Estaban is right, you know,' he said. 'You do need a man.'

'But you come when you can.'

'Not often enough, I am afraid. There should be someone here all the time. Mr Estaban, I believe you applied for employment here? Do you still wish it?'

'Yes.'

'Tell me about yourself.'

'This is Lord Wyndham,' Jane explained. 'He is one of the Hadlea Children's Home trustees.'

Paolo told Mark the same story as he had told Jane. 'I can manage horses and I can manage children,' he ended.

'I thought of buying the pony and trap for the Home,' Jane put in. 'I think I am going to need it.'

'Good idea. I'll make an offer to Sir Edward on behalf of the trustees.' He turned back to Estaban. 'Where are you staying?'

'At an inn along the Lynn road.'

'Go and fetch your things. You can start straight away. And you boys, take these empty plates back to the kitchen and stay there until I decide what punishment to give you. You can start by grooming Bonny and my horse.'

They obeyed and Mark and Jane were alone. He shifted to sit beside her and put his hand over hers. 'Stop shaking, Jane, my love, it is all over. They are safe and Mr Estaban will be an asset, I am sure.'

'He cannot take your place.'

'I should hope not!'

It was an attempt at humour and she dutifully smiled. 'What have you been doing lately?'

'This and that. Asking questions, groping for a miracle.'

'Miracles almost never happen. We would be unwise to put our trust in miracles.'

'Oh, I don't know…' He could not go on. She had had enough upset for one day and he could not add to it. 'Would you like me to take you home?'

'No, thank you. The trap is here and I ought to wait for Mr Estaban to come back. Besides, I spend little time at Greystone these days. Lord Bolsover is always there, gloating.'

'Don't marry him, Jane, please don't. I could not bear it.'

'Mark, it is not up to you. You will be married to Isabel. And there are some who think I will be doing well for myself, finding a wealthy husband at my age and one with a title, too. I know many of the villagers think so.'

'Surely you don't.'

'It is something I have to bear in mind.'

'I do not believe it.'

She sighed. 'There is no point in going over the same ground again, it will not alter anything. Go home, Mark, please.'

Reluctantly he left her. Like an automaton he climbed into the curricle and picked up the reins. How, when he was married to Isabel, could he endure having Jane so close and yet so far out of his reach? Was she determined to accept Bolsover? He felt nothing but fury towards Sir Edward Cavenhurst and all his clan for bringing her to this pass. He felt fury at Drew, apparently ignoring his letter, probably because Isabel no longer stood high in his affections and he did not want to meet her again. Most of all he was furious with himself for his powerlessness.

The stage had gone from the Fox and Hounds and all was quiet as he turned the corner and set off for Greystone Manor. What he intended to say to everyone when he arrived, he had no idea, but he would burst if he did not tell them how he felt. He hoped it would make Isabel think again. He hardly heard the horse until it was almost on top of him.

'Mark! Hold up! Stop, will you?'

He turned to see Jonathan galloping after him and pulled the horse to a halt. 'How did you know where I was going?'

'Jeremy told me. Come back to Broadacres, Mark. Drew is there.'

'Drew?'

'Yes. He was all for rushing off to Greystone Manor as soon as he arrived, but I persuaded him he ought to talk to you first. It is as well I spotted you or I would have gone on to Witherington and missed you.'

Mark turned the curricle in a farm gate and was soon bowling back to Broadacres with Jonathan riding beside him. As soon as he arrived he sped indoors, leaving his friend to see to the horses. Drew was in the drawing room, enjoying hot chocolate and cake with his mother.

'Drew, where have you been?' he demanded.

'Mark, that is hardly a proper greeting,' his mother said. 'Sit down and have something to eat and drink. I am sure you went out without breakfast this morning.'

He sat down and watched his mother pour him a dish of chocolate. He took it from her, but de-

clined food. He was too tense to eat. He turned
to Drew. 'Did you receive my letter?'

'I did.'

'And?'

'I could hardly believe what I was reading. Of
course I left immediately.'

'But that was weeks ago.'

'Yes, hear me out, will you?'

'Go on.'

'When I consulted the timetables, it seemed
easier to go to London and then out again to Norfolk and that is what I did. On the way I fell to
thinking about what you had said in your letter
and it seemed to me there was something havey-
cavey about Hector Bolsover, something he would
rather we did not know. Where did all his wealth
come from when his estate is a modest one?
Could it all have been acquired from gambling?
Did he cheat on a grand scale? Why would he
want to live in a rural place like Hadlea when he
so obviously enjoyed the attractions of the city?
He does not strike me as a man who would be
particularly sensitive to past family history. Was
he just using it as an excuse?'

'I thought of all that,' Mark put in. 'I went to
London myself and made extensive enquiries of
anyone who might have known him. All I could
gather was that he had never served in the army
though he had spent time in the Peninsula and

that on his return his mother had given him an ultimatum to marry. It appears, whatever else he is, he is an obedient son.'

'Yes. He was born when his mother had given up all hope of having a child. His father died when he was a boy and he has looked to his mother for everything. Her word is law.'

'Go on.'

'I decided to find out what I could before I came on to Hadlea and started with Toby Moore. When I spoke to him before, I felt he was hiding something.'

'I looked for him myself but he was out of town. No one knew where.'

'He was back. No doubt he had run out of generous hosts. I decided to put the fear of God into him.' He smiled. 'He is not a valiant man, Mark.'

'No. Wellington had him drummed out for cowardice. He was lucky not to be shot.'

'It was at that time he met Bolsover, who was living in Lisbon. They teamed up to gamble, not always honestly. Bolsover was married to a Portuguese girl, the daughter of a wealthy count. She inherited a vast fortune on her father's demise and he was busy spending it. When it looked as though the authorities were catching up with them over their sharp practices, he and Toby fled the country and came back to England.'

'What happened to his wife?'

'I'm coming to that. You remember I said I was buying a ship? Well, I had one, a beautiful fast clipper, called the *Swallow*, and it was readying for a voyage to India. I sailed on her as far as Lisbon and found Lady Bolsover. He had beaten her to within an inch of her life and she had fled to her aunt and uncle and, as you can imagine, they are bent on revenge. They sent their son, Juanita's cousin, to England to track him down, but they have not heard from him for some time. I think Bolsover got wind of it and wanted somewhere to hide. Sir Edward's debts and the old family story of Colin Paget gave him the idea.'

'He's married,' Mark said, unable to keep the excitement from his voice. 'He's married already! He can't marry Jane.' He jumped up and wrung his friend's hand. 'Thank you, Drew, thank you.'

'What about Isabel?' Lady Wyndham put in. She had been listening intently, but had taken no part in the conversation. 'And there's Sir Edward's debts. You have solved only half the problem.'

Mark turned to Drew. 'What about Isabel?'

'I intend to go over to Greystone Manor just as soon as I have had a rest. I only returned to England yesterday and am devilish tired. My lady, if you could furnish me with a bed for an hour or two, I would be grateful. I need to be fresh and have my wits about me if I am to persuade Sir Edward to entertain my suit. If it takes money, then money he shall have. I have already told the skipper of the *Swallow* to find Teddy when he arrives in Calcutta and bring him home. That should sweeten Sir Edward up a bit, but, if not Sir Edward, then his lady wife.'

'I must go back to Jane,' Mark said.

'Not tonight, Mark,' Lady Wyndham said. 'You can go to Greystone together tomorrow.' She rang a bell at her side to summon a servant to conduct Drew to a bedroom. As soon as he had gone, she turned to Mark. 'Whichever way you look at it, this is going to cause a huge scandal.'

'I know, Mama, but nothing like the one that might have ensued had I run off with Jane, or if Drew had run off with Isabel.'

'I sincerely hope that you have not been entertaining that idea.'

'I could never have done it, even if Jane agreed, which I am sure she would not.'

'Then, let us hope Sir Edward is amenable.'

The next morning saw the two men, both of them nervous, set off for Greystone Manor. Mark was in a long-tailed coat in blue superfine and pantaloon trousers and Drew in a frockcoat and nankeen breeches buckled below the knee. Both had spent an unconscionable time tying their cravats and adjusting the sleeves of their shirts.

For such a formal visit, they chose to ride in the Wyndham coach, driven by Jeremy.

'Shall we go and frighten Bolsover out of his bed?' Mark suggested as they approached the Fox and Hounds. 'I have a mind to make him crawl.'

'Nothing would give me greater pleasure.'

Mark called out to Jeremy to pull up at the inn and the two young men entered the inn and enquired for Lord Bolsover's room. Two minutes later they flung open the door to see the startled man sitting up in bed with a breakfast tray on his lap.

'What the devil—?' he began, but was cut short when Drew removed the tray and put it on a nearby table. 'Breakfast is over, my lord,' he said. 'It is time to say goodbye. The game is over and we hold all the trumps.'

'I do not know what you are talking about.'

'We are talking about a little matter of attempted bigamy,' Mark said. 'Very much against the law, that is. I know the Prince Regent got away with it, but you are not the Prince Regent.'

'You are talking rubbish.' He was clearly agitated, but with the two men standing over him, one each side of the bed, he could not move.

'The lady's name is Juanita,' Drew said. 'Juanita Estaban as was. I have a copy of the registry entry of the marriage made in the cathedral in Lisbon. Would you care to see it, to refresh your memory?'

'No.'

'No, of course not. You know exactly what it says. You left her for dead and fled back to this country. But are you safe? Did you know your wife's kin are searching for you? Yes, of course you do, that is why you are hiding here. I fancy they would like to know where you are. I would not like to be in your shoes if they find you.'

'You are talking rubbish.' He was clearly agitated.

'Is it bigamy or murder?' Mark queried, addressing Drew. 'Whichever it is, our man is in trouble.'

'He certainly is,' Drew agreed. 'Shall we lock him up until we can take him before the Justice?'

Mark laughed. 'I am the Justice.'

'I had forgot. Is there a lock-up in the village?'

'Yes, close by the church. He will be safe enough there while we send for his wife's relations. Or we could tell his mother. I wonder why he has never told her himself, since she wants him married.'

'Perhaps she does not like Portuguese ladies,' Drew said. 'Some of these old aristocrats are like that, they want good English blood in their line.'

'No, I beg you, no.' Bolsover was shaking with terror.

'Then you have only one course open to you,' Mark said. 'Leave Hadlea, abandon your torment of Miss Cavenhurst and take yourself off where the law cannot find you. I will not answer for the consequences, if you do not. Be on the afternoon stage.'

'If I do not?'

'It is up to you, of course,' Mark said. 'But I should not like to be in your shoes when Estaban finds you.' He turned to Drew. 'Shall we leave him to think about it?'

'You are too lenient, my friend, but as I am anxious to be on my way, let us give him the same chance we would give the fox. Run or suffer the consequences.'

Mark was thoughtful as they returned to the carriage. 'There is a man called Estaban working at Witherington House,' he said. 'It cannot be a coincidence, can it?'

'Unlikely, I should say.'

'He must know where Bolsover is or why would he be here?'

'Not our problem, my friend.' The carriage drew up at the Manor. 'I will leave you to tell Sir Edward the good news. I intend to spirit Isabel away somewhere where we can be alone.'

The door was opened by Sophie, who squealed at the sight of Drew and raced back to the drawing room. 'Papa, Mama, Issie. Lord Wyndham is here and he has Mr Ashton with him.'

Isabel rushed out to the hall and stopped to stare at Drew. 'Is it really you?'

He smiled. 'If it is not, I do not know who else it might be.' He took her hand and bowed over it. 'How are you, sweetheart?'

She looked from him to Mark. 'Mark?'

'Do not mind me,' he said. 'I will go and speak to your parents and Jane.'

'Jane is not here, she has gone to Witherington. She spends all her time there these days.'

He would have liked to have turned round and gone straight to her, but courtesy demanded he speak to Sir Edward and Lady Cavenhurst first. He went into the drawing room and bowed to them both. 'Good morning, Sir Edward. My lady. I hope you will forgive me for arriving so early, but I have good tidings and could not wait to tell you.'

'Sophie said Mr Ashton was with you.'

'So he is. He is talking to Isabel. No doubt they will join us shortly.'

Sir Edward rose angrily. 'You mean you have left them alone together?'

'Yes, but please allow them a few minutes while I explain.'

Sir Edward blustered, but subsided.

'The first thing I have to tell you is that you no

longer have anything to fear from Lord Bolsover. His dastardly past has been uncovered and he has been discredited. He will not be bothering you again. You are out of debt and Greystone is safe.'

'Merciful Lord,' her ladyship said.

'That is indeed good news,' Sir Edward added. 'But how has that come about?'

'Through the good offices of my friend, Mr Ashton. It is he you have to thank.'

'Oh. You had better tell us the whole.'

'I will leave that to Drew, he knows the details. I intend to go to Witherington House to speak to Jane, if you will excuse me.'

'Yes, of course,' Lady Cavenhurst said. 'She will be much relieved.'

He bowed and left, passing Drew and Isabel in the hall. They had their arms round each other and were kissing. 'All yours,' he said, laughing, and went out to the carriage with a lighter heart than he had had for a very long time.

Paolo Estaban was proving an asset. He was young and strong and made himself useful in all manner of ways. He had already identified what needed doing before Jane could ask him. Wobbly shelves, window catches, vegetables to brought in from the garden, Bonny to be groomed, all dealt with as if by magic. And the name Witherington House would soon be painted on the side of the

trap. He had talked to Jane of his home and hinted
of a terrible wrong, but most of the time he kept
his thoughts to himself.

'Tell me about your family,' she asked him one
day when they were working together in the garden. 'Do you miss them?'

'Yes, *senhora*, I do.'

'Tell me about them.'

'I have a father and mother and two sisters and
a cousin who lives with us. She is married to an
Englishman.'

'The officer who brought you to England?'

'No. This man is not an officer. He calls himself a gentleman, but he is no gentleman. He
treated Juanita cruelly and when she confronted
him about his gambling and his mistresses he beat
her so badly she nearly died. I found her and took
her home to my parents. When we went looking
for him we discovered he had gone back to England, taking her fortune with him. Is it any wonder we want vengeance?'

'Do you know where he is?'

'Oh, yes, I know where he is. It will not be
long now.'

'What do you mean to do?'

'I have not made up my mind. I might put a
sword through his evil heart, or I might shoot
him, but I have to have the money first.'

'You must not take the law into your own

hands, Mr Estaban,' she said, thoroughly alarmed.
'Tell the authorities. Have him tried.'

'And do you think they will believe me? They
will say the man has a right to beat his wife and
abscond with her money and jewels. Perhaps he
will have an accident. Or perhaps I will challenge
him to a duel.'

'Oh, no,' she exclaimed. 'Duels are illegal in
this country and you could be killed. Your life is
much too valuable to be thrown away like that.
Tell Lord Wyndham your story. I am sure he will
see justice done.'

He smiled slowly. 'No, *senhora*, I must do what
I must do. Now I go and put these brambles on
the bonfire.'

She watched him as he piled up the bonfire,
took a tinder box from his coat pocket and set
light to the heap. Some of it had been lying there
for weeks and was dry and brittle. There was soon
a good blaze going. She turned to go back to the
house, wondering what to do for the best. She
ought to try to stop him from doing whatever it
was he had in mind. One or other of them would
be wounded, if not killed, and though she had no
sympathy for the Englishman, whoever he was,
she could not stand by and let him be killed. Was
this emergency enough to send for Mark? But
Paolo had so far done nothing wrong and might
even deny his conversation with her. She would

just have to watch him and try to persuade him not to do anything rash.

She looked up to see Mrs Butler coming towards her. 'You have a visitor, Miss Cavenhurst. I left him in your parlour pacing about like a caged animal.'

'Did he say his name?'

'No. But I've seen him about Hadlea village a time or two.'

It could not be Mark, Mrs Butler knew Mark, nor her father, for he would not have withheld his name. There was Mark's friend, Jonathan Smythe, but what would he want with her? Had something happened to Mark? She hurried indoors.

Chapter Thirteen

The last person she expected to see was Lord Bolsover, but that was who confronted her when she made her way to the parlour. 'What are you doing here?' she demanded.

'That is hardly a civil greeting.' He looked a little dishevelled, as if he had dressed in a hurry. His hair was not as carefully combed as it usually was and his cravat was askew.

'I am very busy,' she said. 'Please state your business and be on your way.'

'My business is with you.'

'You have no business with me until after my sister's wedding, and not then if I could think of a way out of it without ruining my family.'

'I am not disposed to wait that long. I must marry and the sooner the better if I am to please my mother. Pleasing my mother is paramount, you see. I do not think we can have the nuptials at Hadlea church, the reverend there is bound to want to call banns or have the bishop's blessing and we don't want all that nonsense delaying us, do we? A simple statement and a consummation will suffice.'

'If you think I will behave in that disgraceful manner, you may think again, my lord. You must wait until my sister is married. I made an undertaking to give you an answer then. Now, please go.'

'The trouble is,' he said, making no move to do as she asked, 'I do not think Lord Wyndham will marry your sister after all, which is a pity. It means I have had to change my plans.'

'What do you mean?'

'I think Miss Isabel has other ideas. I fear she is about to elope with Mr Ashton.'

'I do not believe you.'

He shrugged. 'That is up to you. There will be a terrible scandal, of course. As for Lord Wyndham…' He gave a cracked laugh. 'He will lose both bride and mistress.'

'Do not be ridiculous. You are drunk.' She was terrified, but trying not to show it. If she shouted for help, would someone come to her aid? She opened her mouth to scream, but he clapped his hand over her face, pushing her head hard against the wall.

'I told my mother I had found a suitable bride

and she naturally wishes to meet you.' He grabbed her arm. 'My carriage is waiting.'

'Let me go.' Her head was spinning from the impact with the wall. 'I am not going anywhere with you.'

'Unfortunately, my dear, you have no choice.' He began dragging her towards the outer door. She opened her mouth to scream, but he had anticipated that and put one hand over her mouth and with the other thrust her arm up behind her back. She struggled, but he simply gave another tug on her arm. It was excruciatingly painful and forced her to move ahead of him. He propelled her out on to the garden path and round the side of the house towards his carriage. His driver was standing by it and opened the door. She felt herself being lifted bodily and dumped on the seat. Free of his hand over her mouth, she screamed and went on screaming. He lifted his hand to strike her. Then she saw another hand come up behind him, a hand brandishing a firebrand.

Bolsover abandoned her to deal with this new threat. The only weapon Paolo had was the burning stick and he was faced with two adversaries. He held them off with it, waving it from one to the other and shouting in Portuguese, poking it at them. They were all too close to the carriage for her to leave it. Then the hammer cloth caught fire. In the blinking of an eye, flames licked along the body work and caught the curtains.

The horses panicked and began rearing up, threatening to overtopple the carriage. Pandemonium ensued as other people arrived and tried to beat out the flames. Jane could not see them for the smoke, but she felt sure it was Mark's voice she heard giving instructions. Then someone reached in and pulled her out. She felt herself being carried away from the heat and gently put on the grass some distance away.

She coughed. 'Mark, is it you?'

He sat down beside her. 'Yes, my love. You are safe now,'

'Lord Bolsover?'

'Overcome by smoke. He will recover to stand trial.'

'And Paolo?'

'His hands are burned and his hair singed, but Mrs Butler is looking after him. Are you hurt?'

'No, only a little. I am thirsty.'

'A drink you shall have.'

He picked her up and carried her into the house. 'Bring Miss Cavenhurst a tisane and a drink,' he instructed Mrs Godfrey as he passed through the kitchen to the parlour. He put his burden on the sofa and sat down beside her, putting his arm about her shoulders. 'I only just arrived in time. Estaban could not have held them off much longer and the coach was well alight.'

'He is a brave man. I think he knew Lord Bolsover. He had a score to settle and talked of revenge, but it wasn't revenge after all, he did it to save me.'

'He did indeed.'

Mrs Godfrey arrived with a cordial and a dose of tisane. He thanked her and helped Jane to drink.

'It was dreadful, Mark. Lord Bolsover said he was going to take me to meet his mother and we would not trouble with a church wedding.'

'It is all over, my love. Everything. He cannot harm you now.'

'He has a wife. Paolo told me about his cousin's English husband, but I didn't know he was talking about Lord Bolsover.'

'His lordship was under the impression he had killed her. He fled to England to escape Portuguese justice, but she recovered.'

'He said Issie was going to elope with Mr Ashton.'

He laughed. 'No, I do not think they will do that. Unless I miss my guess they will obtain the full consent of Sir Edward.' He paused to kiss the tip of her nose. 'We are free to marry, Jane, my darling. That is, if you will have me.'

'Of course I will, but the scandal...'

'There are to be no buts, Jane.'

'Oh, Mark.' Her head lolled on his shoulder as the tisane took effect. He smiled and kissed the top of her head and held her close. They would have plenty of time to talk when she woke. For the moment he was happy to sit with her sleeping body in his arms and contemplate a rosy future at home with the woman he loved.

Everything had been explained and mulled over at Greystone Manor as everyone gave their own version of events. Lord Bolsover, his face badly scarred by the fire, had retreated to live with his mother, hidden from society, and Paolo Estaban had gone back to Portugal satisfied with his vengeance. Even the scandal was reduced to a simple murmur. It had been made known that Lord Wyndham and Miss Isabel Cavenhurst had agreed to end their engagement by mutual consent and that was followed a few weeks later by an announcement of the betrothal of Miss Isabel Cavenhurst and Mr Andrew Ashton and that of Baron Wyndham of Broadacres to Miss Jane Cavenhurst, eldest daughter of Sir Edward and Lady Cavenhurst of Greystone Manor.

The announcement had been made at a musical recital given at Broadacres by Lady Wyndham. All her aristocratic friends had been invited and it was made clear to them that the evening was in aid of the Hadlea Children's Home and that they were expected to donate generously. It was a glittering affair, with everyone dressed in their finery to listen to the best musicians and soloists in the country. They had not been forewarned of the announcement and it was greeted with delighted surprise and congratulations all round. Several hundred pounds were raised for the orphans, who now numbered fifteen. The master and housekeeper had arrived at Witherington House, and so had a teacher, an enthusiastic young graduate Mark had found.

The villagers of Hadlea greeted the news of the double engagement with much relief and no surprise. As far as they were concerned, it was something they could all have predicted weeks before.

Two weddings took place on the same day at St Peter's church to which they were all invited. Isabel wore the wedding gown Jane had made for her and Jane made another for herself in a rich cream satin. The wedding breakfast, held at Greystone, was the splendid affair Isabel had hoped it would be. The house had been refurbished, not because Drew had paid for it, though he was willing to do so, but because Teddy had come back from India a rich man. On the voyage out to India he had had time to think about his life and where it would lead if he did not mend his ways and, remembering what Drew had said about making his fortune in trade, had turned his back on the card table and tried his hand at commerce. His arrival on the eve of the weddings had made the happy day even happier.

'Well, Jane, my love,' Mark said later that night. 'We had our miracle, didn't we?'

'Only because you and Drew made it happen.' She was sitting up in the four-poster bed at Broadacres, watching him undress. Dispensing with maid and valet, they had begun undressing each other, little by little, until she was naked and he was wearing only his trousers. It was then she became shy and he stood up to divest himself of the last stitch of his clothing. Then he tumbled on to the bed beside her.

'Are you happy with our miracle?' he asked.

'I could not be happier.'

'Oh, but I think you can and I shall show you how, my lovely wife.'

She laughed a little nervously as he reached out for her, but then forgot to be nervous as he pulled her to him and began kissing her and stroking her gently and tenderly until she was roused to ecstasies of delight, responding so naturally that he was enchanted. It was a long time before they spoke again and by then they were sated and drowsy and the words 'I love you', said by him and repeated by her, were said in a sleepy murmur.

* * * * *

HISTORICAL

IGNITE YOUR IMAGINATION, STEP INTO THE PAST...

My wish list for next month's titles...

In stores from 2nd May 2014:

☐ Unwed and Unrepentant — Marguerite Kaye
☐ Return of the Prodigal Gilvry — Ann Lethbridge
☐ A Traitor's Touch — Helen Dickson
☐ Yield to the Highlander — Terri Brisbin
☐ Return of the Viking Warrior — Michelle Styles
☐ Notorious in the West — Lisa Plumley

Available at WHSmith, Tesco, Asda, Eason, Amazon and Apple

Just can't wait?

The Regency Ballroom Collection

A twelve-book collection led by Louise Allen
and written by the top authors and rising
stars of historical romance!

Classic tales of scandal and seduction in
the Regency ballroom

**Take your place on the ballroom floor now, at:
www.millsandboon.co.uk**

0214/MB458

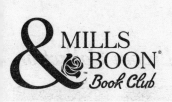

Join the Mills & Boon Book Club

Want to read more **Historical** books?
We're offering you **2 more** absolutely **FREE!**

We'll also treat you to these fabulous extras:

- 🌹 **Exclusive offers and much more!**

- 🌹 **FREE home delivery**

- 🌹 **FREE books and gifts with our special rewards scheme**

Get your free books now!

**visit www.millsandboon.co.uk/bookclub
or call Customer Relations on 020 8288 2888**